Bedside Manners

"Let me help you sit up. Then I will give you some medicine for the pain and your fever," the Earl of Weymouth said to Beth.

After several seconds had passed, she spoke to her makeshift surgeon. "Weymouth, you have the strangest expression on your face."

"Gaping like a landed flounder, am I?" He tried to ease through the awkward moment. "Earlier today I helped you sit up by grasping your arms above the elbow as I raised you, before I removed your bullet. I can't do that now. Unless . . ." He narrowed his eyes, considering the idea that had just popped into his brain.

"Unless what?" asked Beth.

"Unless I hold you around the waist and lift you."

"Do you hesitate because you think it won't work?"

"No, I think it will work very well if you can keep your left arm stationary." He felt a flush creeping up his face. *Gad, almost thirty and he was blushing like a schoolboy!* "I hesitated because you aren't wearing a riding habit and . . ."

She glanced up at him. "I am not missish—well, in some respects—but I am not a feather-headed schoolroom miss."

When he lifted her, Beth didn't swoon, but she certainly felt something when Weymouth wrapped his hands about her waist. Something slightly less shocking than a lightning bolt, yet potent enough to radiate all the way to her toes . . .

A Scandalous Journey

Susannah Carleton

A SIGNET BOOK

SIGNET
Published by New American Library, a division of
Penguin Putnam Inc., 375 Hudson Street,
New York, New York 10014, U.S.A.
Penguin Books Ltd, 80 Strand,
London WC2R 0RL, England
Penguin Books Australia Ltd, Ringwood,
Victoria, Australia
Penguin Books Canada Ltd, 10 Alcorn Avenue,
Toronto, Ontario, Canada M4V 3B2
Penguin Books (N.Z.) Ltd, 182–190 Wairau Road,
Auckland 10, New Zealand

Penguin Books Ltd, Registered Offices:
Harmondsworth, Middlesex, England

First published by Signet, an imprint of New American Library,
a division of Penguin Putnam Inc.

First Printing, September 2002
10 9 8 7 6 5 4 3 2 1

 REGISTERED TRADEMARK—MARCA REGISTRADA

Printed in the United States of America

*To Nancy Lantz,
for loving and believing.*

*To Melissa Jensen and Barbara Metzger,
for their friendship, guidance, and encouragement.*

*To Tim and Andrew Jones,
for their love and support.*

Chapter 1

George Winterbrook, Earl of Weymouth, was not a happy man. He'd been knocked on the head, abducted, rolled in a dusty carpet, and carried aboard a yacht. Now back on dry land, he was God only knew where, trussed up like a Christmas goose, gagged, blindfolded, and hungry. And he had no idea why. Oh, he knew why he was hungry, of course—he hadn't eaten since the previous afternoon—but he could think of nothing that might explain the rest of his condition. According to the chimes of a nearby clock, he had been tied to this wooden chair with its demmed hard seat for more than two hours, and he was getting angrier by the minute. A large, hungry, angry man was not likely to be a pleasant guest. A large, hungry, angry man who couldn't move or speak posed less of a problem to his unknown host, George supposed.

A door opened behind him, and several people entered the room. One, a man from the sound of his heavy tread, came to stand beside the chair to which George was bound. Another, a woman, he thought, moved farther into the room and seated herself a few feet in front of him. The third person, a small man or a large woman, he couldn't decide which, crossed the room and opened a door. The aroma of coffee, eggs, and sausage drifted into the room when he—or she—returned.

As George wondered whether they were going to feed him, or torture him by not feeding him, the man beside his chair bent over and began, not very gently, to remove the rope that bound his hands. Optimistically, George decided that he would get breakfast, which would give him the opportunity to interrogate his captors. He might not get any answers, but he was going to ask questions.

After the cord around his wrists was removed, the man began fumbling with the knot securing the blindfold. Maybe, George thought, he had been too optimistic. Perhaps the man was going to snatch him bald instead. As the blindfold loosened, a familiar female voice said, "Well, well, my lord Weymouth, how nice of you to join our little party."

George groaned silently and braced himself for the sight of Lady Arabella Smalley, who had pursued him for nearly a year with the determination and ferocity of a pack of hounds hunting a fox. There she was, right across the table, a petite, voluptuous blonde of thirty, wearing a dressing gown more suited to a brothel than a respectable breakfast parlor. Not caring for the sight, he glanced around the room. From the wainscoting to the sideboard to the needlepoint cushions on the chairs, it seemed familiar. He knew he had been here before, more than once, but he could not identify the house. *Damn! Where the hell was he?*

Finally the gag was removed. "I don't recall receiving an invitation to this party. If I had received one, I would not have accepted."

"You are the guest of honor, Weymouth. Surely you would not refuse to attend a party in your honor."

George closed his eyes, lightly rubbing his eyelids. "Obviously you thought I would do just that. That is why you had me abducted, is it not?"

"I did not have you abducted."

"Well, someone did, and as the hostess of this so-called party, you seem the most likely candidate."

Arabella picked up her serviette and placed it in her lap. "Nevertheless, I am not responsible for your presence here."

"Then who is?" he all but demanded. "And why?"

"All in good time, Weymouth. All in good time."

Her taunting smile infuriated him. "I think now is a very good time."

"And I say it is not," she snapped. "Eat your breakfast; perhaps it will put you in a better humor."

George picked up his fork. If the next eighteen hours were going to be anything like the eighteen since he had been abducted—and Arabella's presence was a guarantee against any immediate improvement—enduring them would require all the strength he could muster. After one bite, though, he shoved the plate aside, stomach roiling. "Why *am* I here? What is the purpose of this so-called party?"

"You are here to get married, Weymouth. The party is to celebrate our wedding."

George choked on a sip of coffee. The footman standing beside his chair obligingly slapped him on the back.

"Arabella, I wouldn't marry you if you were the last woman on earth."

"I will remind you of those words later today"—she smiled smugly—"after you have made me your wife."

"Given your intentions, you cannot expect me to believe you are not responsible for my presence here." *Did she take him for a fool?*

"My cousin brought you here."

"Your cousin?" George knew her father had no siblings, but he did not know her late mother's maiden name.

"My second cousin, actually."

"Why?"

A frown creased her brow. "Why what?"

His jaw clenched, he asked, "Why did your cousin bring me here?"

"Because he knows I want to marry you, and he wants to give me my heart's desire."

George did not know why Arabella had chosen him as her bridegroom, but her heart was not involved. He was also well aware of the penchant of the women in her family to trap men into marriage. But things were different now than when she'd snared his good friend Sir Robert Sidney in parson's mousetrap. Perhaps she needed to be reminded of the differences, and to hear a few home truths.

"If you think to claim I have compromised you because we are here alone, allow me to remind you that a woman whose husband divorced her because of her repeated and flagrant infidelities doesn't have a reputation that can be ruined."

"I don't intend to claim anything of the sort," she retorted, her smile gone. "Nevertheless, you *will* marry me today." The resolution behind her words resounded through the room.

"Just how do you intend to bring that about? With a pistol?" Not caring for the sneering tone that had entered his voice, George paused, rubbing his temples against an incipient headache. "No clergyman in England would perform a wedding in which one party was so obviously unwilling, and even if you have found one and have a special license, the marriage could easily be annulled on the grounds of coercion."

"Ah, but we aren't in England, Weymouth; we are in Scotland."

It was useful, if daunting, information, but their location was beside the point. He crossed his arms over his chest and waited for the rest of her explanation.

"If necessary, you will marry me more or less at gunpoint. The minister—"

Exasperated, he growled, "What do you mean, more or less at gunpoint? One is either at the business end of a pistol or one is not."

"I mean that a gun will be present, but the minister won't be aware of it. The clergyman in question is my uncle, and he doesn't believe in forced marriages."

"How very obliging of him," George said dryly, his heart and his hopes for a quick escape sinking at the mention of a gun. "What is to prevent me from telling your uncle that you are threatening me into marriage? Or from arguing that you aren't a suitable bride for a man of my rank and position?"

"You won't do that, Weymouth. Under the circumstances, you will find me an unexceptional bride."

When pigs fly! Silently he counted to ten, then twenty, fighting confusion and rising unease. "Where are we, Arabella, and why are you doing this?"

"We are in Scotland, a rather remote area of Scotland." The smirk that accompanied her words, coupled with the matrimonial noose she threatened, had his hands itching to slap her, even though he had never struck a woman in his life. "I am doing this because I need money and because I want to regain my position in Society."

"Your father has money. And marrying me won't restore your social position; you are a divorced woman."

"My father cut my allowance when Robin divorced me.

He refuses to pay my debts." Her voice rose to almost a shriek.

Irritated, George shifted in his seat. Well, he tried to. It wasn't possible to alter one's position when one's torso and legs were tied to a chair.

Arabella smiled at him. "You are one of the most eligible men on the Marriage Mart. All the old tabbies love you. If we married, they would eventually accept me." Her switch from whining to wheedling swayed him not a whit.

"No, they would not." As she opened her mouth to argue, he forestalled her. "It isn't worth brangling over. Neither of us can prove our opinion is correct."

"But, Weymouth—"

"Shut up, Arabella!" Amazingly, she did. Sulking but silent, she glared at him from across the table. George grabbed at the remnants of his fleeting temper and attempted to marshal his thoughts. His mind elsewhere, he drank some coffee—and grimaced because it was cold. To gain a few seconds to ponder her machinations, he reached for the coffeepot. The footman standing by his chair grabbed the pot and filled the cup.

"Let me see if I understand the situation correctly. You propose that you and I will marry today, at gunpoint if necessary. The minister, who doesn't believe in forced marriages, won't realize the weapon is present. You claim—a claim as yet unsubstantiated—to have arranged things in such a way that I won't protest my unwilling compliance to your outrageous demand." George paused a moment as his temper soared anew. "What is to prevent me from marrying you today, then having the marriage annulled on the grounds of coercion?"

"You won't have the marriage annulled for the same reason that you will agree to it in the first place," she stated with calm conviction.

Through gritted teeth, he inquired, "And that reason is?"

"Your so-called niece."

A frown creased George's brow. "Are you referring to Isabelle?"

"If Isabelle is the name of the brat my sister foisted upon your hapless brother after she compromised him into marriage, then I am, indeed, referring to her."

The frown deepened. "What does Isabelle have to do with any of this?"

Arabella's malicious laugh sent a shiver up his spine. "Isabelle has everything to do with this, Weymouth. If you don't marry me today, or if you marry me and later annul the marriage or make any attempt to dissolve it, neither you nor your brother will ever see the child again."

Every muscle in his aching body stiffened. "Dear God—"

Arabella had few scruples, and no morals, but the deficiencies in her character had never directly affected him or his family before. Her sister had been cut from the same cloth, and had nearly destroyed his brother, but Isabelle had saved him. David had fallen in love with the child a few hours after her birth, and her existence had given meaning and purpose to his life for the past three and a half years.

George relaxed his clenched fists and tried to think rationally. "I doubt David would allow you into his home. Certainly he would not permit you to walk out the door with Isabelle."

Arabella laughed again, this time with glee. "I didn't walk through the door to get her, but I have her all the same."

"What? You have Isabelle? How the devil did you manage that?"

"Yes, I have her. My cousin's men snatched the brat when she and your brother and her governess were out for a carriage ride. They brought the governess along, too, but she hasn't regained her senses. They must have hit her too hard."

Bloody hell! He fought to keep his expression impassive and his voice even, not wanting Arabella aware of his burgeoning fear. "Isabelle doesn't have a governess. Perhaps you kidnapped the wrong child?"

"I have my sister's child, Weymouth. She is the image of Marie at that age, although better behaved. I assumed the woman to be a governess, since she was traveling with your brother and the child in a closed carriage, but perhaps she is your brother's mistress instead."

George didn't think his brother had a mistress, but he refused to respond to the jibe. "Where is David?"

"I have no idea where your brother is. Jamie's men left him in Hampshire." She opened her mouth to say more, then shook her head and clamped her lips together.

He wondered what she wasn't saying. Wondered, too, how her cousin was involved, and his identity. George desperately needed a plan, but bound to the chair as he was—and bound by a deathbed promise to his mother to always take care of his younger brother—his choices were limited. *The devil or the deep blue sea.*

"If I marry you, what guarantee do I have that you will return Isabelle to David and never go near her again?"

"One of the articles in the marriage settlement could state that if you marry me today and make no attempt to annul or dissolve the marriage, I will return the brat to your brother."

"You will have to do better than that, Arabella. Much better," George declared, formulating and discarding plans as he sorted through the meager information he possessed. "If I must rivet myself to you to ensure Isabelle's happiness—a Smithfield bargain if ever there was one—I shall require iron-clad guarantees that she is safe from you. Now and forever."

"I will think on it while I dress," she muttered, rising from the chair. "You think about your niece."

"Consider, too, that the fetters of marriage bind both parties."

"Hmph." With one hand on the doorknob, Arabella turned back to give orders to the manservant. "Will, stand guard over his lordship." Then she stormed from the room, slamming the door behind her.

With a stifled scream Beth Castleton awoke from a bad dream with a racing heart, a pounding headache, and a shiver skating up and down her spine indicating that all was *not* well.

The nightmare wasn't the fiery one that had tormented her since the deaths of her parents and sisters five years ago, but it had been equally vivid. A tree across the road, a man jumping down from a carriage on the other side of the obstacle, a highwayman hitting the man over the head, felling him, a little girl tumbling from the carriage crying for her papa, and Beth herself screaming at the highwayman as she clambered over the tree trunk to comfort the little girl.

Beth shook her head to dispel the dream's effect, then moaned when the rhythmic hammering at her temples segued from andante to presto. Cautiously, she eased herself into a sitting position against the headboard, pulled the blankets up around her shoulders, and looked around the dimly lit room. Although not large, the chamber was comfortably furnished. A candle burned on the nightstand, next to a clock that indicated it was nearly eight o'clock. No light penetrated the heavy blue velvet draperies at the window, so she wasn't certain if it was morning or evening. She was wearing a nightgown, although not one of her own, and the fire in the grate was mostly embers. Morning, she concluded decisively.

Her surroundings were pleasant enough, not at all the sort of thing to cause nightmares. It wasn't the bedchamber in her suite at Castleton Abbey, her uncle's home in Buckinghamshire where she had lived for the past year, nor was it the room she had recently occupied at a house party in Hampshire. Beth could not recall ever having seen this room in her life.

Of course you have seen this room before, ninny; you went to sleep here last night. You may have been exhausted and not remember, but you can easily solve this little puzzle.

It was hard to think with her head feeling as if miniature miners with pickaxes were trying to tunnel their way out through her temples and the back of her head, but Beth did her best. She remembered the Dunnley house party, their early morning departure. The change of horses at Basingstoke, then at Reading. Then a sudden halt, the coachman's cry about a fallen tree . . .

No, that was in the dream, not on the journey home.

She tried to remember what she and Aunt Julia had talked about in the carriage, if her great-aunt had mentioned visiting someone on the way home. All she recalled was a long and rather convoluted conversation about needlework, sharing a pot of tea at the coaching inn in Reading, then the carriage stopping . . .

No, that was in the dream.

The nightmare had affected her strongly, strangely. Beth

pinched her arm sharply to test if she was awake or still dreaming, jerked reflexively from the pain, then cradled her aching head in her hands.

A quiet knock sounded at the door. Before she could call "Enter," a woman came in carrying a pitcher of water, her eyes downcast as if watching where she placed each foot. She was followed by a man carrying an armload of firewood. As the man built up the fire, the woman placed the pitcher on the washstand. Beth watched in silence, scrutinizing the pair. The man was about five-and-twenty, she guessed, the woman perhaps a decade older. Judging from their attire, the man was a footman and the woman was a lady's maid, but their features were unfamiliar. Beth was absolutely certain she had never seen either one of them before.

The footman finished his task and left the room. The maid poured water into a bowl, wet a cloth, and turned toward the bed, her gaze still downcast.

"Who are you?" Beth asked. Her voice sounded strange, rather scratchy, as if she had been ill.

"Ah, my lady, ye are awake at last! I hae been sae worrit aboot ye." The woman's lilting Scottish brogue provided no clue to her identity.

Beth studied the maid's face, the red hair drawn neatly back into a knot, the sad brown eyes, the pert little nose, the pale skin marred by a thin jagged scar over the left cheekbone and a vivid bruise on the right. "Who are you?"

"I be Moira Sinclair, my lady. I hae been takin' care o' ye for the past few days."

"Have I been ill?"

"Nay, not ill, exactly. Ye suffered a nasty blow on the head and hae been out like a snuffed candle e'er since." The maid placed the cool, damp cloth on Beth's forehead.

"Ah . . . How many days? And how did I injure my head?"

"Four days or maybe five. I lost track whilst takin' care o' ye. The doctor left ye some powders for the headache. Said ye were certain to hae one when ye woke. I will fix them for ye in a minute. Would ye like tea or, mayhap, some breakfast?"

Her mind reeling, Beth stared at the maid in disbelief. "I have never heard of anyone being unconscious for so long." But it explained her sore head and, perhaps, why she was having difficulty differentiating between fact and dream this morning.

" 'Tis unusual, but my uncle had a patient who was senseless for months."

Impossible as that seemed to Beth, she dropped the subject to pursue other matters. "I want the headache powder, please, and the answers to some questions."

The maid walked to the dressing table and began mixing something into a glass of water. "I dinna ken if I can answer yer questions, my lady, but I will try."

"I am not a 'my lady,' simply Miss Castleton. Are you Miss or Mrs. Sinclair?"

"Just call me Sinclair, Miss Castleton."

"If that is how you prefer to be addressed, then of course I shall. It seems a bit rude to me, though; in America, servants are addressed by their first names."

"Ye may call me Moira if ye like, miss. 'Tis been a verra long time since last I heard my given name." The wistful tone in the maid's voice could be heard clearly, even through a pounding headache.

"Very well, Moira." The woman brought the doctor's remedy, and Beth drank, eager for relief. "Where are we?"

"At a house called Gull Cottage, miss. Very near the sea it is."

"The sea!" Beth gasped. Had John Coachman taken a wrong turn and ended in southern Hampshire instead of Buckinghamshire? "Where did we travel from and how long did it take to get here?"

"I came from London, miss, by boat. The journey seemed to take days, but I was verra sick all the while. I dinna ken where ye traveled from."

The maid was not a font of information, but Beth persevered. Perhaps she had not yet asked the right questions. "Moira, please sit down so you can be comfortable while we talk." The Scotswoman looked surprised but pulled a chair close to the bed and sat down, her hands folded in her lap. "How long have I been here? I do not remember this place, nor do I remember traveling here."

"Ye were unconscious when ye arrived, Miss Castleton. I daresay 'tis why ye dinna remember."

"How did I receive the blow on the head? Was I in a carriage accident?"

"I dinna ken how ye hurt yer head, miss. Whatever 'twas, it happened before ye came here."

"Was I supposed to arrive here? That is, was I an expected guest or am I here because I was injured?" Beth hoped that the doctor's remedy would take effect soon. It was difficult to think when her brain felt as if it might explode any minute. "Oh! Aunt Julia. Is Lady Julia Castleton awake yet, Moira?"

"Yer lady aunt is nae here, miss. And I dinna believe ye were expected, because there was nae chamber prepared for ye."

"My aunt isn't here? But we were traveling together!" More puzzled than before, Beth swallowed hard, fighting to control her fear, and tried to think of other, pertinent questions. "Who owns Gull Cottage? For whom do you work?"

"I dinna ken who the owner is, miss, but 'tisn't my employer. I work for Lady Arabella Smalley."

"I am not acquainted with Lady Arabella."

The maid mumbled something in Gaelic.

"What other guests are here, Moira?"

"None here now, miss; the storms hae delayed them, I reckon. Turrible storms we've had, all the week. Guests are expected this morn, but Lady Arabella has nae mentioned their names to me."

"What an awkward coil! I don't know where I am, how I came to be here, or where my great-aunt is, and I don't know my hostess." Beth sighed. "Well, I daresay Lady Arabella will be able to tell me most of that. I would like to speak with her as soon as possible." She shifted restlessly against the headboard. "Are there other houses nearby? People who might be sheltering my aunt?"

"Nay, miss, there is nae other house in sight."

The shiver returned, snaking up and down Beth's spine. "I am beginning to have a bad feeling about this. A very bad feeling."

"Would ye like a bit o' breakfast now, Miss Castleton? Perhaps ye'll feel better after ye hae eaten."

"Yes, please, Moira. I hope that you are correct."

Beth removed the cloth from her forehead. It hadn't eased her headache, and it kept sliding down over her eyes in a most annoying way. "I would like to take a bath after breakfast. Would you have a tub and hot water brought up, please?"

"Aye, miss, that I will. Shall I fetch yer breakfast and arrange yer bath now or do ye hae more questions?"

"Now is fine, Moira. I cannot think of anything else to ask at the moment." Rubbing her temples, she added softly, "I can hardly think at all."

When the maid left the room, Beth got out of bed. The chamber spun around her like a vortex. Dizzy and disoriented, she reached out blindly, by sheer good luck grabbing the bedpost. She closed her eyes and rested against the smooth, polished wood until she regained her equilibrium. Then, holding on to furniture and the wall, she walked to the window. Looking out, she saw a gray sky, heavy with clouds, and a swath of gorse-filled lawn ending at a rock-strewn beach. She could hear, faintly, the sound of waves breaking on the shore. One thing was certain: she wasn't in Buckinghamshire. Nor in Hampshire, either northern or southern. Pondering the mystery of her present location, she staggered back to bed. Lud, her head hurt.

An hour later she sat in front of the fire, clad in a dressing gown, while Moira dried her hair. The maid's brisk toweling had revealed a large lump on the back of Beth's head, a lump that was once again throbbing in rhythm with her temples. During her bath, she had learned that she'd arrived without any luggage, but that was the only new information she had acquired. A fact as inexplicable as the absence of her great-aunt.

The Scotswoman spoke, startling Beth from her musings. "Yer hair is dry, miss. Stand up, please, so I can dress ye."

The blue carriage dress had been new, and her favorite, but despite the careful cleaning and pressing, it looked . . . shabby. "Moira," Beth fretted, "I must speak with Lady Arabella now. I need to know what has happened."

"Aye, miss, I ken that well, but Lady Arabella isna . . . she doesna take well to interruptions." The maid's hands twisted in her apron. "Please, Miss Castleton. Please wait."

Beth touched Moira's bruised cheek with a gentle finger, her eyebrow raised in question.

"Aye, miss." Tears pooled in the sad brown eyes.

Footsteps sounded in the hallway, then a door banged against a wall and a female voice screeched, "Sinclair!"

Moira stiffened, then hurriedly buttoned Beth's dress. "I must leave, miss. Why don't ye go to the book room and wait for her ladyship. I will tell her that ye wish to speak with her."

"Where—"

"Turn right at the foot o' the stairs. The book room will be right in front o' ye, at the end o' the hallway," the maid explained in a rush as she walked to the door.

"Very well, Moira. I will wait for Lady Arabella in the book room," Beth said, resigned to a wait. "Thank you for your help this morning."

The Scotswoman smiled and bobbed a curtsy. " 'Twas a pleasure to serve ye, Miss Castleton."

A clock in the hallway had chimed four quarter hours, and George's temper had soared forty notches, before Arabella returned. His appeals to the footman to be untied had been met with stubborn refusal. His wish to be moved to a different room, uttered in the hope that seeing more of the house would enable him to determine where he was and to formulate an escape plan, had been ignored. And his request to visit the necessary had produced a chamber pot—and a deal of embarrassment for both himself and the footman.

George was nearly certain that Arabella would carry out her threats. Not absolutely sure, but he didn't want to put it to the test. He feared that the gun forcing him to the altar would be aimed at his niece. Sweet, innocent Isabelle, the joy of his brother's life. George silently cursed Arabella, in three languages. If only he had an ally, someone who would protect Isabelle, come what may. He had failed his brother, and broken his promise to his mother, four years ago. He would never do so again.

The moment Arabella entered the room, George demanded, "Have you come to your senses? Are you ready to give up this scheme and release my niece and me?"

The vixen laughed. "I am in full possession of my senses, Weymouth. And I am not at all prepared to release you or your niece. Not until after we are married."

"There are a number of holes in your plan. My primary concern is the guarantee that Isabelle and David will be safe from your machinations. Until you have satisfied me on that count, do not mention marriage again," he snapped, scowling fiercely.

"The only hole is that I haven't yet thought of a way to ensure the child's safety. I hadn't expected that you would make such an unreasonable demand and—"

"Unreasonable! If you think that is unjust, then you had best rethink your wish to marry me because you are certain to find the rest iniquitous."

George took a deep, calming breath. "That is far from the only flaw in your scheme, but since the others are to my advantage, I shan't bring them to your attention."

Arabella frowned. "I will have to think on this some more. Why don't you visit with your niece until my uncle arrives."

She turned to the footman. "Will, tie his lordship's hands and cover his face with that hood we used yesterday. Then take him to the child, wherever she may be, and stand guard outside the door."

"Her is in the book room," the man replied in broad Yorkshire tones.

Temper soaring, George protested, "Damn it, Arabella, I cannot see Isabelle with a hood covering my head!"

"Just go, Weymouth," she wailed, querulous as a child. "I cannot think with you shouting at me."

Will rebound George's hands, pulled a heavy black hood over his head, then untied him from the chair. As he was escorted down the hall, George smiled, pleased that his demand about Isabelle's safety was such a conundrum for Arabella. With a bit of luck—well, a small miracle—his bachelorhood would be intact at day's end and his niece would be safe.

The footman herded him into a room and closed the door. "Isabelle, it's Uncle George. How is my favorite girl?"

"If Isabelle is a little blonde cherub about four years old, she is asleep on the sofa," a woman replied in lilting accents.

George's flaring hope faded when he recognized the voice. His prayer for an ally had been answered, and he had been granted a prodigiously intelligent one. But still he was doomed. The probability of his niece knowing the square root of three hundred sixty-one was greater than that of Miss Beth Castleton helping him.

Chapter 2

Beth took Moira's advice and went to the book room to await her hostess. Entering the room, she stopped abruptly, her heart racing as furiously as her head was pounding. Lying upon a sofa, sound asleep, was a little girl about four years old—the child in her dream. Had it been a nightmare or had it actually happened?

Question piled upon question until her head was reeling. Beth paced the room, trying to fit facts together. After a quarter of an hour, she admitted defeat; she didn't have enough facts to fill a thimble. Restless, she prowled the room, reciting theorems and working out the proofs in her head. " 'A body remains in a state of rest or constant velocity, both constant speed and direction, when no external force acts on it.' Sir Isaac Newton's First Law. 'The net force on a body is the product of its mass and the acceleration produced: F equals ma.' Sir Isaac again, his Second Law." *Where am I? How did I get here? How long have I been here?*

Beth shook her head sharply, then rubbed her temples at the ensuing jolt of pain. It was foolish to worry over questions she could not answer. After she spoke to Lady Arabella, she would have the information she needed. But how was she, Beth Castleton, an American whose first venture into Society had been something of a disaster, to deal with Lady Arabella, the daughter of a high-ranking peer? Beth knew the rules governing Society, but she was not yet comfortable with its ways. She was uneasy in crowds, shy with strangers, disinclined to chatter, and uninterested in gossip. The fact that she was five or six years older than most of the young ladies making their bows didn't help either. *Stop acting like a ninny! You won't meet Lady Arabella in a crowd, and she won't care how old you are.*

"Where was I? Oh, yes. 'Whenever two bodies interact, the force on the first body due to the second is equal and opposite to the force on the second due to the first.' Sir Isaac's Third Law." *Did the carriage really stop because of a tree across the road or was that just a dream? Who is the little girl?*

Beth clenched her fists. Theorems were not having their usual calming effect. More stringent measures were required. "Prime numbers. One, two, three, five, seven, eleven, thirteen, seventeen." She rattled off the first set quickly as she paced around the perimeter of the room. Her steps slowed as she considered each odd number, determining if it had factors. "Twenty-three, twenty-nine, thirty-one, thirty-seven, forty-one, forty-three, forty-seven." Ten strides down the outside wall, six steps across in front of the hearth, four paces back up, detour around the table. "Fifty-three, fifty-nine, sixty-one, sixty-seven . . ." *Where is Aunt Julia? Does Uncle Charles know what happened?*

The clock on the mantel chimed softly. Beth glared at it, wondering how much longer she would have to wait for Lady Arabella. "The square root of two hundred seventy-three is . . . 16.53. The square root of three hundred fifty-seven is . . . 18.89. The square root of four hundred sixty-one is . . ."

Suddenly, the door to the book room opened, and a male voice rich with affection said, "Isabelle, it's Uncle George. How is my favorite girl?"

"If Isabelle is a little blonde cherub about four years old, she is asleep on the sofa," Beth replied, turning toward the door.

A very tall, broad-shouldered man wearing the standard gentlemen's attire of blue coat and buff pantaloons, both rather wrinkled, and a very unstandard black hood over his face was standing just inside the door. He did not respond to her comment about the child.

Beth swallowed hard. "Who . . . who are you? What do you want?"

"Miss Castleton?" the apparition queried in a mellow baritone. "What are you doing here?"

She shivered violently, then pulled her shawl more closely around her shoulders. "You know who I am?"

"I would recognize your charming accent anywhere. I am Weymouth. We met at Dunnley's house party."

Weymouth! Oh, she remembered the arrogant earl. Beth would count it a blessing if she forgot the humiliation of their first encounter before her dying day. He had strolled into the drawing room at Dunnley Park hours late, a scowl on his face and the dust of the road on his boots. She hadn't heard all the conversation between Viscount Dunnley and the earl, only the end of it. After ascertaining that Weymouth had brought his cello, the viscount had asked the earl to play a duet with "the lovely and talented Miss Castleton." His toplofty lordship had looked across the room at her, said "I think not," then turned on his heel and left the salon. The next morning at breakfast he had requested an introduction, polite as a parson, as if he had never given her the cut direct.

Despite Weymouth's initial attitude and the fact that whenever he was near a meadow full of butterflies took flight in her stomach, Beth had been drawn to him like iron filings to a magnet. He was intelligent and witty, they shared a love of music, and she had enjoyed the violin and cello duets they had eventually been persuaded to play. She ought to dislike such an arrogant, condescending man. She *did* dislike him. "I remember you, Lord Weymouth. What are you doing here and why are you wearing that hood?"

"I am here because I was abducted."

"Abducted!" Beth shivered again but not from cold. "For what reason and by whom?"

" 'Tis rather a long story, Miss Castleton." She could hear fatigue, and something else, in his voice. "To answer your other question, I am wearing the hood because Arabella would not allow me to see my niece unless I wore it."

"And how are you supposed to see her wearing it?" Beth asked, amused by the illogic. "Is your niece an angelic-looking, curly-haired blonde about four years old and, oh, an inch or two taller than three feet?"

"Yes, that description fits Isabelle. Is she all right?"

Beth walked to the sofa. "She does not appear to be injured, if that is what you are asking, but she is very deeply asleep." Placing a hand on the child's forehead, she assured him, "She isn't feverish, though."

"Thank you. What are you doing here, Miss Castleton?"

"I am in this room waiting to speak to Lady Arabella, but I have no idea how I came to be in this place."

"Do you know where we are?"

"No, my lord, I do not. According to the maid who attended me this morning, I suffered a blow to the head and have been unconscious since I arrived. We are near the ocean, though, or perhaps the Channel. I saw a rocky beach from the window in my bedroom. The sky was very dark, too, as if it is going to storm."

"Well, unless the ship that brought me here traveled in circles, we aren't near the Channel." He paused, tilting his head slightly. "I think you are right about the storm; the wind is very strong."

"Lord Weymouth, would you please take off that hood? It makes you look quite sinister."

"I am sorry for that, ma'am. Unfortunately, I cannot take it off; my hands are tied." He raised his arms so that she could see his wrists.

"Oh my! Would you allow me to remove it?"

"Yes, of course. I am quite certain that isn't what Arabella had in mind, but I haven't the slightest objection to thwarting her plans. I would welcome any assistance you can give me."

Beth eyed him warily, wondering what sort of aid he had in mind. "May I help you to a seat so that I can remove that hood?"

George heard the swishing of her skirts as she walked toward him. Gallantly, he extended his arm.

"Thank you, my lord, but I think it would be best if I escort you. You know what they say about the blind leading." He could hear the smile in her voice. "If you recall, although I am tall for a woman, I have not your lofty inches, so—"

"Lofty?" he quizzed. "Oak trees are lofty. I am merely four inches over six feet."

"And I am four inches under six feet," she retorted with some acerbity, "so you will need to shorten your stride to match mine."

He inclined his head with mock gravity. "I shall do my best."

"We are going to take four steps forward." Grasping his left arm just above the elbow, she suited action to words.

"Now, we turn ninety degrees to the right." George had never heard a lady give directions in geometric terms. The rich, melodious tones of her voice brought to mind his father's violin—or hers—played in the middle register, but the precision of her instructions made him think of his father's mathematical treatises.

"Next, we take three steps forward." It was strange to be escorted by a woman, but her brisk competence was reassuring. "Now, turn ninety degrees to the right." She released his arm and stepped a pace away from him.

"I misjudged your height. You need to step forward about four inches." After he had done so, she said, "I think that will do. The sofa you are about to sit on is lower than most. The seat is about three inches closer to the floor than that of a dining room chair."

"If I fall on the sofa in an ungainly heap, will I injure Isabelle?"

Miss Castleton choked on a giggle. "No, Lord Weymouth, you will not. Your niece is on the sofa facing this one."

"What are you chuckling about?" He had never heard her laugh, but it was a lovely sound, even if it was more nervous than mirthful.

"The image of such a Corinthian as yourself falling awkwardly onto the sofa."

"Rejoicing at my comeuppance, are you?"

"No, my lord, not at all." She grasped his elbow. "You move so gracefully that I cannot imagine you sprawling on the sofa in an ignominious heap."

George was pleased by the compliment, although he wished she found his character equally admirable. He had been attracted to her when they first met, but she did not hold him in esteem. She appreciated his musical talent, but that seemed to be the only thing about him that pleased her. It was almost as if he had offended her in some way—except that was impossible.

In response to her gentle tug on his arm, he lowered himself to the sofa. He was glad she had warned him about the height—or lack thereof—of the seat. Just as he was wondering if she had misjudged the length of his legs, his backside made contact with the sofa.

He heard her walk behind him. Then she said, "I will see if I can remove this hood. While I am doing that, I would like you to tell me what is going on here."

George sighed, wondering where to begin. Stalling for time, he asked, "You truly have no idea how you came to be here?"

Her fingers brushed against his nape where the knot secured the hood, sending a shiver down his spine. "I know very few facts. The maid gave me some information and . . . Well, I can speculate a bit, but I am not entirely certain if those things happened or if I merely dreamed them."

He was not sure what she meant by that last remark and chose to ignore it. Logic was the only way to solve this problem. "What do you know to be true?"

"I know three things for certain. First, that I suffered an injury to my head: I have a bruise on my temple, a large knot on the back of my head, and a pounding headache. Second, that we are near the ocean or the Channel; earlier I could hear the waves pounding on the shore. Third, the view from my bedchamber window doesn't look like any part of Buckinghamshire or Hampshire I have yet seen."

"That is all?" George was appalled, and skeptical, but managed to keep his tone even.

"Yes. Now you understand why I am so confused, and why I am eager to speak with Lady Arabella."

He didn't think talking with Arabella would clarify the situation for the valiant American girl, but he refrained from comment.

"The maid told me a deal more. I assume what she said is true, but I don't know it to be factual." Miss Castleton's fingers ceased their gentle tugging on the knot for a moment. "What day is it?"

"It is Sunday the fourteenth of February, I believe."

"Sunday!" Her tone conveyed her shock at that bit of information. He heard her take a deep breath. "Moira said—that is the maid's name, Moira Sinclair," his intrepid ally explained. "Moira said I injured my head before I arrived here and that I have been here for four or five days. The last thing I remember clearly is having tea with Aunt Julia in the inn at Reading while the horses were changed. That was Monday, early in the afternoon." Her fingers stilled again. "Assuming it took a day or two for me to travel from there to wherever we are, I have, indeed, been here for four or five days."

She resumed her self-appointed task. "Next, the maid told me she had traveled here from London, by boat. The journey seemed to take days, she said, but she was very sick the entire time.

"Ahha!" she exclaimed, a note of triumph in her voice, "I think I have figured out this knot."

George was still skeptical. "Why did the maid tell you all this?"

"I asked questions and she answered them." Obviously his companion thought that was perfectly logical, but he wanted to know why the woman had provided answers. "Moira said Aunt Julia is not here, and that she—the maid, that is—did not believe I was expected because there was no chamber prepared for me."

Interesting, George thought. But how had Beth Castleton gotten tangled into this mess and mistaken for Isabelle's governess?

"The only other thing Moira told me," Miss Castleton said, after a tug on the knot that nearly choked him, "was that I am the only guest here, although two are expected today. If you arrived this morning, you must be one of them. But," she added, a note of distress in her voice, "if the little girl is the other, then the rest of what I believe happened cannot be true."

George reviewed his conversation with Arabella. "I was told that you and Isabelle came here together. And I did, indeed, arrive this morning. Very early."

"Oh! I just remembered something else. Moira said this house is called Gull Cottage, and that it isn't owned by Lady Arabella."

"Gull Cottage! No wonder the dining room looked familiar. How very audacious of Arabella."

"Are you acquainted with Lady Arabella, sir? Do you know where we are?"

"Yes, I know Arabella. Unfortunately. We are near Drummore, Scotland, on the Mull of Galloway. Gull Cottage was one of my grandmother's dower properties." Escape from the cottage was possible. It would not be easy— the windows were small and narrow, and there were few doors—but it was possible. For Miss Castleton and Isabelle. Escape from the peninsula was another matter entirely, especially in light of the approaching storm. If they could steal a horse or carriage from the stable, they could get a start, then seek shelter when the storm broke. Failing that, they would just have to hide—and the stable was the only building within a mile of the cottage.

"Lord Weymouth?"

His companion's query interrupted his plotting. Probably a good thing, since he was getting ahead of himself; she had not yet agreed to help him. "I am sorry, Miss Castleton, I fear I was woolgathering. What did you say? And, please, call me Weymouth."

Without saying a word, she walked around the sofa and stood in front of him. She unwrapped the ties from around his neck, placed her hands on top of his head, and pulled off the hood. He looked up at her, at the tall, slender, lovely young lady with golden brown hair and cornflower blue eyes who might be his salvation. And saw, again, the face that had been haunting his dreams.

Beth removed the hood and looked down at the earl. He was as handsome as she remembered, with his deep blue eyes and sable brown hair. She hadn't noticed before that there was a bit of silver mixed with the brown at his temples. His hair was tousled from the hood. Absentmindedly, she reached out and smoothed it into its usual, neat style.

Realizing the impropriety of her action, she blushed. "I apologize, Lord Weymouth. I—"

He interrupted to say, gallantly, "There is nothing for which you need apologize, Miss Castleton."

"I . . . I, um . . ." Looking away from the probing but kind blue eyes, she attempted to gather her scattered thoughts. She needed to tell him about her dream. She ought to have done that while he was wearing the hood, so she wouldn't have to watch those beautiful eyes turn scornful. As her gaze skittered around, looking everywhere but at his face, she realized his hands were still tied.

She dragged an ottoman to the sofa. "I shall work on the ropes binding your hands while I tell you something I think may have happened."

Seating herself in front of him, Beth attacked the knots in the rope. "This morning, just before I awoke, I had a strange dream. The little girl on the sofa was in it. Is she your niece?"

He started at the question, then looked over her head at the child lying on the facing sofa. "Yes, that is my niece. Her name is Isabelle."

"Well, your niece was in my nightmare. If she and I arrived here together, then what I dreamed may have actually occurred. I . . . I . . ." Beth bit her lip. How could she explain without looking a fool?

"Just explain your dream as if you were telling a story."

She took a deep, calming breath. "About twenty or thirty minutes after the change of horses at Reading, there was a tree that had fallen across the road. Our coachman stopped. I looked out the window and saw, on the other side of the tree, another carriage stopping. A man, a gentleman, jumped down and walked forward to talk to his coachman. Another man, a highwayman or ruffian, hit the gentleman on the head, and he fell to the road. As I was climbing out of our carriage to see if I could aid him, Isabelle tumbled out of the gentleman's chaise calling for her papa."

Beth tugged harder on the knot over his wrist. "John Coachman helped me clamber over the tree trunk. As I approached the other carriage, the highwayman grabbed your niece from where she knelt beside her papa. I yelled at the ruffian, and John shot at him, John hit him in the leg, and he dropped the little girl and ran into the woods bordering the road. I picked up the child and comforted her. Her father was still breathing, so I told her he would be fine. Someone else shot at John." She lifted her head and looked at the earl. "That is all I remember."

"I suspect you were hit on the head by the same person who fired at your coachman. That person, whoever he might be, apparently is responsible for your presence here. Arabella believes you are Isabelle's governess, but the first highwayman would have known you were not traveling in the carriage with David and Isabelle."

Beth was amazed at his calm acceptance of her story. "David is your brother?"

"Yes," Weymouth answered, his eyes troubled. "He is four years younger than I. He lives in Oxfordshire, about twelve miles north of Reading."

"He truly was alive when last I saw him."

"Thank you, Miss Castleton." The smile appeared in his eyes before it touched his lips.

Flustered again, Beth looked down at the rope and worked on unraveling the knots. "How did you come to be here, Weymouth? You said earlier you were abducted. Who would do such a thing, and why?"

He squirmed on the sofa, glanced over at his niece, then began to speak.

Moira stood at the top of the staircase and looked down into the hall. Seeing no one, she scampered down the stairs, then walked quickly to the tiny butler's pantry. Espying the majordomo within, she entered and closed the door. "Henry, the young lady awoke this morn. Miss Castleton she is, and verra nice. We must do something to save her and the bairn from whate'er Lady Arabella and her cousin are plottin'."

"I overheard their plan this morning, when Lady Arabella was having breakfast." The disgust in Henry's voice was clear as a bell. "They intend to force Lord Weymouth into marriage. The little girl is his niece. If his lordship doesn't marry Lady Arabella today, she will take the child and hide her away somewhere. His lordship and his family will never see the child again."

" 'Tis wicked Lady Arabella is! We must save the wee lassie. Can we help them get away from here?" Moira beseeched with voice and eyes.

"I have been thinking on it, and I have an idea. Where is her ladyship now?"

"In her chamber."

"And Tom?"

"With Lady Arabella."

"Do you think they will be up there for long?"

"Hmph," Moira snorted. "Ye know the answer to that as well as I do."

Henry walked to the window and looked out. "No sign of the ship, so we don't have to worry about Sir James for a while." He thought for several seconds, tapping one finger against his jaw. "Let's take a tea tray to the book room. Lord Weymouth and the young lady are there. We can tell them we are willing to help them, and I will explain my idea to his lordship."

"Ye're a gud man, Henry Moreland."

"Moira, I want you to leave with them. Lady Arabella will be very angry if her scheme doesn't work, and although I cannot predict how Sir James will react, I doubt he will be happy. I would feel much better if you were safely away from here."

"I will go with Miss Castleton, and gladly. She is a sweet, kind lady. But," Moira fretted, "how will they escape?"

"Do not worry until we have talked with Lord Weymouth. He may have a plan, too."

"Ach! Dinna worry, he says. How can I do aught else?" Henry patted her hand. "Tell me about Miss Castleton whilst we wait for the kettle to boil."

Beth stared at Weymouth in astonishment, her mind whirling. His tale of abductions, forced marriage, threats, and a deathbed promise sounded like the plot from a Minerva Press novel. A bad one. But he clearly believed Lady Arabella would do as she had threatened, and he wasn't a man to fly up into the boughs needlessly.

"I . . . I . . ." Beth shook her head, uncertain what to say, then resumed work on the knots in the cord binding his wrists. She knew he was looking at her; she could feel his gaze.

"Miss Castleton, will you help me?"

"Of course I will. No one should be forced into marriage, and no child should be torn from her family. But what can I do?"

"Will you take my niece away from here? If I know Isabelle is safe, I can refuse to marry Arabella."

"I am willing to try, Weymouth. Do you want—"

Beth started when the door opened. Glancing over her shoulder she saw Moira and a manservant—the butler, judging from his attire—enter the room, the latter carrying a tea tray. The maid closed the door as the man set the tray on a table.

"Lord Weymouth, Miss Castleton, we have come to offer our assistance," the man said.

"You are Lady Arabella's servants but you wish to help me?" The earl's tone was incredulous.

"Yes, my lord. We work for Lady Arabella, but we don't share her morals."

" 'Tisna right what she is doin'," Moira exclaimed.

Beth glanced at Weymouth and voiced the question she saw in his eyes. "What do you think you can do to help his lordship?"

The butler introduced himself and Moira, then crossed the room to stand in front of Beth and the earl. "Shall I try my hand at that knot, miss?"

"If you like. I am having a hard time with this last one." She stood and stepped away, seating herself at the end of the sofa on which Isabelle slept.

The servant—Henry Moreland by name—sat down, looked Weymouth in the eye, then went to work on the rope. "I was thinking that I could order the carriage made ready, with his lordship's portmanteau and the child's on it. Some of Lady Arabella's things would have to be put on there, too, so the groom would think the order came from her ladyship. Then, miss, you and Moira could carry the little girl out to the carriage."

"Ye will hae to make Will come into the house, Henry," Moira interposed. "He would think it strange that I was in the coach before Lady Arabella."

"What about Miss Castleton's luggage?" Weymouth queried.

"She doesna hae any."

Beth looked at Henry. "Who will drive the carriage? And how do you plan to get Lord Weymouth into the coach without Lady Arabella knowing of it?"

"You or his lordship will have to drive the carriage, miss. Will is both groom and coachman, and he is loyal to Lady Arabella."

"Sailing would be better," the earl declared. "We would get to London more quickly, and there would be less chance of pursuit. Is there a boat we can use?"

"The yacht that brought you here has left, my lord. When it returns, Sir James—Lady Arabella's cousin—will undoubtedly be on it. You need to be gone before then, and I don't know of any other boats about."

Weymouth muttered something under his breath. Beth did not know if his grumbling was due to the lack of a sailboat or Sir James's probable involvement in his cousin's scheme, but it did not matter. They had to work with the resources they had.

"Back to Henry's plan," she said, her tone cheerful and optimistic. "How large is this carriage and how many horses?" Thanks to her grandfather's lessons, Beth could drive a team, but she was more comfortable with a pair.

" 'Tis Lady Arabella's traveling chaise, miss. Four horses."

Weymouth looked at her, one eyebrow raised in question. "Can you drive a carriage, Miss Castleton?"

"Yes, but I have never driven four in hand for long distances. Only a stage or two."

"You are a lady of many talents."

She blushed at the compliment but continued plotting their escape. "Moira, would you be willing to travel with me and take care of the child? And accept a position as my lady's maid afterward?"

"Oh, aye, miss. Gladly." Moira's smile beamed like a candle in the dark.

Beth glanced at the butler, who still worked on the knots binding the earl's wrists. "Do you intend to travel with us, Henry? And I don't believe you ever answered my question about Lord Weymouth."

"I would be pleased to travel with you, miss, but only if we can get his lordship safely away. If we can't, I will stay and help him."

The manservant looked the earl in the eye. "I just don't know if we can get you into the carriage, my lord. I thought, if we could get the child safely away, you would have a reason not to marry Lady Arabella today. She and her cousin will likely send Tom and Will chasing after the child. You can follow the ladies later, on horseback."

"It is a very good plan, Henry," Weymouth stated. "I will see you well rewarded for this day's work."

"Well, my lord, if you should happen to be needing a footman, that would be reward enough."

"An underbutler is what you will be if this succeeds."

"Thank you, sir." Henry's smile reached from ear to ear. "There," he said a few moments later, untying the rope from the earl's wrists. "I will order the carriage made ready now, my lord. I don't know how much longer Lady Arabella will remain abovestairs. If she comes down before the carriage is ready, perhaps you can argue with her until we get Miss Castleton, your niece, and Moira into the carriage and away."

Weymouth chuckled. "I think I can provide sufficient distraction."

The butler bowed formally, then walked to the door. "Moira, you had best go pack your things, and the child's."

"Aye. I will return as soon as e'er I can, Miss Castleton." After a quick curtsy, the maid followed Henry from the room.

Weymouth crossed to the tea tray and poured two cups. He brought one to Beth, where she sat next to the still sleeping Isabelle, then seated himself on the facing sofa. "It seems almost too good to be true, doesn't it? Do you think it could be a trap?"

"I believe Moira wants to help. She is afraid of Lady Arabella, with good reason. Henry seems sincere, and I count it in his favor that he will not leave until you are safe, but that could be a ruse. You must make the decision to trust them or not, Weymouth. You have the most to lose."

Frowning, he curled his fingers around the teacup and set the saucer aside. "Who taught you to drive a team? Could you drive one for a long distance?"

"My grandfather taught me." Beth smiled in remembrance. "I think I could drive a team for most of a day, if the horses worked well together. But if I have to work to keep them up to their bits, my arms will tire and I won't be able drive as long.

"The main problem is that I have only the vaguest notion of our present location. As for getting from here to London"—she shrugged—"I would drive east until I found a main road going south, I suppose."

His frown eased, almost becoming a smile. "That will work, but you must go north from here to get off the Mull, the peninsula. Then east until you reach the road to Carlisle, then south to London."

"It would be much better, Weymouth, if we can get you into the carriage. I—"

Suddenly, Isabelle awoke, catapulted into Beth's lap, and threw her arms around Beth's neck. "Pretty lady, you are finally awake!"

Beth placed her cup and saucer on the table next to the sofa, then hugged the little girl. "Yes, Isabelle, I am awake and so are you."

"What, Isabelle? No hugs for your Uncle George?"

Isabelle bounced off Beth's lap and scrambled into her uncle's outstretched arms. "Uncle George! You must save me from the mean lady."

"I will, little one. Miss Castleton, the pretty lady, is going to help."

"Good. Else that bad man might hurt her again."

"Which bad man?"

Isabelle wrinkled her nose. "The black-haired, ugly one. Tom. He hurted her head when she was helping Papa and me."

Weymouth settled the child in his lap. "Listen to me, Isabelle. In a little while, Miss Castleton is going to take you to a carriage. A maid will go with you. When it is time to leave this room, you must not say anything—not even one word—until you are in the carriage. You must be a very good girl and do just as Miss Castleton and Moira say. They will take you to Grandpa, and he will take you home to your papa. Do you understand?"

The child nodded solemnly. "Isn't you going to come, Uncle George?"

"I . . . I . . ." The earl looked at Beth, his gaze beseeching.

"Isabelle, your Uncle George will come with us if he can, but he might have to stay here to make sure the mean lady and the bad man don't chase after us. If Uncle George can't come with us today, he will ride as fast as he can to catch up to us tomorrow."

"It will be better if Uncle George comes with us," Isabelle declared. Beth wholeheartedly agreed.

"I will come today if I can, little one," Weymouth promised. "If not, I will catch up to you tomorrow."

The book room door opened, and Moira entered. "Nearly ready, m'lord." She walked over to Isabelle and whispered in her ear. The child nodded, climbed from her uncle's lap, and took Moira's hand. "We will be right back. Er, Miss Castleton, would you like to come with us?"

"No, thank you, Moira, but please bring my pelisse when you return."

"Aye, miss, that I will."

The earl stood. "Miss Castleton, thank you for helping me."

Beth rose to stand in front of him. "I have not done anything yet."

"You are doing a great deal, and a good deed, by spiriting my niece to safety. When you reach London, take her to my father, the Marquess of Bellingham."

"You will be with us long before we reach London."

"I will join you as soon as I can. If I can," he added ominously.

"Weymouth, you are frightening me!"

"I don't mean to, but it is best to face facts. I may not be—"

Moira and Isabelle slipped into the room. "Quick, miss, put on yer pelisse. Henry says 'tis time to get in the carriage."

As Weymouth assisted Beth into her wrap, someone pounded on a nearby door. Angry voices resonated in the hallway just outside the book room.

Chapter 3

$\mathcal{T}$he reactions of his companions to the commotion in the hallway demonstrated their character and experience, George believed. Isabelle scampered to his side and clung to his leg, whimpering softly. Moira's eyes opened wide. She put the back of her left hand against her mouth, as if to prevent any sound from emerging, and looked to Beth Castleton for direction. The American girl tensed, then took Isabelle's hand in one of hers and held out the other to the maid.

"If anyone enters," his intrepid ally whispered looking at the Scotswoman, "we shall say we are going to take Isabelle for a walk before the storm breaks."

Moira nodded, her expression easing, and Miss Castleton glanced up at him. "Weymouth, will you make your stand now or later?"

"Later, if at all possible," he answered quietly.

"Then perhaps you should sit in that chair by the fireplace and read a book. It wouldn't do to look as if you are plotting an escape."

Henry's voice joined the others in the hallway. "Good morning, Reverend Southwick, Sir James." His next words were chiding. "Tom, why haven't you taken her ladyship's uncle to the parlor and offered him refreshments?" The voices faded as the speakers moved down the hall.

Miss Castleton took a deep breath, then looked at the maid. "Should we go out to the carriage, do you think?"

"I dinna ken, miss." If the valiant American weren't holding Moira's hand, the terrified Scotswoman would be wringing her hands.

Miss Castleton walked to the door, eased it partially

open, looked out, then closed the door quietly. "I don't see anyone in the hall," she reported when she rejoined them.

This was the best opportunity they were likely to have. Handing her his purse, George instructed, "Go now. And go with God."

"In the event we stray from the right roads and you can't find us, you will need money for your own travel."

Acknowledging the wisdom of her words, he removed sufficient funds to cover a journey to London, then gave her the purse.

She placed it in her reticule, then looked up at him, a question in her eyes.

"Go now," he repeated. "Wait five minutes for me, then leave. If anyone comes out of the house, leave immediately."

His valiant ally nodded, but her expression was still troubled. Bending down, she put her arm around Isabelle. "Little one, it is time to go. Say goody-bye to your uncle, then you must be quiet as a mouse until we get into the carriage. When we walk outside, I will hold one of your hands and Moira will hold the other. Moira and I will take good care of you until Uncle George comes."

"I will be good," his niece promised in a whisper. She looked up at him, and he knelt to hug her. "I love you, Uncle George. Hurry up and come to the carriage."

George swallowed, but the lump in his throat remained. "I love you, too, Isabelle. I will join you in the carriage if I can. Otherwise I will catch up to you tomorrow. Be a good girl until I get there."

"I will, Uncle George."

After giving his niece another hug, George stood. Isabelle immediately reached for Miss Castleton's hand. She smiled at the child, then glanced up at him. "We will wait five minutes."

He watched them walk to the door. "Thank you, Miss Castleton."

As she glided through the portal, she smiled over her shoulder at him. It was a very wobbly smile.

Beth walked with Moira and Isabelle toward the front door of the cottage. She was glad it was only a few steps from the book room door; the bones in her legs seemed to have turned to water. A woman's voice joined the male voices in the parlor. Lady Arabella, undoubtedly. That didn't bode well for Weymouth getting to the carriage, Beth thought, sighing.

Moira eased the front door open, and they stepped outside. The sky was still gray, the clouds dark and heavy. The wind was brisk and rather chill. A carriage was standing in the drive, four horses in harness, and a groom at the leaders' heads. *Darn and double darn!*

"Moira," Beth breathed, "tell the groom he is needed inside the house."

"Will," the maid called, "Henry needs you inside."

"I can't go inside. I must hold the horses." The man's accent was very broad.

"I could hold them for you." Beth gave Isabelle's hand a squeeze before releasing it and walking toward the groom.

The groom scratched his chin. "I reckon that would be all right."

Beth rubbed the nose of the near leader. "They are beautiful animals. What are their names?"

He told her the names and characteristics of each animal. When he began detailing their pedigrees, Moira reminded him that he was needed inside.

"Right. Thank ye, miss." The groom bowed awkwardly. "I will be back as quick as I can."

As soon as Will entered the house, Beth told Moira to get into the carriage. The maid lifted Isabelle inside, then climbed in herself. As Beth clambered up to the box, she realized she was missing a vital piece of information. Weymouth had told her to go north until she was off the Mull, but the clouds completely obscured the sun and she had no idea which direction was north. After checking that the reins were secure and the brake was set, she climbed down then opened the carriage door. "Moira, on which side of the house does the sun rise in the morning?"

The maid's blank expression indicated her answer before she spoke. "I dinna ken, miss. I havena been outside until today."

"Uncle George will know," Isabelle piped up.

Beth smiled at the little girl and queried the maid. "Was it bright in my room in the mornings?"

"I dinna open the draperies. I feared the light would hurt yer eyes."

Beth looked at the sky again, to no avail. "I do not know which way is north. I will have to go back inside and ask Lord Weymouth or Henry. You and Isabelle stay here and be very quiet."

"Aye, miss, that we will."

"I won't talk until you come back, pretty lady," Isabelle promised.

Beth brushed a finger against the child's cheek, then closed the carriage door.

Walking quickly toward the house, Beth studied the large, L-shaped structure. Idly, she wondered if the short leg of the L, which contained the entry hall and the book room, had been a later addition to the house. She climbed the three front steps, then quietly opened the door.

After easing the door shut, she stood in a shadowed corner of the entry hall looking and listening. She didn't see Henry or George. Nor Will or the "black-haired, ugly" Tom. She much preferred to avoid an encounter with the latter two men, as well as with Sir James. Voices raised in anger came from the direction of the parlor. She recognized George's mellow baritone, Lady Arabella's rather shrill soprano, and the rounded, rolling bass tones of another man. The minister, perhaps. That deep, mellifluous voice should be preaching in a cathedral, not arguing in a remote country parlor. She couldn't hear Henry or Will, nor the unknown Tom and Sir James. If any of the four were in the room, they were silent witnesses to the argument raging there.

She couldn't stand here like a ninny; the five minutes had nearly elapsed. She would have to search out Henry to get the answer to her question. Beth took a deep breath, squared her shoulders, and walked farther into the house.

She sidled along the wall, past the book room and the turn toward the parlor, then quietly opened a door on the left. The dining room. Empty. Next to it was a small pantry. Also empty. She heard clattering pots and French imprecations in the kitchen. Definitely not Henry's voice, and she had no wish to encounter the cook.

The parlor was the only other room on this floor, unless a small room lay beyond the kitchen. Since Henry was unlikely to be found in that hypothetical room, she would have to brave the parlor. Beth's heart sank to the vicinity of her knees as she pondered the best approach. A bewildered innocent disturbed by the noise should do the trick, she thought. A few hours ago she had been exactly that. *Dear God, please help me pull this off without endangering Isabelle or George.*

Rubbing her aching temples, Beth headed toward the parlor, then stopped abruptly. Would a concussed, confused innocent wear a pelisse inside the house? Probably not, she concluded, unbuttoning hers and slipping it off. Carrying it over her arm, she approached the large salon.

Henry emerged from the kitchen, placed a large tea tray on the hall table, and stood quietly in the shadows beneath the staircase. He didn't have anything so definite as a plan, but he was determined to do whatever he could to help Lord Weymouth. Bringing tea into the parlor might provide a useful distraction. Especially, Henry thought with a grin, if he dropped the heavily laden tray. He listened to the escalating argument, waiting for an opportune moment.

His eyes nearly popped from their sockets when he saw Miss Castleton approach the parlor. Will had said that Moira, the young lady, and the little girl were taking a walk. Instead of tooling the carriage up the Mull as she should be, Miss Castleton was strolling toward the salon as if escape were the farthest thing from her mind. Frowning, Henry watched her, wondering what had gone wrong.

Rubbing her temples, she stood to one side of the open doors as if studying the scene within. Perhaps she, too, had a plan to help Lord Weymouth. Henry believed the earl would prefer Miss Castleton to be driving his niece toward London instead of assisting his escape. But she wasn't, so Henry resolved to do whatever he could to get Miss Castleton and Lord Weymouth out to the carriage and safely away.

As he watched, her expression changed from scrutinizing to bewildered, and she stepped into the open doorway. "What in the world is going on here?"

Miss Castleton looked and sounded as confused and innocent as a child. It was a plan of sorts, Henry supposed. He carried the tea tray across the hall and took up her previous post beside the doors.

At the sound of Miss Castleton's voice, Lord Weymouth,

Lady Arabella, and Reverend Southwick fell silent. The three of them, as well as Tom and Sir James, turned to look at her. His lordship's expression was anguished.

"What is going on here?" Miss Castleton rubbed her temples. Henry wondered if she still suffered from the headache or if she was only pretending.

"Who are you?" inquired Reverend Southwick. "I am sorry if our noise disturbed you."

"I am Miss Castleton. And, yes, your shouting is distressing. Why are you arguing?"

"Our disagreement is no concern of yours," Lady Arabella snapped, her tone dismissive.

"Allow me to escort you to a quieter room, miss," Lord Weymouth said as he walked toward Miss Castleton.

"She don't need no escort, yer lordship," Tom stated. "And you ain't leavin' this room."

"You cannot order Lord Weymouth about," the clergyman admonished.

"I can and will," the dark-haired man sneered, pulling a pistol from the pocket of his jacket. "This little beauty gives me the right."

"No, Tom!" Lady Arabella and Sir James shouted in unison, clearly displeased.

"What . . . what . . ." Reverend Southwick blanched at the sight of the gun.

Lord Weymouth was nearly at the door. It was now or never, Henry decided, before someone was hurt. Carrying the tray, he stepped into the room. "Here is your tea, my lady." As he passed the earl, Henry muttered, "Take Miss Castleton and leave now, my lord."

George watched, astonished, as the manservant stepped between him and the pistol Tom brandished. George didn't want Henry sacrificing his life, but it was too late to do anything about it now except take the generously offered opportunity to escape. As Arabella and Sir James berated Tom and the clergyman remonstrated with Arabella, George advanced to Beth and extended his arm. "May I escort you to another room, Miss Castleton?"

Two steps and they would be in the hallway. His heart in his throat, George took the first stride.

All hell broke loose in the room behind him.

The pistol barked. Beth Castleton gasped and crumpled

against his side. Glancing down at her, George saw blood spilling from a wound high on her back, near her left shoulder. He scooped her up in his arms and ran down the hall toward the front door. Arabella screamed, Reverend Southwick fussed, china shattered, and Tom bellowed, "Git outta me way." *Good man, Henry!* George shifted the burden in his arms and pulled open the door.

He raced down the steps and across the drive to the carriage. It appeared empty, but Moira pushed open the door from inside. She crouched on the floor, her body cradling his niece. George laid his valiant ally on the rear-facing seat. "Miss Castleton has been shot. Left shoulder." He gave the maid his handkerchief and tore off his cravat. "Make a pad and try to stop the bleeding. When we are safely away, I will stop and we can do a better job of it."

Isabelle was wide-eyed and trembling. He tousled her curls. "Help Moira take care of the pretty lady, little one; I have to drive the carriage. Hang on tight," he added with a wink. "I'm going to spring 'em."

He slammed the carriage door and mounted the box just as the front door of the cottage crashed open. Grabbing the reins, he released the brake and glanced over his shoulder at his pursuers. Henry ran toward the coach, two great-coats and a bundle in his arm. Tom stood in the doorway, reloading his pistol. George reached down, pulled Henry onto the box, then gave the horses their heads.

Chapter 4

*T*he horses careened down the drive. George wanted to put as much distance between them and Arabella's pistol-wielding footman as he could. As quickly as possible. He knew the bouncing of the carriage would be painful for Miss Castleton, and hard on Isabelle and Moira, but a bit of jostling—well, quite a lot of jostling—was better than dying. Tom was ready and willing to use that gun again.

George glanced at Henry, shivering on the box beside him. "Put your coat on, man. Then you can take the reins while I put on mine."

Henry blanched. "I can't take the reins. I've never driven aught but a gig."

"Put your coat on. Then you can help me into mine."

Accustomed to obeying orders, the servant donned his coat. "Er, how will you put your coat on, my lord? Without giving me the reins."

"One arm at a time." George grinned, exuberant at their escape. "I want a straight section of road to do it, though."

A few moments later he spoke again, his tone serious. "Henry, I thank you for what you did in there. It was very brave, and very foolish, of you to step between Tom and me, but I thank you."

"It wasn't so brave or foolish as all that, my lord. I knew Tom wouldn't shoot me. I hoped to throw off his aim so you and Miss Castleton could leave the room."

"You succeeded. Instead of putting a ball in my heart, Tom hit Miss Castleton in the shoulder."

Henry moaned. "Miss Castleton was shot?"

"Yes. We need to find a safe place to stop. And a sur-

geon. There may be one in Portpatrick or in Glenluce. I
know there is one in Newton Stewart.''

"How far from here are those places?"

"Portpatrick is twelve or fifteen miles from here. Glenluce is about fifteen miles beyond that and Newton Stewart
another fifteen to twenty miles.''

"I think, for Miss Castleton's sake, we should try Portpatrick."

"How many men will Arabella and her cousin send chasing after us?" George's tone was urgent.

Henry's voice, in contrast, was decidedly smug. "There
are only an ancient coach, two equally ancient carriage
horses, and two hacks in the stables. One is quite old, the
other is Lady Arabella's hunter. Will is a good horseman,
but he's too heavy for either animal. Tom doesn't ride, at
least not that I've ever seen, but the horses are up to his
weight. Lady Arabella may chase after us on her hunter,
but I imagine they will harness up the coach—and it, by
some quirk of fate, is missing several of the pins that hold
the wheels on the axles.'' He patted his pocket and grinned.

George chuckled and settled the horses into a canter.
"Did you really drop the tea tray?"

"Indeed I did. It made quite a satisfactory mess. And I
threw the tray at Tom before I ran out of the room.''

"You are a good man, Henry. I am pleased to have you
in my service, but it may be necessary for you to learn to
drive before you begin your new duties. Or to help Moira
take care of Miss Castleton and my niece.''

"I am willing to learn, my lord, or to help Moira.''

A mile or so later George shifted all the reins to his right
hand. "I would like your help in putting on my greatcoat
now. Left arm first." After several precarious minutes, and
a great deal of shifting about, the coat was, more or less,
in place. Then, the task accomplished, George inquired,
"Been a valet, have you?"

"Not a valet, no, but I was a batman in the army."

"What regiment and whom did you serve?"

"The Ninth Dragoons. I served Captain Gardner.''

Surprised that Henry hadn't named an infantry regiment,
George's gaze darted to his new servant. "I was a major in
the Sixteenth Dragoons. Are—''

Moira pushed open the trap. "Lord Weymouth, the

bleeding hae slowed a bit, but Miss Castleton needs a surgeon. The ball, 'tis still in her shoulder."

George swore silently but fiercely. "The nearest town is ten or twelve miles away. Will Miss Castleton be all right until then?"

"I reckon she will hae to be. How long a time, m'lord?"

"Perhaps an hour and a half."

Moira mumbled something in Gaelic. "I shall do my best to make her comfortable. If ye see a stream or well, some water would be verra helpful."

"Henry will watch for water. How are you and my niece holding up?

"The bairn is worrit about Miss Castleton but happy to be wi' ye. I am glad to be serving Miss Castleton and nae Lady Arabella. Thank ye for bringin' me wi' ye."

"You owe your thanks to Miss Castleton, not me."

"To the both of ye, I think," Moira said, then closed the trap.

Neither man spoke for several miles. George broke the silence when he could no longer suppress the question that had been puzzling him for nearly an hour. "Why the devil did Miss Castleton come back into the house?"

"I don't know, my lord. You could have knocked me over with a feather when I carried the tea tray into the hall and saw her walking toward the parlor. I thought something must have gone wrong, but I couldn't figure out what it was." Henry scratched his head. "I still can't.

"It was the most amazing thing." The manservant's voice was warm with admiration. "Miss Castleton stood to the side of the parlor doors, rubbing her forehead and . . . studying the people in the room, I suppose. Then, all of a sudden, her expression changed to one of befuddlement. When she stepped into the room and asked what was going on, she appeared as confused and innocent as Miss Isabelle. Too different from the decisive young lady in the book room to be real, I thought."

His expression pensive, Henry suggested, "Perhaps it was a ruse to get you out of the house, but I thought Miss Castleton understood that she was to take your niece and Moira away whilst I assisted you."

"I am certain that Miss Castleton understood that she was to take Isabelle and Moira to safety. I told her to wait five minutes for me, but to leave immediately if anyone came out of the house."

A slight frown creased George's brow. "I am as perplexed as you are, and you can be certain I will ask her about it later. I don't know Miss Castleton well, but this seems out of character. She is independent and rather prickly, but far from foolish. Dauntingly intelligent, in fact."

"I have known some scholarly men who had no sense of how to go on in the world, but in the book room Miss Castleton seemed quite needle-witted."

George nodded. He'd been impressed by her logic as she plotted their escape. "I believe she is."

"Moira might know why Miss Castleton came back inside."

"Perhaps, but I prefer to ask Miss Castleton."

The two men sat in silence for the next few miles. George pondered where they could hide while Miss Castleton recovered from her injury. Arabella and her cousin, or whomever she sent after them, would check every town with a posting inn. Ergo, they couldn't stay at an inn. He ran through a list of his friends and relatives, seeking one with an estate or hunting lodge in this area. His father had an estate north of Dumfries, but that was nearly a hundred miles away. Wrexton! Well, he was Elston now, but that didn't change the fact that the man had a hunting lodge near Newton Stewart. There was a fishing lodge, too, even farther west. *Think, George, think.* Stranraer. Hawthorn Lodge, about a mile west of Stranraer.

He gave himself a mental pat on the back before turning to his companion. "I just remembered that a friend of mine has a fishing lodge near Stranraer. We can stay there for a few days until Miss Castleton recovers enough to travel."

"Is Stranraer closer than Portpatrick? Or more likely to have a surgeon?"

George consulted a mental map of western Scotland. "They are both about the same distance from here. And, I imagine, about equally likely to have a doctor. It is only five miles or so from Stranraer to Portpatrick. If there isn't a surgeon in Stranraer, I will send someone to Portpatrick to inquire there. The advantage to Stranraer is that we won't have to stay at an inn. Arabella and Sir James, or whoever they send chasing us, will check all the inns."

"The posting inns, certainly. I wonder," Henry mused, "if Tom knows he hit Miss Castleton. If so, they may seek out surgeons, asking if they have treated a young lady who was shot."

"That is a chance we will have to take."

"What if . . ." Henry swallowed then squared his shoulders. "What if there isn't a doctor or surgeon in Stranraer or Portpatrick?"

"We will cross that bridge if we come to it." George knew his expression was grim, but Henry was well aware of their perilous situation. "We could travel on to Glenluce, but it isn't any more likely to have a surgeon than Portpatrick. I know there is a doctor in Newton Stewart, but that is too far away.

"If worse comes to worst, I can try to remove the ball from Miss Castleton's shoulder. I did it in the Peninsula after our surgeon was wounded, but I never expected to do such a thing again." George shuddered. "Does Moira have any skill at doctoring?"

"I don't know about doctoring, but she makes salves and tisanes. She has a box of herbs and such, but I don't know if she brought them here."

"Let's hope she did."

George slowed the horses to a walk as they approached a crossroads. "Does that signpost indicate the road to Stranraer or Portpatrick?"

"Portpatrick three miles to the left, Stranraer four miles straight ahead."

He set the team in motion along the road to Stranraer. Moira opened the trap. "How much longer, Lord Weymouth? Miss Castleton fainted aboot a mile back."

"About half an hour. We are going to a fishing lodge owned by a friend of mine. It will be more comfortable for Miss Castleton, and safer for all of us. We will stop once more to inquire the surgeon's direction. By then we will be only a mile from the lodge."

" 'Tis a good idea, the lodge," Moira opined before closing the trap.

A frown pleated Henry's brow. "Do Lady Arabella or Sir James know your friend? Would they think to look for you there?"

"Arabella knows Elston, but I would be very surprised

if she knows of his Scottish properties. Of course," George added, both voice and expression rueful, "I would not have expected her to know about Gull Cottage, either."

"It isn't one of her father's estates?"

"No. It is one of my father's."

That remark having rendered Henry speechless, George returned to his planning. He needed to send word to his brother that Isabelle was fine and with him. And inform his father that his heir was alive and well but temporarily detained in Scotland. Miss Castleton would want to write her uncle. If she wasn't able to do so, he would do it for her.

He didn't think there would be servants at the lodge. A caretaker, probably, but more than that was unlikely. They needed food, too, and fodder for the horses. *Damnation, things were getting complicated.*

"Henry, does Moira cook?"

"Some, I reckon; most women do. And I can cook a nice pot of stew."

"I am a dab hand at eggs and bacon," George said, "but that and sandwiches are about the extent of my culinary skills."

"Between the three of us, we should be able to put food on the table, even if it isn't quite what you and Miss Castleton are accustomed to."

When they reached the town of Stranraer, George was delighted to realize that he remembered the way to the lodge. He had worried that he would have to ask, which would increase the chances of Arabella and Sir James finding them. George stopped at The Thistle and sent Henry in to ask the surgeon's direction.

George's stomach knotted at the glum expression on the manservant's face when he scrambled back up on the box. "There isn't a doctor or surgeon in Stranraer, my lord. They had a doctor, a good one apparently, but he died a few months back. There is a surgeon in Portpatrick, but the innkeeper says he is a drunkard not fit to treat a dog. He didn't know if there is one in Glenluce."

"Damn!" George tooled the horses out of the inn's courtyard and set them along the road to the lodge at a brisk trot while Henry relayed the bad news to Moira. Halfway to the lodge, the storm broke, the rain coming down in torrents.

"Devil take it, can nothing go right!" George hunched his shoulders and lowered his chin, wondering when he and his hat had parted company. Probably two days ago, when his abductors cracked him over the head.

"What's amiss, my lord? Other than the fact we are getting very wet."

"That plus the fact that we need food and fodder. I doubt that there are many provisions at the lodge."

"I can ride back into town later and get what we need."

"I daresay you will have to. I, apparently, will be acting the surgeon." George swore again. "If Miss Castleton doesn't have a good reason for coming back into the house, I am likely to take off her head."

"No you won't," Henry stated with calm conviction.

"What makes you so sure of that?"

"If it wasn't for Miss Castleton, you might well be married to Lady Arabella now. Things were not in your favor when Miss Castleton entered the parlor."

"Very true. Tom was about ready to use that pistol to force me in front of the minister and to persuade him to perform the ceremony. But the marriage wouldn't have been legal."

"Because you were forced into it?"

"Yes." George glanced to the right, looking for the lodge gates.

"Wouldn't you have to prove that? If you said you were coerced and Lady Arabella said you weren't, it would be your word against hers."

"The witnesses would know I did not marry willingly. The minister, too."

"If you think Tom would speak in your favor, you'd best think again. I doubt Reverend Southwick and Sir James would, either; Lady Arabella is, after all, their relative."

George feathered the turn between the gateposts marking the entrance to Hawthorn Lodge. "All things considered, I will ignore Miss Castleton's head and concentrate on her shoulder."

"I knew you would, my lord."

"Our luck may have taken a turn for the better. The lodge appears to be occupied."

"We will find out when we knock on the door," said the pragmatic Henry.

George stopped the carriage in front of the house, then secured the reins and set the brake. Before he could descend from the box, the front door opened and Higgins, formerly Elston's batman and now his valet, descended the steps carrying an umbrella.

Higgins peered at him through the downpour. "Lord Weymouth?"

"Yes, Higgins, it is I. Is Elston here?"

"Yes, sir, he is. He didn't mention he was expecting you."

"He didn't know I was coming. Hell, I didn't know myself until about an hour ago."

"My lord?" Higgins clearly was puzzled by that remark.

"It is a long story—and not a pretty one." George opened the carriage door, helped Moira out, hugged his niece and swung her down, then lifted Miss Castleton, who was still unconscious, and carried her into the house. Higgins herded Moira, Henry, and Isabelle inside. When George entered, Robert Symington, the Marquess of Elston, was standing in the hall.

"George, this is an unexpected surprise!" Elston smiled, unflappable as ever, looking as if unexpected visitors, including unconscious, bleeding ones, were an everyday occurrence.

"A pleasant one, I hope." George forced a smile, but knew it was a poor effort.

"Yes, of course. Are you going to introduce me to your companions?"

"The lady in my arms in Miss Beth Castleton. She has been shot and still carries the ball in her shoulder. The little cherub is my niece, Miss Isabelle Winterbrook." Seeing Elston's upraised eyebrow, George returned a surprised look and introduced the servants. "The lady holding Isabelle's hand is Moira Sinclair, Miss Castleton's maid. And the man standing beside me is Henry . . . um . . ."

"Henry Moreland, my lord." His new underbutler bowed to the marquess.

"Let's get you settled into rooms." Elston led the way up the stairs.

"Robert, what do you know about the surgeon in

Portpatrick?" George's immediate concern was his valiant rescuer. Anything else—everything else—could wait.

"Only that he is said to be a drunken sot not fit to treat man or beast."

"Did the innkeeper tell you that?"

"No, my housekeeper." The marquess's eyebrow rose again.

"The innkeeper in Stranraer told us the same thing," George explained. "There isn't a doctor or surgeon here, so we must either call in the surgeon from Portpatrick or remove the ball from Miss Castleton's shoulder ourselves."

"Mrs. Maxwell may have experience with that sort of thing. I do not recommend the man from Portpatrick."

"I hope Mrs. Maxwell is an expert. I don't fancy acting the surgeon again."

"Again? Have you done it before?" Elston's tone reflected his surprise.

"Yes, in Spain, after the regimental surgeon was wounded."

"Good God." The marquess opened a door at the top of the stairs. "Put the young lady in here, George. Higgins, ask Mrs. Maxwell to come up."

"Yes, my lord, as soon as I show the little girl and her maid to a room."

George gently laid Beth Castleton on the large tester bed. "Henry, would you bring our things in from the coach?"

"Yes, my lord. Let me light the fire first. Er, what about the extra things we put on?"

George frowned. "What extra things?"

"If you recall, we included some of her ladyship's things to fool the coachman."

"Bring those in as well. Miss Castleton may be able to use some of them."

When the fire was crackling in the grate, Henry left the room. Elston, his brown eyes bright with curiosity, turned to George. "I hope you plan to give me a round tale, my friend."

George ran a hand through his hair. "Sometimes, Robert, truth is stranger than fiction."

Chapter 5

❧

*B*eth woke to the sound of men's voices and a burning pain in her left shoulder. Once again, she was in a strange room, but this time there was a familiar person in it. Weymouth. He and a man she didn't know were standing near the hearth. The stranger was a fine figure of a man, an inch or two over six feet, with the same broad shoulders and slim hips Weymouth had. His hair was darker, though—black as sin her grandmother would have called it—and his eyes were chocolate brown. He was a good-looking man, with a broad forehead, patrician nose, and lean cheeks, but he wasn't as handsome as the earl.

There shouldn't be men in her bedchamber. She opened her mouth to say so but the only sound that emerged was a moan. Both men immediately turned toward her.

Weymouth crossed the room and sat on the edge of the bed, then took her right hand in his. "How do you feel, Beth?"

"Shoulder . . . hurts."

As he opened his mouth to ask another question, a short, plump woman with a round face, bright brown eyes, rosy cheeks, and gray hair bustled in carrying a tray full of bandages and little bottles. She was followed by a short, wiry man with a large kettle of water and what appeared to be a doctor's satchel. He dropped the satchel in the corner, placed the kettle on a hook over the fire, then left the room.

The woman, whose apron and cap proclaimed her the housekeeper, set the tray on a table near the bed then came to stand beside the earl. "Mr. Higgins said the young lady has been shot?"

"Yes. The young lady is Miss Castleton." The housekeeper curtsied and smiled at Beth as Weymouth continued his explanation. "The ball is still in her shoulder and must be removed immediately. Have you any experience with doctoring?"

All the color left the housekeeper's cheeks. "No, Lord Weymouth, none at all. I . . . I come over faint whene'er I see blood. I can offer my uncle's satchel, though."

"Your uncle's satchel?" Clearly Weymouth was as puzzled by that remark as Beth herself was.

"My uncle was the surgeon in Stranraer until he died a few months back. He carried the satchel when he made his calls. I thought there might be things in there you could use." The woman pinned the earl with a stern look. "You are planning to do this yourself and not call in that butcher from Portpatrick, right?"

"Yes." The word was accompanied by a sigh. "Perhaps you will entertain my niece so that Miss Castleton's maid can help me?"

"Indeed I will. Children are one of life's pleasures," the housekeeper pronounced. "I will send the maid in straightaway, my lord."

As soon as the housekeeper departed, Henry entered. He dropped a portmanteau near the armoire. "Where shall I put your things, Lord Weymouth?"

"The room across the hall," the stranger directed. As he turned back toward the bed, he met Beth's gaze and bowed. "Elston, at your service, ma'am."

"Beth Castleton. Thank you . . . for taking . . . us in." It was hard to breathe, harder still to think clearly through the pain.

Elston's left eyebrow arched at her words. He hadn't expected her accent, Beth supposed. His reply, however, was as elegant and urbane as the man himself. "My pleasure, Miss Castleton. We will have the opportunity to become acquainted while you recuperate."

After a sweeping glance around the room, he turned to Weymouth. "What can I do to help?"

"I need another kettle of water to boil the doctor's instruments."

"Boil them?"

"To clean them. The regimental surgeon believed that

disease and infection could be spread by dirty hands and instruments."

"Certainly dirt and grime won't aid healing," Elston commented as he walked to the door.

Weymouth squeezed her hand, which he was still holding. "Beth, the only surgeon nearby is a drunkard. General opinion is that he isn't fit to treat a dog." He took a deep breath. "I am going to remove the ball from your shoulder, with Moira's help. I have done it before, in the army, but—

He broke off as the Scotswoman entered the room. "Mrs. Maxwell is givin' the bairn a wee nuncheon and will stay wi' her until I return. How can I help ye, m'lord?"

"The first thing to do is get Miss Castleton undressed."

The maid stared at Weymouth, her eyes wide with shock.

"Moira," Beth explained, "his lordship . . . isn't going to do . . . anything improper . . . only remove . . . the ball . . . from my shoulder."

" 'Tis improper for him to even be in yer bedchamber," Moira huffed.

"So it is . . . but he cannot . . . do his doctoring . . . from the hallway. Your presence . . . will maintain . . . a semblance . . . of propriety."

Weymouth grasped Beth's arms just above the elbow. "Let me help you sit up so that Moira can remove your dress."

Elston entered with another kettle of water, took one look at the group by the bed, and, with a strangled "I will be in the hall if you need me," beat a hasty retreat.

The removal of her gown was excruciatingly painful. Beth bit her lip to keep from moaning. When she was down to her chemise, petticoat, and stockings, Weymouth moved to the hearth, his back to the bed. As he pulled off his coat, he told the maid to finish undressing her, lay her on her stomach, and cover her with the sheet. Then he sorted through the doctor's satchel, dropping various instruments into the pot of boiling water.

When she was undressed and lying down again, Beth sighed in relief. Her ordeal was far from over, but at least she would be stationary for the rest of it.

Moira crossed to the hearth. "Lord Weymouth, we need

an oiled cloth so we dinna ruin the sheets. And some laudanum for Miss Castleton."

He jutted his chin in the direction of Mrs. Maxwell's tray. "Is there an oiled cloth there?"

"Aye, and laudanum."

"Is there brandy or whiskey?"

"M'lord, ye canna be thinkin' of drink now!"

"Not for me," Weymouth said, the amusement threading his voice a marked contrast to Moira's scandalized tone. "I will use it to clean the wound."

"Well, there are nae spirits here."

"Robert," he called, "I need some brandy or whiskey and a large kitchen knife."

Elston peeked into the room. "Have you a preference for one over the other?"

"Whiskey, if you have it."

The marquess replied in the affirmative and departed on his errand. As Moira approached with the laudanum, Weymouth washed his hands with what looked to be lye soap. After instructing the maid to do the same, he carried a pan of water and a cloth to the bed. Beth was comforted by his calm demeanor as he seated himself and began washing her shoulder.

George swore silently. The wound was a horrendous mess, with gun powder and bits of fabric from Beth's dress clinging to the edges—and likely inside, too. The pistol ball had ripped through the muscle in her shoulder. He couldn't see the ball, probably because it was lodged against the bone. If that was the case, it was going to be devilishly hard to remove. And incredibly painful for Beth. If they were both lucky, she would faint early in the operation and not regain consciousness until after he finished.

"Moira, please take the instruments from that pot of boiling water and lay them on a clean cloth on the tray by the bed."

"Where shall I put the bandages and such that are on the tray now?"

"Put them on the dresser until we need them."

Elston returned with a decanter of whiskey. "Do you need anything else?"

"Undoubtedly, but I cannot think what." When their

host left, George crossed the room and picked up a clean cloth, the whiskey, and a short leather strap he had found in the surgeon's satchel. Returning to Beth, he sat on the side of the bed and handed her the strap.

"What do . . . I do . . . with this?"

"Bite on it instead of on your lip. This whiskey is going to sting like the dickens." He saturated the cloth, placed his right hand on her right shoulder to hold her in position, then laid the whiskey-soaked cloth over the wound.

She jerked against his restraining hand, breath hissing between her teeth and tears streaming from her eyes. "I am sorry, Beth." Her skin was as soft as a rose petal. Startled at such an improper thought, George realized he was rubbing her uninjured shoulder with his thumb. But he didn't stop. She needed soothing and he . . . well, he could use a bit of comfort himself. His thumb continued its stroking as he asked the question that had troubled him for hours. "Why did you come back into the house this morning?"

"The clouds . . . obscured the sun. I couldn't tell . . . which direction . . . was north. Moira didn't know. I came back . . . inside . . . to ask you . . . or Henry."

"As simple as that." George rubbed his chin with the back of his left hand—and nearly fell off the bed when the pungent whiskey fumes hit his nose. "I take it you couldn't find Henry."

"No. I looked in . . . all the rooms . . . except the kitchen . . . but could not . . . find him. I was—"

"You can explain the rest later. Does it hurt to talk?" The ball was too high to have hit her lung, but something was causing her to space out her words.

"Hurts to breathe. Pulls . . . my shoulder."

Frowning as he puzzled over that, George removed the whiskey-soaked cloth. The sooner he began, the sooner he would finish. "It would be helpful to us both if you fainted." He tried for a humorous tone but didn't quite succeed.

"I shall endeavor . . . to oblige you," his patient said, a thread of laughter in her voice.

"Moira, sit on the other side of the bed. Put your hands on Miss Castleton's right shoulder and hold her down. Keep her as still as possible."

The maid seated herself, smoothed Beth's hair, and placed her hands on their patient's shoulder. " 'Twill be over soon, lass."

George picked up the forceps. "Beth, turn your head toward Moira."

Ten minutes later, Beth had fainted and he was sweating like a pig. The pistol ball was wedged tight against the bone. As he cleaned bits of cloth and debris from the wound, he pondered the best way to dislodge it. Finally, the wound was clean; all that remained was to extract the ball.

The damned thing didn't want to move. George was determined that it would. Beth's shoulder was bleeding profusely, the forceps kept slipping. Stubbornly but patiently he tried again and again. Finally, using one of the surgeon's scalpels to push from the back and the forceps to pull from the front, he worked the ball loose. A few more tugs with the forceps and it was out. George wiped the sweat off his brow with his shirtsleeve.

"Are ye going to . . . I dinna know the English word, heat the knife and put it against the lassie's skin to stop the bleedin' and close the wound?"

"I had considered that. It would be the best way, and the easiest, but it will leave a nasty scar and be very painful for Beth as the burn heals."

"Better some pain and a nasty scar than to die because the wound becomes . . . Ach, I canna think in English when I am upset."

Every joint in George's body protested when he stood up. As he laid the knife in the fire to heat the blade, Moira said, "The lassie willna complain about the scar. She is verra lucky ye were here to do this."

"*Lucky?* If not for me, she wouldn't have been shot."

"Ye canna say that, m'lord." Moira's tone conveyed her shock at his self-accusation. "Ye mustna e'en think it. Lady Arabella and Sir James might hae done far worse to the lassie, and to your niece, if ye hadna been here."

Shuddering at the thought, George washed his hands. "Perhaps." When the blade was white-hot, he bent and picked up the knife, then walked back to the bed. "Hold her shoulder again, Moira. She may feel this even though she is unconscious."

He took a deep breath then placed the glowing blade

against Beth's shoulder. As the smell of burning flesh assailed his nostrils, he had to steel himself not to pull the knife away too soon. Finally, it was finished. He sighed in relief, as did Moira, and again mopped the sweat from his brow.

The maid lightly touched his arm "Ye're a gud man, Lord Weymouth."

"Right now, I am an exhausted one."

"Go lie down for a while. I will sit with the lass."

"We need to put a cold compress on that burn. And to watch for fever."

"Aye. I will take care of her. Rest now, so ye can watch her tonight. 'Tis more likely she will be feverish then."

Weary to the bone, George stumbled across the hall and fell onto his bed. He was asleep almost as soon as his head touched the pillow.

Moira tidied the room and examined the vials the housekeeper had left. There was willow bark for fever, chamomile, comfrey, and more. No one brought cold water. There was hot water in abundance, but that wasn't what she needed. Biting her lip, she fretted over whether she should ring the bell or go down to the kitchen. She didn't want to leave her mistress, but she was only a servant and had no right to order anyone about. Finally, after checking her patient, she opened the door and stepped into the hall.

Lord Elston was standing a few feet away, talking to the servant who had greeted Lord Weymouth when they arrived. "Mrs. . . . ah, is there something you need, ma'am?"

Moira curtsied. The marquess was an intimidating man, tall, dark, and rather aloof. "Moira Sinclair, m'lord. I need a pan of cold water, if ye please. The colder the better."

"Higgins will get it for you." The marquess nodded to his servant. "You need only ring, and someone will bring whatever you require. Your job is to nurse your mistress."

"How large a pan of water do you need, Mrs. Sinclair?" the man Higgings inquired.

"A basin full will do for now."

As Higgins went off on his errand, Lord Elston surprised her by continuing the conversation. "How is Miss Castleton? Was Weymouth able to remove the pistol ball?"

"Aye, he did a grand job of it. Better than many a surgeon would hae done. Miss Castleton fainted early on, but she is sleepin' now. 'Tis the best thing for her. The poor lass will be in a deal of pain when she wakes."

"I imagine so. If there is anything you need, just tell someone and I will send to the apothecary in town."

"Thank ye kindly, m'lord."

Higgins returned with a basin of water. As she turned to leave, the marquess inquired, "Where is Weymouth?"

"I believe he is asleep." Moira twisted her hands in her skirt. "Is it possible for Mrs. Maxwell to watch the bairn until Lord Weymouth can sit wi' Miss Castleton?"

"The bairn? Ah, George's niece. Weymouth's man is with the child now." Moira was astonished when the marquess explained further; perhaps he wasn't as aloof as he appeared. "I have only three servants here, Mrs. Sinclair— Higgins, Mrs. Maxwell, and a maid—but we shall all do whatever we can to help."

"Thank ye kindly, Lord Elston." Bobbing another curtsy, she took the basin of water and retreated to the sickroom.

Sometime later, Mrs. Maxwell brought her dinner. The housekeeper sat with her while she ate, asking a lot of questions about Miss Castleton and how she had been shot. Not knowing how much her mistress and Lord Weymouth would want told, Moira said only that she hadn't seen the shooting and didn't know how it had happened. Which was true, but not at all what the housekeeper wanted to hear. Mrs. Maxwell's next question was interrupted by a quiet knock on the door, prefacing the entrance of Lord Weymouth.

Moira put down her napkin and began to rise, but the earl waved her back into her seat. "Finish your meal."

His long legs quickly covered the distance from the door to the bed. "How is our patient?"

"Still asleep, m'lord. It worries me that she hasna awakened yet."

He placed the back of his fingers against Miss Castleton's cheek, checking for fever, then lifted the compress to examine her shoulder. The sight of the burn was too much for Mrs. Maxwell, who hurriedly excused herself, saying she would return later for the tray. As the door closed behind the housekeeper, Moira sighed and leaned back in the chair.

"Asked a lot of questions, did she?"

"Aye. 'Tis just curiosity, but I didna know what ye wanted told. I said I hadna seen the shooting. Fortunately, ye came before she asked much about Miss Castleton."

"Probably a good thing, since I don't imagine you know much about your new mistress."

"I know she is a sweet, kind lady." That was the most important thing as far as Moira was concerned. "And verra brave. She is an American, I think, although her accent is different from others I hae heard."

Searching for additional facts, she reviewed her early morning conversation with Miss Castleton. "I know she was traveling with her aunt before she came here, and she was verra worrit this morn because she doesna know what happened to that lady."

Moira placed her teacup on the table and her tray on the floor. "The poor lassie only came to her senses this morn and now this. 'Tisna right."

"No, it isn't right or fair that Miss Castleton should have suffered so much at Arabella's hands. But she did. Now we must do all we can to make her well, then return her to her family." Lord Weymouth sighed. "I must write her uncle and tell him what has happened."

"M'lord, I think . . ." Moira's hands fisted in her skirt.

"Go on, please."

"If Miss Castleton were my niece, I would be happy just to know that she is safe and well. If I learnt she had been shot and I wasna able to see her and nurse her back to health, I would fret myself to flinders until I saw her again."

"You are a wise and thoughtful woman, Moira Sinclair."

Blushing, she ducked her head. "Thank ye, m'lord."

A knock on the door spun George around and brought the Scotswoman to her feet. Henry peeked inside, his face a study in dismay.

George suppressed a sigh. "What's amiss?

"Lord Elston requests that you join him for dinner, and Miss Isabelle is tired and wants to be put to bed." The manservant gulped a breath, then continued more calmly. "I haven't been around children much. I don't know how to put a child to bed, at least not a little girl."

Thankful that there was no real disaster, George pondered how the three of them could best meet both requests and watch over Beth. "Moira, will you stay with Beth while I put Isabelle to bed and eat dinner?"

"O' course I will."

"Thank you. Henry, tell the marquess I will join him in about twenty minutes."

"Yes, my lord. Right away, sir." Henry spun on his heel and marched to the stairs.

Thirty minutes later, George's hair looked like he had been pulled backward through a bush, his cravat was damp and decidedly limp, and he was convinced that nannies and nursery maids were worth their weight in gold. Tucked into bed, her eyes at half-mast, Isabelle was demanding a bedtime story. And he couldn't remember a single one. "Once upon a time . . ." He cleared his throat and hoped for inspiration. "Once upon a time—"

The door opened and a maid entered, bobbing a curtsy. "Me name's Janet, m'lord. Mrs. Maxwell sent me up to sit with the wee lassie so ye can have yer dinner."

George kissed his niece good night. "Janet will tell you a story, Isabelle." Divine intervention was even better than inspiration.

Chapter 6

During dinner George told Elston all that had happened: The abduction of Isabelle and Beth six days ago, his own yesterday, Arabella's threats, her cousin's involvement, Moira's and Henry's assistance, and the escape to Hawthorn Lodge and safety. Robert now knew the entire story and, staunch friend that he was, had been appropriately outraged, appalled, and amused during the recounting. Neither man could figure out Sir James's motives. He was reputed to be a bit mad, but George did not know if the scheme had been Arabella's idea or her cousin's, only that Sir James had arranged the abductions. Robert was of the opinion that something should be done to stop the miscreants, but George thought it best to let sleeping dogs lie. Arabella was, unquestionably, a *chien,* but he could not bring her to book for the crimes she and her cousin had committed without airing a lot of dirty linen in public. Not to mention ruining Beth's reputation and, possibly, Isabelle's.

Over the port, which Robert drank deeply while he himself merely toyed with a glass, George tried to determine what was troubling his friend. Robert shrugged it off as a case of midwinter blue-devils, but George knew it was more than that. The old marquess had died in a hunting accident in December, but George didn't think that was the cause of his friend's melancholy; Robert and his father had often been at loggerheads over the years.

Pondering the matter, George trudged up the stairs. Even if he couldn't discover the cause, he would do everything in his power to put Robert in better frame before they left for London. At the top of the stairs, he turned toward his room, then remembered that he was to sit with Beth during the night. Dragging a hand through his hair, he tapped on her door and entered.

Moira was sitting in a chair near the bed, dozing over some mending, but roused at the sound of his footsteps. "Miss Castleton awoke about seven o'clock, m'lord. I gave her a few drops of laudanum for the pain and a dose of willow bark for the fever. She drank some barley water but wouldna take any broth."

He crossed to the bed and placed the back of his fingers against Beth's cheek. She was feverish, but not alarmingly so. "Did she speak to you?"

"Aye. She asked, first, if Isabelle was safe. Then she wanted to know where we are. When I told her, she remembered meetin' the marquess earlier today. She doesna remember bein' shot or comin' here."

"Many soldiers don't remember being wounded." He lifted the compress from Beth's shoulder. The skin was raw and blistered but looked about as he expected. There were no indications the wound was festering, but it was too early for that, really. A basin of water with small chunks of ice bobbing on the surface sat on the bedside table. He soaked the cloth before replacing it on Beth's shoulder.

As he listened to Moira's instructions on when and how much laudanum and willow bark Beth should be given, and washing her face and hands with cold water if the fever rose, he studied the garment the Scotswoman had fashioned for her mistress's convalescence. It looked like a man's nightshirt—or as if it had been one before Moira's scissors had gotten to it. The neckband and right sleeve were intact, but the left sleeve and the left side of the back of the shirt had been removed. The body of the shirt was, presumably, intact below the blankets. It was cleverly contrived to preserve Beth's modesty while allowing them to treat her shoulder with compresses and salves. He complimented the maid on her ingenuity and received a shy but pleased "thank ye" in return.

"Moira, allow me to remove my coat and get a book, then I will sit with Miss Castleton." He walked to the door and across the hall to his room, unbuttoning his coat as he went.

Someone, Henry or Higgins, had unpacked his portmanteau. His dressing gown was draped across the counterpane; his slippers were on the floor beside the bed; the book he had been reading, *Sense and Sensibility*, was on the nightstand. After removing his coat, cravat, and waistcoat, he pulled on his dressing gown. He eyed his slippers longingly, but he couldn't remove his boots without the aid of his valet or a bootjack—neither of which was present. Moira wouldn't object to a few minutes delay while he rang for Henry or Higgins.

As he crossed to the bellpull, he heard a man's voice in the hallway and altered direction to the door. Henry was asking Moira if she needed more ice or water. The maid answered in the affirmative, and Henry turned to leave, but George delayed his departure, requesting the manservant's help in removing his boots. Then, his feet clad in slippers, George sent Henry on his way and went to relieve Moira.

The house was quiet save for the soft ticking of the ormolu clock on the mantel and the crackling of the fire in the grate. Reaching the end of a chapter, George's mind drifted from the story he was reading to the day's events. It had been a stroke of luck for him, and for Isabelle, that Beth had been mistaken for his niece's governess and abducted along with the child. Even more astonishing was Beth's unhesitating acquiescence to his request for assistance, especially since she had, apparently, disliked him on sight. Oh, she had played pretty duets with him at Dunnley's house party, but that had been because their host had asked her, not because she enjoyed his company.

George wasn't a vain man, but he knew women found him attractive—or were attracted to his fortune and future title—and that his manners were better than most of his contemporaries. Beth's manners were excellent as well. She had been friendly and politely patient with his rattle-pated young cousin and his absentminded great-uncle, the two most trying members of the house party, but not so with him. Although she had never been rude, her frosty acknowledgment of their introduction over the breakfast table had set the tone for all their encounters. Until today.

Today she had been different. She had been frightened when she first saw him, hooded as he'd been, then a bit . . . wary, perhaps. After that, wary or no, Beth had been extraordinarily helpful. She had removed the hood, untied his hands, agreed to take Isabelle to safety, helped plan their escape, and winkled him out of Arabella's clutches. Henry had helped with the latter—indeed, they would all still be at Arabella's mercy if not for the redoubtable Henry—but Beth was the one who had been shot.

George hoped that the fact that he had been the one to remove the pistol ball from her shoulder, would ameliorate Beth's aversion. He knew, although he wasn't certain how or why, that she would not blame him for her injury. Perhaps during her convalescence he could figure out the enigmatic Miss Beth Castleton.

He wanted more. Beth was one of the most interesting women he had ever met. They shared a love of music and—if his ears had not deceived him this morning—mathematics, enjoyed riding and dancing, and preferred convivial conversation over social chitchat. He wanted her friendship, but he would settle for understanding her.

An anguished moan brought him to his feet. Beth writhed on the bed, tears spilling from her closed eyes. "No! Nooooo!" A nightmare.

George placed the back of his fingers against her cheek. Her fever had risen a bit, but that wasn't unexpected. If he woke her, she would be free of the dream and he would be able to dose her with willow bark. "Beth. Wake up."

Seating himself on the edge of the bed, he tried again. "Wake up, Beth. It is only a dream." Still no response. Placing his hand on her uninjured shoulder, he shook her gently. "Beth. Wake up, Beth."

The muscles under his hand relaxed. She looked over at him, her eyes still unfocused. "You had a nightmare, Beth. Whatever it was, it cannot harm you."

She turned as if to roll onto her back. With a gentle but firm hand he stopped her when she was lying on her right side. "Don't roll over onto your back."

She blinked several times but didn't move. "Why ever not? And what are you doing in my bedchamber, Weymouth?"

"You were shot in the shoulder this morning. We removed the ball and patched you up, but if you roll onto your back, your wound will protest. Vociferously, I imagine."

"I was shot? By that footman of Arabella's, I suppose. I thought he was aiming at you."

George hid a smile at her disgruntled tone. "He was, but Henry threw off his aim."

"How did he do that?"

"By stepping between me and the footman."

"Good heavens! He deserves a medal for bravery. Or foolishness."

George smiled down at her, pleased that her thoughts mirrored his. "Exactly what I told him—after I thanked him, of course."

"Of course." A frown pleated her brow. "I remember . . . I think I remember Moira saying that we are at a hunting lodge owned by one of your friends." She moved her left hand toward her face, then stopped abruptly, her breath hissing between her teeth.

With fists and jaw clenched, she battled the pain. To give her time to conquer it, he explained, "This is Hawthorn Lodge, one of the Marquess of Elston's estates."

"He was in here . . . earlier today . . . wasn't he? A tall . . . dark-haired man . . . dressed in . . . a black coat." The words were forced out between gritted teeth.

"Yes, that was Elston. Let me help you sit up, then I will give you some medicine for the pain and for your fever." He reached out his hands then, dumbfounded, dropped them.

After several seconds had passed, Beth spoke, her voice nearly normal. "Weymouth, you have the strangest expression on your face."

"Gaping like a landed flounder, am I?" He tried to ease through the awkward moment.

The hint of a smile tilted one corner of her mouth. "Possibly. Are you going to tell me what is amiss?"

"Earlier today I helped you sit up by grasping your arms above the elbow and holding them against your body as I raised you. You were lying on your back then, before we removed the ball. I can't do that now, and no alternate method has occurred to me. Unless . . ." He narrowed his eyes, considering the idea that had just popped into his brain.

"Unless what?"

"Unless I hold you around the waist and lift you as if I were assisting you onto a horse."

"Do you hesitate because you think it won't work?"

"No, I think it will work very well if you can keep your left arm stationary." He felt a flush creeping up his face. *Gad, almost thirty and he was blushing like a schoolboy!* "I hesitated because you aren't wearing a riding habit, and I feared you would think my suggestion shockingly improper."

"Weymouth, your presence in my bedchamber is shockingly improper." Her voice was tart. "Since I didn't swoon at finding you here, I am unlikely to do so now, knowing you are helping me." She glanced up at him, then continued in a milder tone. "I am not missish—well, I am in some respects—but I am not a feather-headed schoolroom miss."

"You are neither bird-witted nor empty-headed, O Ancient One." His hands spanned her waist, his thumbs about touching. "Keep your left arm still."

Beth didn't swoon, but she certainly felt something when Weymouth wrapped his hands about her waist. Something slightly less shocking than a lightning bolt, yet potent enough to radiate all the way to her toes. He lifted her as if she were light as thistledown, half turned her in midair, then sat her down and reached behind her to pile the pillows against the headboard.

"Lean back against the pillows but be careful of your shoulder. Wait. Let me put this compress back on." He picked up a cloth lying on the blankets, immersed it in a basin of water then placed it over her shoulder.

She shivered. "It is cold."

"Cold is the best thing for burns."

"I have burns from being shot?"

"No, you have a large burn where we cauterized the entry wound."

"That makes much more sense." She thought for a moment about what he had said, then and earlier. "You keep saying 'we'—we removed the ball, we cauterized the wound. Who is we?"

"Moira and I."

Incredulous, she gaped at him. "Moira? The Moira who is my new maid removed a pistol ball from my shoulder?"

"No, I did." Weymouth rushed on, his words nearly tumbling over themselves in his haste. "I told you before we began that the only surgeon nearby was a drunken sot and that I was going to remove the ball from your shoulder. Told you I had done it in the army."

Beth frowned, trying to recall their earlier conversation. "I remember something about the doctor being a drunkard not fit to treat a dog, but not the rest." When she noticed his alarmed expression, she added, "I have no objection to your having done so, Weymouth. On the contrary, I am very grateful to you." Thoughtfully, she studied him. "Were you really a surgeon in the army? I would have thought you a dashing Hussar or Dragoon officer."

"I was a major in the Queen's Light Dragoons. But for a time after our regimental surgeon was wounded, I took on his role and performed a number of surgeries under his direction."

"Good heavens. Did all the officers do so? I can't imagine most of the army officers I know performing surgery."

"I was chosen to do it because I am known to have a gift for treating horses."

"Surely there must be significant differences between treating horses and performing surgery."

"There are." He stood abruptly. "Now, young lady, it is time for your medicine."

"I apologize if I distressed you by asking about it, Weymouth."

"You didn't." He turned away and reached for a glass on the nightstand.

Beth didn't believe him, but since it was clearly something he preferred not to discuss, she sought a new topic of conversation. "How far are we from Gull Cottage?"

"About fifteen miles."

Only fifteen miles? "Aren't you worried that Lady Arabella and her cousin will find us?"

"I would be if we were staying at an inn; since we are not, I think it highly unlikely that they will." He poured water from a pitcher into the glass, then added several drops from a small bottle.

Beth thought she understood his intent. "While we are safely holed up here, Lady Arabella's men will dash toward London looking for us?"

"Yes." He handed her the glass. "Sooner or later, when

they don't find any sign of us, they will realize that we aren't ahead of them. Who knows what they will do then?"

She sniffed the contents before she drank. Laudanum. "Are there a number of different roads we could take from here to London?"

"There are several different routes a traveler could take, but most would use the Great North Road."

"Since Arabella's men could wait along the Great North Road for us to pass by, I imagine you don't plan to travel that route." He poured something from another little bottle and gave it to her. "What is this?"

"Willow bark. For your fever. And no, we won't take the Great North Road."

Beth swallowed the medicine and raised her right hand to her forehead. She was either feverish or her hand was very cold. Probably both. "How far is it from here to London?

"About five hundred miles. Perhaps a bit less."

"Considering the state of the roads this time of year, it will take us almost a fortnight to reach London, won't it?"

At his answering nod, she sighed. "Uncle Charles and Aunt Julia must be frantic with worry. If I wrote a letter to let them know I am safe and well, would it reach them before I do?"

"Yes. I will hire a messenger to deliver your letter, as well as several I need to send." George dragged a hand through his hair then sat in a chair beside the bed. "I had thought to borrow a horse from Elston and send Henry off with the messages, but we need him here."

Before she could question him, he explained. "Elston has only three servants here: Higgins, who serves as butler and valet; Mrs. Maxwell, who is both cook and housekeeper; and a maid named Janet. We have only Moira and Henry. Someone has to be with Isabelle all day, someone needs to be with you all day, and someone needs to sleep part of the day so they can sit with you at night. I—"

Indignant, she exclaimed, "It isn't necessary for someone to sit with me all day. Or all night."

"It won't be necessary later in your convalescence, but it is until the fever breaks."

"Weymouth, really, it is not—"

"Don't argue, Beth. Please."

He sounded so weary that she ceased protesting. "Who will watch Isabelle during the day?"

"Henry and Moira mostly, although I will take a turn, too. Moira will want to be here with you, but an hour or two in the morning and afternoon with Isabelle will benefit both. I can't quite picture Henry in the role of nurse"—his blue eyes twinkled—"so I will sit with you when Moira is with Isabelle in the afternoon. And also at night."

He rubbed one knuckle against his lower lip. "Beth, would you have any objection to entertaining, or being entertained by, Elston for an hour or so each day? In the afternoon, most likely."

"I have no objection, but I can't imagine the marquess in the role of nurse, either."

"Not as a nurse, just as a companion. Something is bothering him, although he denies it. If you would talk with him, or play chess or cards with him, it might divert him from whatever he is brooding over."

"I am willing to try."

"Thank you. Then Elston can sit with you in the afternoon while Moira is with Isabelle and I am sleeping."

Beth wrinkled her nose. "I think being shot has affected my memory. Didn't you say you would take Moira's place in the afternoon?"

A smile teased one corner of his mouth. "I said that originally, but then I thought of Elston and I changed my mind."

"Hmph. And men say women are fickle."

Weymouth chuckled softly. "I will take Moira's place in the morning, Elston in the afternoon. That will work better, actually; I can spend the morning with Elston and sleep between luncheon and dinner."

Beth stifled a yawn. "How long do you intend for us to stay here so that Lady Arabella and her searchers get far ahead of us?"

"We will stay here until you are fit to travel. At least a week."

"You needn't wait so long on my account. I can rest in the carriage as easily as here."

"No, you can't. Not yet, at least. You don't realize the extent and severity of the burn on your shoulder. If you can endure the cloth of your dress rubbing against it in a week, I will be exceedingly surprised."

"Oh, my dress. It looked shabby enough, despite Moira's efforts, after my abduction. She will have her work cut out for her to repair the hole from the pistol ball. I daresay there might be a bloodstain, too."

Weymouth shifted in his chair, stretching his long legs out in front of him and crossing them at the ankle. His movement tumbled a book from the arm of the chair to the floor. "You lost a great deal of blood, Beth. That is another reason we will stay here at least a week; you need to build up your strength." He leaned over to pick up the book.

She didn't want to argue with him about the length of her convalescence. He was so very different tonight, much more friendly and approachable than the toplofty man she had met at Dunnley's house party. She much preferred this side of his character—and hoped to see more of it. "What are you reading?"

"*Sense and Sensibility* by A Lady."

"That is one of my favorite novels! I do hope she will write others, don't you?"

"I have read only a few chapters, but I like it very well."

Beth suppressed another yawn. "It is the strangest thing. I slept for five days after being knocked on the head and for several hours today, but I am quite sleepy now." She pushed away from the headboard, keeping her left arm rigid against her body by wrapping her forearm around her waist.

The earl stood and looked down at her for a moment. "Sleep is the best thing for you. It gives your body a chance to heal." Leaning down, he grasped her around the waist again, lifted and turned her, then laid her down on her right side.

"Will you read to me, Weymouth?"

He dipped the compress in the basin of water then placed it on her shoulder and tucked the blankets around her. "Sleep now. I will read to you tomorrow, if you like."

"You could read to me until I fall asleep." She snuggled her cheek against the pillow.

"So I could," he said, a hint of amusement in his voice as he settled into his chair and picked up the book. "Mrs.

Dashwood and her daughter have arrived at Barton Cottage and have just made the acquaintance of Sir John and Lady Middleton."

"I remember. They call to invite Mrs. Dashwood, Elinor, and Marianne to dinner at Barton Park."

"Exactly so." His voice deepened a shade. "Chapter Seven. 'Barton Park was about half a mile from the cottage. The ladies had passed near it in their way along the valley, but it was screened from their view at home by the projection of a hill. The house was large and handsome; and the Middletons lived in a style of equal hospitality and elegance. The former was for Sir John's gratification . . .' "

Beth drifted off to sleep to the sound of Weymouth's rich baritone.

Chapter 7

❧

*B*eth woke late the next morning. Moira was sitting in the chair beside the bed, mending. "Good morning, Moira."

"Good day to ye, Miss Castleton. How are ye feelin' this morn?" The maid set her sewing aside, crossed to the bed, and placed her hand on Beth's forehead.

"My shoulder hurts, but I expected that. Am I still feverish?"

"Aye." Moira frowned. "Ye need to be sittin' up to take yer medicine. If I place a pillow so yer shoulder will be cushioned when ye roll over, can ye sit up?"

"I think so, although I may need your help."

The maid walked around the foot of the bed, positioned the pillow, then retraced her steps, her eyes narrowed thoughtfully. Beth clamped her left arm rigidly against her side, her right hand holding her left elbow in place, took a deep breath, and rolled over onto her back. Moira held out a hand, and Beth grasped it, allowing the maid to pull her up into a sitting position. She piled the pillows against the headboard, and Beth sank back against them, feeling she had earned her breakfast. The Scotswoman picked up a bottle from the nightstand, poured out a dose, and gave it to Beth.

"I am very thirsty, Moira. May I have something other than that bit of willow bark to drink, please?"

"Aye. Ye need to drink when ye hae a fever." The maid picked up the compress, which had fallen on the quilt, dipped the cloth in the basin, and replaced it on Beth's shoulder. "Would ye like water or barley water?"

Beth wrinkled her nose. "I would much prefer tea."

"Drink a glass of barley water, then ye may hae tea."
Moira poured out a glass and handed it to her. "Is yer
shoulder painin' ye? Do ye want some laudanum?"

"It hurts, but it isn't really painful. I don't need the laudanum now."

Moira mumbled something in Gaelic as she walked to
the bellpull.

When it came a short time later, the tray with Beth's tea
and breakfast was carried in by the earl, not by the maid
who had answered the bell. He sent Moira off for her own
tea and an interlude with Isabelle.

"Good morning, Weymouth."

"Good morning, Beth." He placed the tray across her
lap. "Mrs. Maxwell sent you tea and toast for breakfast.
How are you feeling this morning?"

"I feel quite well, all things considered."

The earl settled his long frame into the chair beside her
bed. "I sent off letters to your uncle, my brother, and my
father early this morning."

"Thank you for writing to Uncle Charles for me." Beth
handed her companion a cup of tea, studying him. "Are
you as tired as you look?"

"Probably." He rubbed a hand over his face. "I will sleep
this afternoon."

"I hope you will." She sipped her tea. "How many chapters in *Sense and Sensibility* did you read last night?"

"Four or five. The ladies met Colonel Brandon, and Wil-
loughby rescued Miss Marianne, then came to call the
next day."

They discussed the characters in the book, then went on
to other novels they had read and enjoyed. Beth drifted off
to sleep in the middle of the conversation, surprised at the
similarities in their likes and dislikes.

She awoke several hours later, feeling quite chilled.
After attending to her most pressing needs, Moira dosed
her with willow bark and gave her a glass of barley water.
When the maid reported that Isabelle had been asking to
see "her pretty lady," Beth encouraged a visit. The three
of them were engrossed in a game of spillikins when a
knock on the door presaged the entrance of Weymouth's friend.

"Good afternoon, Lord Elston." Beth smiled at her visitor.

"Good afternoon, Miss Castleton. I hope I am not disturbing you." The marquess carried a pack of cards and a cribbage board.

"Not at all, sir. Moira and Isabelle have rolled me up, horse, foot, and guns." The game finished, Beth hugged the little girl, then sent her competitors off for a nap. As they left the room, Beth motioned Lord Elston to the chair beside the bed.

The marquess appeared discomposed so she sought to put him at ease. "Lord Elston, it is very kind of you to entertain an unexpected, unknown guest."

"It is my pleasure, Miss Castleton. And you are no longer an unknown guest, since George introduced us."

As Beth remembered it, Lord Elston had introduced himself, although the earl had been present. "Have you known Weymouth a long time?"

"Almost twenty years. We entered Eton at the same term and have been friends ever since." The marquess crossed one long, elegantly clad leg over the other. "You have a lovely accent. May I ask in what part of America you live?"

"I lived in Virginia, just outside of Charlottesville, until fifteen months ago. Now I live here—in England, I mean—with my great-aunt and uncle."

"The Earl of Castleton is your uncle? And Lady Julia your great-aunt?"

"Yes. The earl is also my guardian."

"I wonder why we haven't met before." The hint of a smile tilted one corner of Lord Elston's mouth. "I believe I am in Lady Julia's good graces."

"I was in mourning for my grandparents last year during the Season."

"My condolences, Miss Castleton. My father died a few months ago. It is . . . difficult, is it not?"

Beth sighed. "It was for me. Their deaths were sudden, which made them harder to accept. Was your father's death unexpected or had he been ill?"

"He died in a hunting accident, riding a new horse neck or nothing over an unfamiliar run."

"My condolences to you. Were you and your father close?"

"I loved and respected him, but sometimes I wonder if I really understood him."

Something in his voice made Beth think this lack of understanding was troubling him. "Why do you say that, sir?"

The marquess waved a hand. "It is nothing, Miss Castleton." After a moment he spoke again, his tone social and urbane. "George thought you might enjoy a game of cards or chess."

"I play chess, but my grandfather claimed I wasn't a good opponent because I did not take the game seriously enough. I do enjoy cards, though. Especially cribbage and whist."

"Shall we play a game of cribbage?"

"I would enjoy that. But I warn you in advance, sir, in the past day or so I have developed a regrettable tendency to fall asleep in the middle of conversations, no matter how interesting the topic or witty the speaker."

Lord Elston nodded as he dealt out the cards. "I shan't hold it against you, ma'am. Will you be making your come-out this Season?"

"That was Aunt Julia's plan, but the machinations of Lady Arabella and her cousin may have put paid to it." Beth discarded two cards to the crib.

"How so?"

"I imagine an abduction tarnishes a young lady's reputation."

The marquess played his first card. "I daresay it would, if it were widely known. Lady Julia and Castleton aren't going to trumpet it about, and Weymouth and I won't say anything, so who is to know?"

"Lady Arabella and her cousin, of course, as well as anyone my uncle has searching for me." Beth pegged her points for the hand. "The worst part, for me, is not knowing if my aunt and uncle have any idea what happened to me."

Lord Elston's arcing brows conveyed his surprise. "Worse than being shot?"

"Yes. That is a physical injury, painful but bearable. The worry is an emotional pain, less easily controlled and, for me, harder to endure."

He shuffled the cards, then dealt for her. "You are very

wise, Miss Castleton. Would you think me terribly rude if I asked how old you are?"

"Not terribly so." She smiled at Lord Elston, who chuckled, then played her first card. "I am three-and-twenty."

"Since you would never be so rude as to inquire, I will tell you that I, like George, am nine-and-twenty." The marquess played his cards and pegged, his brow creased in thought. "George's birthday is in a few days. Perhaps we should have a party if you are still here then. What say you, ma'am?"

"I think it an excellent idea. What day is Weymouth's birthday?"

"The twenty-first of February."

"He told me last night that we would stay here for at least a week." Beth frowned. "Is today the fifteenth or sixteenth?"

"It is Monday the fifteenth."

"May I do something to help plan this party?"

"Just recuperate so you can act as hostess. That is, if you wouldn't mind." The cool, composed marquess looked, and sounded, rather hesitant.

"I would be honored, Lord Elston."

"Tomorrow afternoon we can plan more. For now, you need to rest."

"But we haven't finished our game!"

"You may finish trouncing me tomorrow, Miss Castleton." With a twinkle in his eyes, he added, "I lost three games of chess to George earlier. A man shouldn't have to suffer more than that in one day."

Beth fell asleep marveling at how the marquess's smile transformed his face from austere to boyishly engaging.

George sat in Beth's room, a book open in his lap but his thoughts on his patient. The wound was healing well, with no indication of festering, but Beth's fever had risen steadily for the past two days. Before Moira left, she reminded him that fever was normal after surgery. But the Scotswoman was dreaming of heather in the Highlands or some such thing while he sat here worrying.

Beth had drifted in and out of consciousness all day. She had been asleep when he came in three hours ago, and slept still. He was almost tempted to wake her so he could dose her with willow bark. Old Dr. MacInnes, the surgeon in his regiment, claimed sleep was the great healer. That might well be true, but Beth had been sleeping like a babe and her fever continued to rise.

He dragged a hand through his hair, then he set his book aside, stood, and bent to feel Beth's forehead. *Was she warmer than the last time he had checked?* Seating himself on the edge of the bed, he freshened the compress on her shoulder. Then, taking another cloth from the basin of cool water on the nightstand, he wiped her face and hands. It was all he could do for now—and it was frustrating as hell.

Too worried to sit still, he paced around the room. This was all his fault. His and Arabella's and Sir James's. If Arabella hadn't decided she wanted to marry him, and if her cousin hadn't concocted such a bizarre scheme to give her her heart's desire, and if they hadn't kidnapped Isabelle to force his compliance, and if he hadn't asked Beth to spirit his niece to safety, then she would be snug in her bed at Castleton Abbey—without a hole in her shoulder, a burn, and a fever.

He would make it up to her, George resolved. Somehow, he would repay her for all she had done for him, and suffered because of him. He would introduce her to all his friends and acquaintances. Surely several of them would realize what a wonderful girl she was and want to marry her. On second thought, he would only introduce her to the friends who were worthy of her. That narrowed the list of potential husbands drastically, but—

"No. Noooooo!" George whirled on his heel. Beth was thrashing about on the bed, her face contorted by some strong emotion and tears streaming down her cheeks. "Noooooo!" Another nightmare.

Perching on the edge of the bed, he placed his hand on Beth's right shoulder and shook her gently. "Wake up, Beth. It is only a dream."

She burrowed into the blankets, lying quietly but sobbing as if her heart were broken. He stroked his hand up and down her back, hoping to calm her until he could wake her. "Beth, wake up. Everything is fine. Wake up, Beth."

Her body went rigid beneath the quilts, the crying ending on a gasp. "Weymouth?" Despite the tremor in her voice, her thoughts were coherent enough to recognize his voice.

"Yes, it is I." His hand soothed along her spine. "You had a nightmare, Beth, but everything is fine. Nothing can hurt you now."

She nodded jerkily, then wiped away tears with the back of her hand.

He handed her his handkerchief. "Let me help you sit up. Do you want something to drink?"

"Yes, please."

She was still far from composed. He tried to soothe her with his voice now. "I am going to lift you like I did the other night. Do you remember that?"

"Yes. I will keep my left arm still."

"Good girl." Standing, he drew the covers down to her hips, wrapped his hands around her waist, then lifted and turned her and sat her down almost against the headboard. Keeping one hand between her back and the ornately carved wood, he used the other to pile the pillows behind her. Beth pulled up the blankets, her eyes downcast. He replaced the compress on her shoulder, wondering why she was avoiding his gaze.

He reached for the cloth he had used earlier to wipe her face and hands, dipped it in the basin, then handed it to her. "Wipe your face, my dear; it will help you feel better."

As she scrubbed away tearstains, he poured a glass of barley water then traded cloth for glass. He measured out a dose of willow bark, and she took that as well, docile as a child.

Why wouldn't she look at him? "Would you like something to eat, Beth?"

"No, thank you. I am not hungry."

"Would you like something else to drink? Some tea, perhaps?"

"No, thank you." She smoothed the blankets with the right hand.

"Tell me about your dream."

That got more of a response. Her eyes jerked up to his, then down to her lap. "I . . . I . . ." She shook her head.

He sat down and covered her restless hand with his own. "Tell me," he commanded. "Was it the same dream you had two nights ago?"

She huffed out a breath. "Probably. There isn't much variety in my nightmares, just the same two over and over."

"Tell me." His voice was gentle, a request this time. "If you tell them, sometimes they lose their power."

"I should be so lucky." Her tone was caustic.

He hooked a finger under her chin, forcing her to meet his gaze. She capitulated to his unspoken demand with a sigh, closing her eyes for a moment. "I will tell you, but I would like another glass of that wretched barley water first."

After drinking her fill, she leaned back against the pillows. "I don't know which nightmare I had tonight. It was either the dream about the fire that killed my parents and sisters or the one about the carriage accident in which my grandparents died."

When her hand resumed its agitated movement, he grasped it between both of his. As he groped for words, his famed address having deserted him in the face of such devastating losses, she spoke again. "I didn't see the fire or the accident, but I have dreamed of them since they happened. And the dreams are always the same.

"Strangely enough, I first had the dream about the fire the night it occurred. I was at my grandparents' home, had been there for a week, helping out while my grandfather was confined to bed after injuring his knee. My screams woke the household. Late the next day we received word about the fire, and that my parents and sisters were dead."

He squeezed her hand, offering comfort and encouragement. "I am sorry for your loss, Beth. When did they die?"

"Five years ago last November."

"And your grandparents? I assume you lived with them after your parents died?"

"Yes. Until they died last year. It was—" Her voice was choked with tears.

He smoothed her fingers against his palm, easing the tensed muscles. When she regained her composure, he requested, "Tell me about the other dream."

Her eyes bleak, Beth complied. "My grandparents had gone to a dinner party at Monticello, Mr. Jefferson's home. I was invited but didn't go because I'd twisted my ankle the day before when a horse I was schooling over jumps refused a fence."

She took a deep breath. "It had snowed earlier in the day; the roads were wet but not icy. Mr. Jefferson wanted my grandparents to stay overnight, but they refused. It was the anniversary of my parents' and sisters' deaths and my grandparents wanted to come home. To be with me if I had the nightmare about the fire."

Tears spilled from her eyes. "Something startled the horses, and they bolted. The carriage slid off the road and into a ditch. Both my grandparents were killed."

Raising her eyes to his face, she said, "They died because of me."

George gathered Beth into his arms, cradling her against his chest as she sobbed out her grief. He rubbed his cheek against her hair and his hand along her spine, murmuring words of comfort she was too distraught to hear. *God, she had suffered so much. She had lost everyone, everything.* Oh, she had Lady Julia and the earl, and he didn't doubt they loved her, but she had only known them for about a year.

She was burdened with guilt—misplaced guilt. He knew a thing or two about that, having dragged a load of his own all through the Peninsula. He had finally come to terms with his; perhaps he could help her do the same.

Long minutes later, she lay weakly against him, drained of tears. His shirt front was soaking wet, as was the back of her nightrail. *The back of her nighttrail?* George smoothed her hair from her brow, then brushed the back of his fingers against her cheek.

Her fever had broken. Finally. *Thanks be to God.* Beth would begin to recover her strength now. To heal, physically. And, he hoped, emotionally.

He realized, suddenly, that neither of them had said anything since she finished telling him about her dreams. As he searched for something to say, Beth spoke. "I am sorry, Weymouth. I am generally not a watering pot."

He heard embarrassment, or perhaps nervousness, in her voice. "You need not apologize, Beth. Mourning the loss of loved ones is natural, not shameful." His hand continued stroking along her spine. "Besides, your tears have had a beneficial result tonight. Your fever has broken."

"Good. I am tired of drifting off to sleep in the middle of conversations." There was a hint of returning spirit in her voice.

He stood, cradling her against his chest, and walked to

the hearth. He seated himself in the chair there, Beth sideways across his thighs. "Your nightgown is damp. We will sit here until it dries, then you can go back to sleep."

"I am perfectly capable of sitting here by myself."

"Of course you are. But since the front of my shirt is as damp as your gown, we will share the chair so we can both dry."

"I am too tired to argue with you, Weymouth."

"Good. I want you to listen to me instead."

She glanced up at him then, but returned her gaze to the fire without saying a word.

"Beth, do you remember our conversation at Gull Cottage when I told you about the promise I made my mother before she died?"

"Yes. You promised you would always take care of your brother. You would have married Lady Arabella to keep Isabelle safe because of that promise."

He nodded. "I broke that promise once—or thought I had. And I suffered agonies of guilt because of that failure."

She looked at him questioningly but didn't speak. "Four years ago, the Season David met Arabella's sister, Marie, I was in the Peninsula. He wrote to me, waxing eloquent about his lady love. I knew Marie, knew she was as incapable of loving anyone as Arabella is, so I warned David to be careful. Marie trapped him into marriage, presented him with a child that wasn't his, then eloped with a lover."

George plunged on. "I believed I had failed him, that—"

"You didn't fail him." Beth placed her hand on his shoulder. "You warned him, but he chose not to heed your warning. Your brother made a decision, and he is responsible for it. Not you."

He covered her hand with his. "Yes, David made his own choice. Just like your grandparents chose to return home to you. We may not like the consequences of those decisions, but we are not responsible for them."

She bowed her head. Nearly a minute passed before she spoke. "Thank you, Weymouth."

They sat in silence for a time, gazing into the fire. When exhaustion claimed Beth, slumping her spine, he carried her back to bed. She was asleep before her head touched the pillow.

* * *

The rest of the week passed rapidly. Beth enjoyed the time she spent each day with Weymouth, Elston, and Isabelle. The little girl was a delight, lively and good-natured, always with a hug for her "pretty lady." Elston had become a friend. If she had met the marquess in Society, Beth knew that his elegance and reserve would have tied her tongue in knots. Here, however, her injury and the paucity of servants had destroyed some of the social barriers. Elston had entertained her with cards and stories, fetched and carried trays for her, and sent into town for foods to tempt her appetite and build up her strength. He had also presented her with a length of cloth Mrs. Maxwell had found in a trunk in the attic, which Moira had made into a simple gown for her mistress.

Weymouth, too, had become a friend. He had cared for her when she was ill, helped her deal with her grief and guilt over the deaths of her parents, sisters, and grandparents, and entertained her for hours on end. Beth wished she knew whether his chivalrous attitude was normal or due to the fact she was a damsel in distress. She had not forgotten their first encounter, but she was willing to be convinced that his behavior that evening may have been atypical. Time would tell.

Sunday evening they celebrated the earl's birthday. Mrs. Maxwell created a sumptuous dinner, Elston provided champagne, and Weymouth was now the proud owner of a pearl stickpin of Elston's he had always admired, a pen wiper made by his niece (with help from Henry), and a handkerchief Beth had embroidered, somewhat awkwardly, with his initial. They ended the evening in good spirits, convinced their journey to London would be as pleasant as their stay in Stranraer.

They were wrong.

Chapter 8

*T*he journey started off well enough. At breakfast Elston surprised them all by announcing he would travel with them, at least as far as Brough, where an estate problem required his attention. Weymouth could ride with him, the marquess offered, leaving more room for Beth, Moira, and Isabelle in their carriage.

When he learned that Henry had never handled a team and the earl would have to drive, Elston was undeterred, offering not only Higgins's services as Henry's driving instructor, but his own in spelling Weymouth as coachman. They left Hawthorn Lodge shortly after nine o'clock, the two peers on the box of Arabella's chaise, Higgins and Henry atop the marquess's traveling coach.

It was a cold, blustery day. The gentlemen were bundled in their greatcoats, with mufflers, hats, and gloves to keep them warm. Weymouth had a hat now, the marquess having provided his second-best curly-brimmed beaver when apprised of the earl's loss. Inside the carriages, the ladies had hot bricks for their feet and every comfort Elston and Mrs. Maxwell could contrive. Beth rode in solitary splendor in Arabella's chise, tucked up with pillows and blankets and Weymouth's copy of *Sense and Sensibility*. Moira and Isabelle also had blankets and a pillow as well as a number of picture books and toys Mrs. Maxwell's sister's niece, a young miss of seven, had deemed too babyish for her own use.

Elston started them off, tooling down the drive, feathering the turn onto the road, then setting the team to a steady canter. The plan was to change horses at Glenluce and drive on to Newton Stewart, spending the night at the marquess's hunting lodge there. It was only twenty-five miles for the day, but the gentlemen deemed it better to stay there than to push on and be forced to rack up at an inn.

The roads were dry and the carriages well sprung, but before they had traveled two miles, Beth wished she was back in bed. At every bump in the road, her shoulder brushed against the squabs. She shifted this way and that, rearranging pillows and blankets, trying to find a comfortable position. Having exhausted all possible seated configurations—and herself—she lay down on the seat. That worked quite well for several miles until a particularly large jolt bounced her onto the floor.

She wanted to be home, at Castleton Abbey. She wouldn't even cavil at being at Castleton House in London, with the Season stretching before her like a racetrack before a Derby contender. To reach either place, she had to endure a carriage ride of about four hundred ninety-five more miles, give or take a few. Resolute, she gritted her teeth and climbed back onto the seat.

By the time they reached Glenluce, she had bitten her lip until it was bleeding. Her shoulder was bleeding, too—a fact she intended to conceal. Unfortunately, the moment Weymouth opened the carriage door, he realized something was wrong. "Little fool, why didn't you say something?"

Ignoring her disclaimers, he scooped her up in his arms and carried her inside the inn. As soon as they were settled in a private parlor, he and Elston left the room, taking Isabelle with them, so that Moira could tend Beth.

"Moira, I need a dose of laudanum, please."

"Ye need to be restin' in bed, nae bouncin' aboot in a carriage." The maid mixed several drops of the pain medicine into a glass of water. "Is it yer shoulder?"

Beth drained the glass quickly, eager for relief. "Yes, but you mustn't tell Weymouth it is bleeding. Just make a pad for it, please."

"His lordship is nae fool, lass. He knows something is amiss."

"He suspects something, but you are not to tell him what it is." Beth was stubbornly determined.

Moira fastened the bandage, then rebuttoned her mistress's dress. "And what are ye going to tell him when he asks why yer lip is bleedin' and ye're white as a sheet?"

Beth studied the toes of her shoes. "I hope he will not ask."

"Hmph." The maid smoothed Beth's hair. "Is it nae more sensible—"

A knock on the door heralded the landlord with their luncheon, closely followed by Elston, Weymouth, and his niece. "I want to be home, Moira," Beth whispered. The maid nodded her understanding as the earl stalked toward them. Moira hastened away to settle Isabelle at the table.

George scrutinized Beth's pale face and pinched features. "How bad is it?"

"I am all right." She studied his cravat—a nicely done Mathematical if he did say so himself—but wouldn't meet his eye.

"No, you are not." He hooked his forefinger under her chin and forced her gaze up to his. "Is your shoulder bleeding?"

She bit her lip, her eyes darting to the side. "Yes."

"Why didn't you say something, Beth?" His tone reflected his lack of understanding—and his frustration.

"I want to be home, Weymouth." She looked up at him, her eyes beseeching him not to call a halt to the journey.

How could he argue against that? He raked a hand through his hair, then offered his arm to escort her to the table. "Let's eat our luncheon."

As Isabelle dawdled over her meal, George stood and walked to the window, motioning for Elston to join him. "Beth's shoulder is bleeding. I suspect the bouncing of the carriage rubs her shoulders against the squabs."

"The pillows don't provide enough of a cushion?"

George sighed. "Apparently not. Or perhaps the friction between the pillows and her dress caused the bleeding."

"Should we stay here for a few days or go back to the Lodge?"

"She is in a great deal of pain but wants to continue. She wants to be home."

"I daresay she does. As a result of her good deed, she has suffered—"

"I know that all too well," George said, rather testily.

"Will you ride inside and hold Beth on your lap so that she can rest without exacerbating her injury?"

Elston looked distinctly taken aback. "Miss Castleton considers me a friend—and I am—but she will not permit such a liberty. At least, not to me. I will drive, you ride with Miss Castleton."

"Thank you, Robert."

When they were ready to leave, George escorted Beth to the carriage, Elston walking beside her. As the marquess mounted the box, George lifted Beth inside.

She looked surprised when he sat next to her. "I thought you were driving this stage."

"I had planned to." Grasping her waist, he lifted her onto his lap, ignoring her startled gasp. "Instead, Robert will drive and I will try to ease your discomfort."

"Weymouth, you needn't do this."

"Am I supposed to ride on the box, pretending I don't know you are in pain?" He untied the ribbons of her bonnet and tossed it on the other seat, his movements abrupt. Then he took a deep breath and exhaled slowly, willing himself to calm. "I can't do that, Beth. You have suffered too much already on my account." He placed his hand on her head, guiding it to rest against his chest.

"You cannot blame yourself—"

"Go to sleep, Beth." He smoothed his hand over her hair, enjoying its silky feel against his palm and fingers. "Sleep so you won't feel the pain."

"This is shockingly improper." It was a statement of fact, not a protest.

"We have violated the canons of propriety many times since we met unchaperoned in the book room at Gull Cottage, but the high sticklers will never know that we haven't kept the line."

She did not reply. Glancing down, he saw she was asleep, her eyelashes like curly-plumed fans against her cheeks. Gently, he traced one with his thumb. He had never noticed that the ends of her lashes were lighter, as if they had been dipped in gold.

Cradling Beth in his arms, he stretched out his legs, propping them on the opposite seat. As the carriage bowled toward Newton Stewart, George pondered the many ways, according to Society's dictums, he had compromised Beth's reputation in the past eight days. If word got out that he had been in a room or in this carriage with her unchaperoned, he would be honor-bound to propose. He had never harmed Beth nor offered her insult, but that wouldn't matter to the gossipmongers. It did matter to him.

George had decided long ago to marry for love or not at all. He knew, and Beth knew, that he had behaved honorably. If her reputation was tarnished as a result of her abduction and subsequent disappearance, he would, of course, offer her marriage. But he would not be able to offer his heart.

Beth woke when the carriage slowed before making a turn. *Lud, she was sleeping in a man's arms!* In Weymouth's arms, she amended, recognizing his scent. She blushed at such a shockingly improper thought. It was the scent of his shaving soap she identified—or so she told herself.

"Your timing is excellent, Beth. We are nearly at Hillcrest Lodge."

How had he known she was awake? Had he seen her blushes? "I slept so long? I am sorry to have been such a poor traveling companion." Hoping her cheeks had lost their flush, she pushed away from his chest.

"You are an excellent traveling companion, although far too stoic." He lifted her from his lap and placed her on the seat beside him. "How is your shoulder?"

"It isn't as painful as it was earlier. Thank you for easing the ride for me."

"What can we do to make the trip less painful for you?"

Beth felt the color flaming in her cheeks again. She could not, she would not, sit in his lap for the entire trip to London. "I couldn't find a comfortable position sitting, even with the pillows cushioning my shoulder. Lying down was much less painful, until a large bump in the road jolted me off the seat. Tomorrow I will lie on the seat and hope for more even roads."

"Elston and I will do our best to give you a smooth ride."

"I know you will, and I appreciate all that you have done for me."

The carriage stopped, halting their conversation. Weymouth climbed down, then turned to assist her. Elston joined them and escorted her up the steps and into the house. They passed the evening quietly, in cards and conversation, teaching Beth to play piquet.

The second day they traveled to Castle Douglas. Posting houses were few and far between, so they progressed slowly to spare the horses. Once they reached Carlisle, Weymouth and Elston said, they would be able to change horses regularly.

It was cold the next morning when they left Castle Douglas. The sky was heavy with clouds. Rain before noon the earl predicted; snow by mid-morning was the marquess's opinion. Beth hoped that the inclement weather, whatever it was to be, would hold off until late afternoon, after they arrived in Dumfries. She didn't want Weymouth, Elston, Henry, or Higgins sitting on the box in rain or snow.

She lay on her side on the carriage seat, blankets and pillows padded about her to keep her from bouncing off if the road was bumpy. She read for a while, but the poor light put an end to that pastime after only a few chapters.

She thought about her traveling companions, Weymouth in particular. His behavior here in Scotland was so very different than in Hampshire. She could not imagine the toplofty earl of the house party removing a pistol ball from her shoulder, nursing her through a fever, or holding her on his lap to alleviate the painful jolting of the carriage. Yet he had done all of that and more. Was his current attitude an aberration or had his demeanor at Dunnley Park been atypical? Beth wished she knew the answer to that question. She liked the man traveling with her; she hadn't liked the arrogant earl.

When the coach stopped after only an hour, she wondered what was amiss. Then, hearing the shouted commands of ostlers, she realized they had reached Dalbeattie. Elston, his cheeks ruddy from the cold, opened the carriage door. "May I join you, Miss Castleton?"

"Please do." Beth struggled to untangle herself from the blankets and sit up.

"You are not to sit up, ma'am. I will not have you injuring your shoulder or in pain on my account."

"Very well." She subsided back onto the seat. "Thank you. Has it turned colder?"

He unwrapped the muffler from around his neck and placed his booted feet on the newly replenished hot bricks.

"I don't know if it has gotten colder or if it merely seems so. George and I decided to switch off every hour. Higgins and Henry will do the same."

"Is Henry able to drive alone?"

"We will see in an hour or so. He was driving when we left Castle Douglas, but Higgins was on the box with him. Higgins thinks Henry can handle the team on his own, at least under normal conditions."

"Perhaps you and Weymouth can ride inside this afternoon."

"Perhaps we can. If the weather holds."

She craned her neck to peer out the window. "Do you still think it will snow by mid-morning?"

"I do."

"I hope you are wrong, sir. I dislike the thought of any of you sitting on the box in bad weather."

A smile tugged at one corner of the marquess's mouth. "Time will tell, Miss Castleton. Given a choice, I would rather drive in light snow than in pouring rain."

They talked companionably for a time, Elston explaining that he was visiting each of his properties to see what, if anything, was required. Beth knew he hadn't much time to tend to business at Hillcrest Lodge, but he assured her he had been able to do what he needed. Shortly thereafter, she drifted off to sleep.

She woke when the carriage slowed again. "Elston, I am sorry to have been so rude as to fall asleep."

"You need rest to recover from your wound and the fever. Besides," he added, a twinkle in his eyes, "how do you know that I haven't been napping, too?" He buttoned his greatcoat, wrapped his muffler about his neck and the lower part of his face, then teased on his gloves. "George will keep you company for the next hour or so." With that he opened the door and jumped down to the road.

"George, you owe me a brandy."

"I will pay up tonight. Watch the off leader; he doesn't seem to like the snow."

Weymouth brushed snowflakes off his hat and the capes of his greatcoat before climbing inside the carriage and settling on the rear-facing seat. "How are you faring this morning, Beth?"

"Quite well. Are you very cold? Would you like a blanket?"

"No, thank you." After removing his gloves, he rubbed his hands together to warm them. "Are you comfortable? Warm enough?"

"I am fine, Weymouth. Has it been snowing very long?"

"Twenty or thirty minutes. It isn't snowing hard now, but I think it may later."

"Oh dear."

George unbuttoned his greatcoat and settled back in the seat. "If the snow doesn't get any worse, we should be able to reach Dumfries today. If not, well, we will cross that bridge if we come to it."

He grimaced inwardly. Clichés were not the way to win the lady's admiration. *Did he want her admiration?* Yes, he realized after half a moment's thought, he did. He wanted Beth's friendship, and to gain it he had to earn her respect. She wasn't the cool, aloof miss he'd met at his cousin's house party—at least, she hadn't behaved like that here in Scotland. He rather thought the lady he was seeing now was the real Beth. He had observed on the Peninsula that character, true character, emerges in adversity.

"I find it much easier to converse with you here than I did at Dunnley Park. Why is that, do you suppose? Is that merely that our circumstances have relaxed the social conventions?" George knew the easing of social restrictions had nothing to do with it. He was the son and heir of a marquess, well schooled in social graces, able to talk with ease to the highest sticklers of the *ton* or the lowliest tradesmen.

Beth swung her legs to the floor and pushed herself into a sitting position. Before he could voice a protest, she said, "Don't fuss, Weymouth. I have been lying on that seat for hours. It won't hurt me to sit up for a time."

She glanced down at her hands and smoothed the wrinkles from her gloves. Just as he began to wonder if she was considering her reply or stalling to avoid the question, she met his gaze again. "I daresay the relaxation of social restrictions is a part of it. Mostly, it is because we are not in the midst of a large group of people. I am rather shy"— her eyes darted to the window—"and I feel like a fish out

of water in a crowd. Social events like the house party are
an ordeal for a social misfit such as I."

A social misfit? Was she suddenly attics to let? "Beth, you
are no more a social misfit than I am!"

"Oh, but I am, Weymouth," she contradicted, looking
him in the eye. "I may be the granddaughter and niece of
an earl, but most people do not realize that. The moment
I speak, they characterize me as 'that American girl.' Not
everyone does so, but my American-ness is only a small
part of the problem. I am a bluestocking by anyone's defi-
nition. I am uninterested in gossip, not good at social chitchat, and five or six years older than the other girls making
their come-outs."

"Ancient, are you?" he teased. "What does that make
me, with seven more years in my dish?"

"It is different for men and well you know it. I am practi-
cally on the shelf, but you are just entering your prime."

He couldn't argue with that. Society had different rules
for men and women, and probably always would.

She huffed out a breath. "I would be considered at my
last prayers in America, too. But there, I knew the people
with whom my family socialized. Here . . . I don't quite
know how to explain it. You have known most of the people in Society all your life. You know which families are
related, who is friends with whom, all of those sorts of
things. I do not. For example, I know that a cousin of
Viscount Dunnley and Captain Middleford attended their
house party, but I have no idea which guest it was. Aunt
Julia would know, but I kept forgetting to ask her."

"I can ease your mind on that score. I am Dunnley and
Stephen's cousin. My mother and their father were sister
and brother." George had learned a great deal with his
question, not the least of which was that he had not properly considered her situation, nor how isolated she must
feel. "I understand that you feel . . . different and discon-
nected, Beth. Have you made many friends here?"

"No." She bit her lip, her pretty blue eyes once again
avoiding his.

"I hope that you consider me one." She nodded but
didn't look at him. "Elston, too. When we reach London,
I will introduce you to people who share your interests. I
know that you like music, and mathematics." Another shy

nod. "Were you really calculating square roots in your head in the book room at Gull Cottage?"

The carriage halted abruptly, rocking Beth back against the squabs. She hissed out a breath, then asked, "Has it been an hour already?"

George quickly buttoned his greatcoat. "No. Something must be amiss." Opening the door, he jumped down to the road. "Stay inside the carriage."

Chapter 9

***

$\mathcal{E}$lston, Higgins, and Henry were standing near Elston's coach. Henry was speaking to the marquess, Higgins nodding in agreement. George wasn't close enough to hear the conversation, but their expressions indicated the news was not good. As he walked toward them, the first word he heard was a heartfelt "Damnation!" from Elston.

George was quickly given all the details. The near wheeler had picked up a stone in the off rear hoof, which Henry hadn't noticed for a time. Higgins had removed it now, but the damage was done. Elston's carriage would have to travel at a walk until they could change teams. If they were in England, the next posting house would be twenty or thirty minutes ahead. This, however, was a rather unpopulated area of Scotland; no one knew how far it was to the next inn.

All four men were of the opinion they should push on, not turn back to Dalbeattie. Elston proposed that Moira, Isabelle, and Henry should join Beth in Arabella's chaise; he and Higgins would follow. Henry felt he should stay with the slower equipage, since it was his fault the horse was lame. Higgins argued that he and Henry should drive the marquess's coach. George wanted to knock their heads together for such quibbling—they were standing in the cold and snow on an isolated moor, for heaven's sake!—but gamely stepped in to referee.

"Robert, it will be a long haul to the next inn at a walk. Are you determined to stay with your rig?"

"I am."

George nodded; he'd expected as much. "Henry, don't lambaste yourself. In weather like this it is difficult to notice a minor change in gait. I know you wish to stay with the marquess's coach, but we must be practical; it will take experienced hands to get that team to the next inn. I have no doubt that you will someday be an admirable whip, but today you and I will take turns driving Arabella's carriage."

Henry agreed with a nod, clearly pleased that he would still be allowed to drive. After a moment's contemplation of the difficulties Elston and Higgins might encounter, George said, "Robert, when we reach the next posting house, I will send a team back to you. Shall we wait for you there or meet you in Dumfries tonight?"

"Let's rendezvous at the Rose and Crown in Dumfries."

"Very well. Before we resume our journey, I suggest we enjoy the luncheon the innkeeper provided. After we eat, Isabelle and Moira can join Miss Castleton."

The suggestion was greeted with approval. Henry and Higgins climbed into the marquess's coach to share the meal with Moira and Isabelle; George and Elston joined Beth.

Over meat pastries and cold chicken, they apprised her of the situation. Realizing how difficult sharing the carriage would be for Beth, George pondered alternatives.

Her melodic voice interrupted his musings. "What is the matter, Weymouth?"

"I am considering how you can share the carriage without sitting upright."

"I don't think that will be possible; it is too cold for you and Henry to stay on the box when you aren't driving. Isabelle may be content to sit on someone's lap, although probably not for long. I shall manage." Beth's sweet smile and her quiet courage hit him in the solar plexus, like the punch Gentleman Jackson snuck under his guard a few weeks ago.

"I shall do what I can to ease the ride for you when I am inside."

She ducked her head. "Thank you, Weymouth, but that won't be necessary."

George felt a stab of disappointment; he had enjoyed holding Beth on his lap. *Lord help him, had he suddenly become a rake?* No, of course not, he assured himself. Beth was a very attractive young lady. He liked her and felt protective toward her, but they were only friends.

"George?"

He returned to the present with a start. "My apologies. I was woolgathering."

"We should resume our journey." The marquess buttoned his greatcoat, wrapped a muffler around his neck, donned his hat, then pulled on his gloves.

"Indeed we should." George, too, prepared to face the cold and snow.

As her companions readied themselves to brave the elements, Beth wrapped the remaining food and placed it in the basket. "Elston, please take this with you in case you are delayed."

The marquess opened the carriage door and jumped down to the road. Reaching back inside for the basket, he gave her one of his rare smiles. "Thank you, Miss Castleton. I will see you in Dumfries." He swept her an elaborate bow worthy of a courtier, then walked toward his coach.

Arabella's chaise seemed much smaller to Beth when Moira, Isabelle, and Henry joined her. The manservant bemoaned his stupidity in laming the horse until the maid hushed him with a firm *"Cuist!"* Isabelle was restless, so they played simple games and told stories to entertain her. Henry and Moira were as fascinated as the child by Beth's tales of America.

After about an hour, they came to a small inn. It wasn't a posting house, so there weren't horses to send back to Elston, but they had a cup of tea to warm their insides while the innkeeper's son replaced the bricks in the coach with hot ones.

When they resumed their journey, Weymouth joined the women while Henry took a turn with the reins. After a searching glance at Beth's face, the earl took his niece on his lap, telling her it was time for her nap, and ordered Beth to lie down on the seat. Isabelle, tired and cross and accustomed to Elston's more spacious coach, pertly informed her uncle that she couldn't go to sleep unless she was lying down. To avert an argument between uncle and niece, Beth, after a quelling look at Weymouth, offered Isabelle the nest of blankets and pillows Moira was preparing on the forward-facing seat. When the maid volunteered to share the seat with the squirming child, the earl helped the women exchange places without saying a word.

His silence was of short duration. As soon as Beth was seated beside him, his left arm reached out, captured her about the waist, and pulled her against his side. She gave him a reproving glare, to warn him not to lift her onto his lap in front of Moira and Isabelle, then laid her aching head against his shoulder with a weary sigh.

"Why, Beth?" he whispered.

"Because Isabelle needs to rest more than I do."

"I don't agree."

"You didn't spend the last hour in here with her, Weymouth. The child needs a nap." Beth's voice had been more tart than she intended. Biting her lip, she repressed a sigh and wished she, too, could lie down.

"She could have slept on my lap."

"Undoubtedly, but she wasn't inclined to do so. This isn't—"

Isabelle interrupted their quiet conversation. "Uncle George, the mean lady said she is my aunt. I don't want Lady Rarabel to be my aunt."

"Lady Arabella is, indeed, your aunt. She was your mother's sister."

"But I don't like her," the child protested, petulantly. "I want a different aunt."

"We cannot choose our relatives, little one. Lady Arabella is the only aunt you have, except for Great-Aunt Tilly and Great-Aunt Caroline. When I marry, my lady wife will be your aunt."

Beth thought he was missing the point of the argument. "Isabelle, you could ask a lady you like to be your honorary aunt."

"What is a ronorary aunt?

"An honorary aunt," Beth emphasized the correct pronunciation, "is a special lady you would like to have as your aunt, even though she is not a relative. You—"

"How do I get her to be my ronorary aunt?

"Miss Isabelle, dinna be interruptin'. 'Tis rude."

"I am sorry, Miss Castleton." The child's rote apology won her a smile from the maid and a mind-your-manners glower from her uncle. "How do I get a lady to be my ronorary aunt?"

"Honorary aunt." This time it was Weymouth who voiced the correction. "You have to say it properly, or the lady you ask will not know what you mean."

The little girl's mouth worked silently for a moment. "How do I get a lady to be my honorary aunt?"

"Very good, Isabelle." Beth smiled her approval. "After obtaining your father's permission, you ask the lady if she would be your honorary aunt. If she agrees—and any lady would be flattered to be asked—she will tell you how to address her and the deed is done."

Isabelle's lower lip protruded in a pout. "But I don't want to wait to ask Papa."

Hoping to avert a tantrum, Beth darted a look at the earl. "I daresay that, in the absence of your papa, your uncle could give his permission."

"Would you, Uncle George?" When Weymouth nodded, a smile lit his niece's face. "Miss Castleton, will you be my honorary aunt?"

The question surprised Beth—and delighted her. She swallowed, trying to dislodge the lump from her throat. "I would be honored, poppet. If your uncle thinks your papa would approve, that is."

Weymouth looked at her, clearly astonished. "Without a doubt," he averred.

Isabelle bounced in her seat. "Does that mean yes, Uncle George?"

"Indeed it does, little one."

Beth smiled at both Winterbrooks before saying, "You may call me Aunt Beth if you like." The little girl catapulted onto Beth's lap, pushing her back against the squabs. She bit her lip to keep from moaning. When Isabelle threw her arms about Beth's neck and kissed her cheek, she gave the child a one-armed hug and returned the salute. Speech was beyond her as she battled the pain in her shoulder.

Brushing the tears from Beth's cheeks, Isabelle asked, "Why are you crying, Aunt Beth?"

Weymouth picked up his niece and returned her to her seat. "Perhaps your Aunt Beth is crying because she is happy." His mild tone was belied by the scowl marring his handsome features. "Or because you bumped her sore shoulder when you jumped on her lap."

"Did I hurt you, Aunt Beth? I didn't mean to. I am very sorry." Tears pooled in the little girl's blue eyes.

Beth's voice was thin, but she managed a halting reply. "I know you didn't mean to hurt me. You will be more careful until my shoulder is better, won't you?"

Isabelle nodded emphatically.

George, all too aware of the tension in Beth's slender frame as she tried to control her pain, rejoined the conversation with an avuncular command. "Isabelle, it is time for your nap." As the child opened her mouth for the inevitable protest, he added, "Miss Castleton wouldn't like her new niece to be cross as crabs."

Without another word, Isabelle snuggled into the blankets and closed her eyes.

George wiped the tears from Beth's face with his handkerchief. "How bad is it?"

"Better now."

He didn't believe her but, ever the gentleman, refrained from calling her a liar. "Do you want some laudanum?"

"No." She shuddered. "It seems to bring on my nightmares."

"Lean against me and use my shoulder as a pillow."

" 'Tis a rock-hard pillow you offer, Weymouth, but I thank you for it."

When he was certain Beth was asleep, George addressed her maid. "Moira, please check Miss Castleton's shoulder as soon as we reach the inn at Dumfries. I need to know how badly this has set her back."

"Aye, Lord Weymouth, I will hae a look as soon as may be." After a searching glance at his face, the Scotswoman said hesitantly, "The bairn dinna mean to hurt Miss Castleton."

He sighed. "I know she didn't, but just sitting in the carriage is painful for your mistress, and Isabelle's demonstration of affection certainly didn't help."

"What if my lady canna travel tomorrow?"

"Then we will stay another night at the inn." With his right hand, George pulled out his watch. "Considering that we haven't found horses to send back to Elston, and likely won't until we reach Dumfries, it will be very late when the marquess arrives. For both his sake and Beth's, I think we should spend tomorrow in Dumfries."

Moira nodded. "I agree wi' ye, m'lord, but I dinna think either of them will."

"Then I will have to play the arrogant earl, won't I?"

A smile twitched one corner of the maid's mouth. "I have nae doubt ye can do it well, m'lord, but Lord Elston outranks ye."

"That he does. And he can out-arrogant me without even trying." George sighed theatrically, a man sorely tried, and Moira's brown eyes sparkled with mirth.

"He is a gud man, the marquess."

"One of the best, and a very good friend. He will agree to a day's delay for Beth's sake, and she, for his."

Sometime later the carriage skidded sideways then came to an abrupt halt. George eased Beth upright and motioned for Moira to take his place. Plopping his hat upon his head, he grabbed his gloves and muffler then opened the door and jumped down, nearly losing his footing when his boots slid on the icy road. *Damn!*

As he buttoned his greatcoat and wrapped the scarf around his neck, he conferred with a shaken Henry. After ascertaining that the horses were not injured, George pulled on his gloves, then mounted the box and took the reins.

With only his thoughts for company, he drove through the whirling snow. He worried about Beth and how much of a toll this afternoon had taken on her, and about Elston, far behind them. All George could do for his friend was send horses back to him—and rely on Robert's good sense and skill as a whip.

They arrived in Dumfries as dusk was falling. George felt cold to his bones after more than two hours on the box, but when the ostlers ran to the weary horses and began unharnessing them, he shouted instructions to send a team back to Elston. The postilions mumbled about being sent on a fool's errand until Henry said he would get a horse and lantern and ride with them. The look in his eye told George that his new underbutler didn't quite trust them to do as ordered. And that he wanted to atone for his earlier mistake. Knowing he wouldn't be able to talk Henry out of going, George didn't even try. He only told his man that if he found Elston west of the little inn where they'd stopped for tea, he should try to convince the marquess to stay the night there. Henry promised to do his best, but his face expressed doubt that he could persuade the marquess to do anything he didn't wish.

Having done all that he could for his friend, George opened the carriage door to hand his ladies out. One look at Beth told him the afternoon had been more of an ordeal for her than he'd imagined. He swung his niece down, told her to stand beside him, and motioned for Moira to descend next. As he assisted her, he watched Isabelle cavorting beside the coach, trying to catch snowflakes on her tongue.

"Miss Castleton is in a bad way, m'lord. Can the bairn play for a wee bit whilst ye get my lady inside?"

"Yes, for a few minutes, if you stay here with her."

"O' course I will, m'lord."

With his niece taken care of, George turned back to Beth. She was curled on the seat with her uninjured side against the squabs, her feet tucked up, and her eyes closed. There was more color in his cravat than in her face, and she hadn't moved since he'd opened the door. *Was she in such pain that she wasn't even aware they had stopped?*

"Beth?" Her eyelids fluttered open. She gazed at him without recognition for a second or two, then closed her eyes again. "Dear God. What have we done to you, sweetheart?" He lifted her into his arms and carried her into the inn.

The innkeeper met him at the door, bowing obsequiously. "Good evening, my lord. Welcome to the Rose and Crown."

"Good evening," George replied mechanically, mentally assigning rooms. "I need three bedchambers and a private parlor. A friend will be joining us later tonight and he, too, will need a room."

"I have only three bedchambers and two private parlors left, my lord. Would your friend be willing to double up?"

"Elston can share my room, if you have space elsewhere for his man and mine. They can double up as well."

"Yes, my lord." The innkeeper held out a quill and indicated the register.

George opened his mouth to say he'd sign later, but feared that would give rise to a number of questions he'd prefer not to answer. He shifted his hold on Beth, balancing her in one arm, and she moaned softly. Grabbing the pen, he dipped it into the inkpot, and quickly scrawled "Weymouth & party."

The landlord picked up three keys and turned toward the stairs. Isabelle skipped into the inn, followed by Moira, and came to stand beside him. Her little forehead scrunched in a frown, she tugged on his coat and asked, "Uncle George, is Aunt Beth feeling better?" just as the landlord inquired, "Is your wife ill, my lord?"

Ignoring the man, George mustered a smile for his niece. "She will, poppet, after she is settled in her bed. Take Moira's hand and follow the innkeeper upstairs. He will show us our rooms."

Several hours later George sat, exhausted, in front of a roaring fire. He'd spent the evening entertaining his niece so Moira could take care of her mistress. Beth's wound had opened again, possibly from Isabelle's demonstration of affection, but more likely from rubbing against the squabs. Beth had drifted in and out of consciousness all evening, her beautiful blue eyes foggy with pain—and laudanum. George wished he could do more for her than watch over her while she slept; he hadn't felt so helpless since the Peninsula.

Glancing down at the book on his lap, he remembered the time at Hawthorn Lodge when she'd asked him to read to her. It had eased her then; perhaps it would have the same effect now. "*Sense and Sensibility*. Chapter Thirty-one. 'From a night of more sleep than she had expected, Marianne awoke the next morning to the same consciousness of misery in which she had closed her eyes.' " He stopped, casting a worried glance at the girl on the bed. Miss Marianne Dashwood's misery had a different source than Beth's, but he wasn't inclined to read about any woman's sufferings. Setting the book aside, he stood and walked to the bed, then touched Beth's cheek with the back of his fingers.

Her eyelids fluttered open. "Weymouth?"

Thank you, God. His knees suddenly weak, George sank down on the edge of the bed and took her right hand in both of his. "Yes, it is I."

"I suppose there is a reason you are in my bedchamber?"

She glanced around the room, a frown creasing her brow.
"And a reason I do not recognize this room?"

"We are at the Rose and Crown in Dumfries. Would you
like something to eat or drink?"

"Turned waiter, have you?"

The hint of a smile accompanying Beth's teasing comment brought him an enormous feeling of relief. *She was
going to be fine. Not tonight, perhaps not even tomorrow,
but the worst was past.* "No, but you missed dinner; I
thought you might be hungry."

"More thirsty than hungry. Some tea would be very nice."

"Barley water would be better." After lifting her to sit
against the pillows, he stood and walked to the dresser.
"How is your shoulder?"

"It hurts. Far more than it has for the past several days,"
she said, equal measures of worry and resignation in her
voice. "If you are proposing barley water as a cure for the
pain, I can assure you, it won't help."

He poured a glassful, then glanced over his shoulder at
her. "Do you want some laudanum?"

"No," she replied, shuddering. "Nightmares."

He crossed to the bed and offered her the glass. "How
much of this afternoon do you remember?"

Her eyes narrowed in concentration. "One of Elston's
horses went lame. Isabelle, Moira, and Henry joined me in
the carriage. We played games and I told stories about
America. You joined us later when Henry drove." Her
forehead wrinkled—and her nose. "Did Isabelle ask me to
be her honorary aunt?"

"Indeed she did. And you accepted. What else do you
recall?"

A delicate blush suffused Beth's face with more color
than she'd had for hours. "I slept with my head on your
shoulder."

"Yes, you did. A rock-hard pillow you called it," he
teased, one finger caressing her rosy cheek. "What else?"

She batted his hand away, like a horse swishing its tail
at flies, then clasped it and entwined her fingers with his.
Frowning again, her gaze swept the room. "N-nothing else.
I don't even recall arriving here."

With his free hand, he rubbed the creases from her brow.
"You were nearly unconscious when we arrived, Beth."

"Was I?" She looked at him through her lashes, her expression puzzled. "I remember I was, um, uncomfortable sitting in the carriage."

"Your wound opened and began bleeding. Tomorrow—"

"How could a cauterized wound open?"

"It didn't. The scar tissue over the burn cracked open and bled."

"Oh." Her eyes darted away from his. "I will be fine by morning, Weymouth."

"I am pleased to hear it, but we won't be traveling tomorrow." Before she could protest, he added, "Elston still hasn't arrived. He and Higgins will need to rest after driving so long, and so late, today."

"Is it still snowing?"

Reluctantly, George untangled his fingers from hers, then rose and walked to the window, shoving the drapes aside. "It is, but not as hard as it was earlier. The roads may be too snow-packed or too icy to travel in the morning."

"It is February, in Scotland. I should think snow and ice are normal this time of year."

"They are," he replied absently, wondering whether Robert, Higgins, and Henry were spending the night at the little inn on the moor. Dropping the drapery, he returned to his chair by the hearth and picked up his book. "Go to sleep, Beth. Sleep and heal."

She turned onto her side and, one-handed, pulled covers over her shoulder. Snuggling her cheek into the pillow, she glanced over at him. "Is that *Sense and Sensibility*? Will you read to me, please?"

George opened the volume and skipped several pages, passing over the travails of Miss Marianne. "I am in the middle of a chapter."

"I don't mind where you start. I know the story well."

"Very well." He quickly scanned the page, then flipped back to find the chapter number. "In Chapter Thirty-two. 'Colonel Brandon's delicate unobtrusive inquiries were never unwelcome to Miss Dashwood. He had abundantly earned the privilege of intimate discussion of her sister's disappointment, by the friendly zeal with which he had endeavoured to soften it . . .'"

Realizing that Beth was asleep, George closed the book, stood, and stretched. Traversing the room one last time, he opened the door to the adjoining chamber where Isabelle and Moira slept, so the maid would hear if Beth called out. Then, weary to the bone, he walked to the other door, opened it, and stepped into the hallway. Locking the door behind him, he trudged down the hall to his own room.

After a day's rest, two days of travel brought them to Elston's property near Brough. They spent the night at his estate, with every comfort the household could provide. Weymouth was very quiet at breakfast, and Beth knew he worried about her shoulder being reinjured, since she would be sharing the chaise again. Elston expressed his concern more obliquely, apologizing for not having an extra carriage to loan them, this estate having been rented for the past decade by a distant relative, recently deceased. Weymouth gratefully accepted the marquess's offer of a horse, saying that he and Henry could take turns driving and riding. When Beth expressed a wish to ride part of the time, the earl told her it would be too much strain on her healing wound. She did not agree, but forbore from arguing.

As they stood in the drive in front of the house, Beth tried to express her appreciation to the marquess. "Elston, I thank you most sincerely for all you have done to help us. I shall miss your conversation—and your friendship."

He took her hand and bowed over it. "It was my pleasure, Miss Castleton. You shall always have my friendship, whether I am present or not, but further conversations will have to wait until I come to London later this spring. I hope you will save a dance for me at your come-out ball."

She smiled shyly as he handed her into the chaise. "I would be honored, and delighted, to dance with you then."

Nine rainy, muddy days later, on the ninth of March, they arrived in London early in the afternoon. Of Lady Arabella and her cousin, they had seen not a trace. She had been several days ahead of them at Carlisle, but they hadn't traveled the Great North Road, and there had been no other reports of her or Sir James.

Beth descended from the chaise in front of Castleton House with the eagerness of a condemned man escaping the gallows. She would be happy not to see the inside of a carriage for at least a week. That wasn't likely to happen, but it was comforting to know she would never again see the inside of this particular vehicle.

Impatient to see her great-aunt and uncle but wishing she were wearing something other than the shabby carriage dress she had worn for the better part of the past month, she accepted George's escort to the door. Moira and Isabelle followed behind them; Henry stood at the horses' heads.

North, her uncle's regal butler, greeted her at the door. His obvious delight at seeing her was more emotion than Beth had ever thought to see on his rather forbidding countenance. Lord Castleton and Lady Julia were from home, he informed her, but expected back for tea. As Beth unbuttoned her pelisse, she introduced Moira as her new maid. North quickly assessed the Scotswoman, then greeted her kindly and promised to introduce her to the household.

George didn't surrender his greatcoat and hat to the butler. *Was he so eager to see the back of her that he wouldn't even stay for a cup of tea? And when had she started thinking of him as George?*

After a quick word to Moira, Beth led her guests to the morning room. A swift glance at the earl showed him more Friday-faced than he'd been since Gull Cottage. Puzzled by his manner and mien, she offered him a chair, which he declined, then shifted her attention to his niece, who sat beside her on the sofa.

"Isabelle, I hope you will visit me before you return home to Oxfordshire."

"May I bring my papa, Aunt Beth? I want you to meet him."

"Of course you may bring your father. I would like to tell him what a wonderful daughter he has."

Isabelle scrambled to her knees and hugged Beth tightly. "I will miss you, Aunt Beth."

Blinking back tears, she returned the child's hug. "I shall miss you, too, sweet girl."

George's pacing halted in front of the sofa. He held out a hand to help her rise. "Beth, I would like to return later this afternoon to speak with you."

What was this? Her expression serene despite her tumultuous thoughts she said, "You are welcome at any time,

Weymouth. A simple 'thank you' seems vastly inadequate. I cannot express my appreciation and gratitude for all that you have done for me."

He turned abruptly, picked up his niece, and strode rapidly from the room. *What in the world had she said to provoke that grim expression?*

Chapter 10

George's scowl as he drove from Grosvenor Square to Portman Square was unrelated to the traffic in Mayfair. Indeed, he barely noticed the other vehicles on the road, threading his way through them with great skill and little thought. Beth's words—"I cannot express my appreciation and gratitude for all that you have done for me"—haunted him. *Did she not realize that her reputation might be ruined because of him?* The blame was not entirely his, of course, but the result of Arabella's desire to wed his title and fortune and Sir James's mad plan to grant his cousin's wish.

Honor demanded that George propose to Beth. He had no idea what explanation the Earl of Castleton and Lady Julia had given for Beth's absence, but the tale they'd told was of little consequence. George knew that he had compromised her reputation, if only in the eyes of their families. He had spent many hours alone with her—from the book room at Gull Cottage to the carriage journey from Stranraer to Brough. Not to mention the several nights he had spent in her bedchamber. He had nursed her then, not offered her insult or debauched her, but if the gossipmongers learned of it, they wouldn't care about such trifling details.

George had thought the knowledge that he'd acted honorably toward Beth would be enough to satisfy his conscience and his honor. He was a bit surprised to find that it was not. He would offer for her this afternoon, after they had talked with Lord Castleton and Lady Julia. It would not be the love match he'd wanted, but it could be a happy marriage. They were friends and had a number of common interests. He rather thought they had similar goals and dreams, as well. In addition to all that, she was lovely, intelligent, well-spoken, and liked children. Yes, it could be a happy marriage.

Arriving in Portman Square, he saw a carriage parked in front of Bellingham House. He could cry craven and pull around to the mews, but he had to face Society sooner or later. It might as well be now, with his niece to tout his heroic rescue. At the thought, he nearly groaned aloud. How could he convince three-year-old Isabelle of the utter necessity of not mentioning Beth's name? He would do his best—and pray it was sufficient.

As he halted the chaise, a groom in his father's livery ran to the leaders' head. "Welcome 'ome, m'lord!"

"Thank you, Jim. It is good to be here."

"Yer lord father will be mighty pleased to see ye."

"And I, him." George descended from the box, then opened the carriage door and lifted Isabelle into his arms. Henry jumped down behind them. "Jim, tell the footmen to unload everything except that small trunk."

"I will see to the luggage, my lord," Henry stated.

"Thank you." George started up the walk, quietly exhorting his niece not to mention Beth's name. Unable to explain the potential problems, he settled for, "You don't want to cause trouble, do you?" Isabelle's reply was a vehement shake of the head just as Hargrave, his father's butler, opened the door.

"Welcome home, Lord Weymouth. And Miss Isabelle." The butler's normally solemn countenance was wreathed in a smile.

"Thank you, Hargrave. Is my father in?"

"Yes, my lord. In the morning room with your aunts and their guests."

"Aunts in the plural?" George helped his niece remove her coat, then doffed his greatcoat and hat.

"Yes, my lord. Lady Matilda and Lady Richard. Lord David is there as well."

"I am in no fit state to be seen—"

Isabelle was not concerned about her uncle's dishevelment—or her own. Upon hearing her father's name, she ran down the hall. "Papa, Papa!"

Before she was halfway there, her father appeared in the doorway, then knelt on the floor and opened his arms. "Oh,

sweet baby!" The joyous reunion brought tears to George's
eyes. His daughter held firmly in one arm, David rose and
embraced his brother with the other. "Thank you, George.
Thank you for bringing her back to me, safe and sound."

The occupants of the parlor watched unabashedly, the
ladies dabbing at their tears with lacy handkerchiefs, the
gentlemen blinking rapidly. Andrew Winterbrook, the Marquess of Bellingham, stood and strode across the room,
both hands outstretched to greet his eldest son. "George,
it is good to have you home."

"Thank you, sir. It is—"

His aunts' arrival halted the conversation. Hugging his
father's sister, Lady Matilda Elliott, George asked, "Aunt
Tilly, what brings you from Northumberland?"

"You do, nephew. I couldn't bear to sit at Bellingham
Castle, waiting for days' old news of your return."

Next he hugged his father's younger brother's widow,
Lady Richard Winterbrook, who served as chatelaine at his
estate. "And you, Aunt Caro? What brings you from
Dorsetshire?"

"You do, for the same reason as Tilly. And before you
ask, all was well at Winterhaven Manor when I left."

Untangling himself from his aunt's embrace, George
made his bow to the guests—Charles Castleton, the Earl
of Castleton and Beth's uncle, and Lady Julia Castleton,
her great-aunt. "Lord Castleton, Lady Julia, I apologize for
appearing before you in all my dirt. I just left your niece
at Castleton House, sir."

The earl, who had injured his hip in a riding accident
many years ago, struggled to his feet with the aid of a
sturdy blackthorn cane. "She is well?"

"Her wound is healing nicely, sir, but she will bear a
scar."

"Miss Castleton was injured?" This from Aunt Tilly.

George sighed. He had hoped that he and Beth could
tell the tale together. "Miss Castleton was shot by one of
Arabella's footmen." Before his aunt could voice another
question, he said, "It is a long story, best told by both Miss
Castleton and myself. She can describe her experiences,
and I, mine." He darted a look at his father and mouthed
the word "dinner."

Bellingham stepped into the breech. "Castleton, Lady

Julia, will you join us for dinner this evening? George and your niece can give us the tale then."

"There is a vote in Lords tonight that neither of us should miss," the earl said, his voice gruff.

"So there is. Would you like to send word for your niece to join us now?"

"Lord Castleton," George interposed, "may I suggest that you send a message to your niece telling her that I will call for her in an hour to escort her here? I daresay she would appreciate a bath as much as I," he added ruefully.

"An excellent notion." Lord Castleton motioned to a small desk. "May I?"

"By all means," Bellingham replied.

The note was quickly written, and a footman dispatched to carry it to Beth. With a bow, George retired to repair his appearance.

An hour later, looking and feeling much more the thing in a blue superfine coat by Weston, buff inexpressibles, a cream-colored waistcoat, clean linen, and Hessians polished to a mirror shine, George was on his way back to Castleton House, accompanied by Lady Julia. The silver-haired spinster was a lovely woman, despite her nearly seventy years, and one of Society's leading hostesses. She was also awake on every suit. Since he didn't want to answer questions until Beth was present, George queried Lady Julia. He learned that she and Lord Castleton had been in London for a sennight, that more and more members of the *ton* were arriving daily, and that Beth had already received vouchers for Almack's, having met, and favorably impressed, Lady Cowper and Lady Sefton during the winter.

Back in Grosvenor Square, George assisted Lady Julia from the carriage and escorted her to the door. A flicker of surprise crossed the butler's face at seeing him again, but North's words were for Beth's great-aunt.

"Lady Julia, Miss Beth has returned!"

"Thank you, North." The formal words were accompanied by a joyous smile. "Lord Weymouth has already given us the good news. Where is my niece?"

"I believe she is in her chamber, my lady. John will inquire." The butler nodded to a footman, but Lady Julia overrode the order.

"No, I will go." She ascended the stairs at a pace more sprightly than stately.

Beth flitted around her chamber, moving objects then returning them to their original positions. *Why has Uncle Charles summoned me to Bellingham House?* 'Twas an unanswerable question for the nonce. Perhaps her relatives and George's wanted to hear of their experiences at the same time. She frowned at the realization that a complete recounting would require the participation not only of George and herself, but also of Moira and Henry. Perhaps even Isabelle. And Aunt Julia and George's brother—what was his name? Daniel? David?—to explain what occurred directly after she and Isabelle were kidnapped.

Walking into her dressing room, where Moira was studying her mistress's wardrobe, Beth said, "I need you to come with me to Bellingham House."

"Aye, miss, to act as yer chaperone."

"That, of course, but if my uncle has summoned me for the reason I think, you may be asked about Lady Arabella's and Sir James's scheme or . . . about our escape and our journey to London."

The Scotswoman paled. "Ye mean I will hae to speak to yer uncle?"

"Yes, and probably to Lord Weymouth's father as well."

The maid wrung her hands. "Miss Castleton, I dinna know if I can."

Beth clasped Moira's hands in hers. "Of course you can. My uncle and Lord Bellingham are not ogres. At least, Uncle Charles isn't. I have never met the marquess, but I cannot believe that he is, either. Do you really think an unkind man could raise a son as charming and amiable as Lord Weymouth?"

"Nae, I reckon not. 'Tis just . . ."

" 'Tis just what?" Beth prompted.

"I am verra uncomfortable around men I dinna know. But I will try, miss, fer yer sake."

A light rap on the bedchamber door distracted them both. "Beth?"

"Aunt Julia!" Beth raced from the dressing room to greet her great-aunt. "I am so happy to see you!" She kissed her aunt's porcelain cheek and returned her affectionate embrace. "I thought you were at Bellingham House."

"I was, darling, but I couldn't wait to see you, so I came with Weymouth to escort you." Her aunt's gaze swept from head to toe. "You look lovely, my dear."

Beth laughed. "Had you seen me an hour ago, your opinion would have been *quite* different."

Aunt Julia arced an eyebrow in inquiry.

"I had been wearing the same dress for more than a month. Except for the times when I was . . . ill. I am sorry to say that, between pistol holes, bloodstains, and mud, my blue carriage dress is beyond repair."

Aunt Julia shuddered, then hugged her again. "How is your shoulder?"

"A bit sore from the jostling of the carriage, but healing well, thanks to Moira and Weymouth."

"Moira?" Her aunt's eyebrow rose again.

"Moira Sinclair, my new maid, who helped us escape from Arabella and her cousin."

"I would like to meet Moira and thank her for taking such good care of you."

"And so you shall." Taking her aunt's hand, Beth led her to the dressing room. "Aunt Julia, this is Moira Sinclair. Moira, this is my great-aunt, Lady Julia Castleton."

Moira curtsied as Aunt Julia said, "I thank you very much for taking such good care of my niece."

" 'Twas my pleasure, Lady Julia."

"We shall talk more later. Now"—Aunt Julia linked her arm with Beth's—"there are a number of people awaiting us at Bellingham House. Not to mention," she added, her delft blue eyes twinkling, "a very handsome gentleman downstairs."

"But, Aunt Julia, I want to know what happened to you after I was abducted."

"And so you shall, darling. At Bellingham House, we will all describe our . . . experiences."

George roused from his contemplation of the best way to describe the plotting of Sir James and Arabella and all its consequences at the sound of Lady Julia's voice. Placing his nearly empty sherry glass on the console table beside his chair, he rose to his feet. When Beth and her great-aunt appeared, his breath caught in his throat.

She was beautiful! George gathered his scattered wits. "Beth, you look lovely. Your dress nearly matches the color of your eyes."

Smiling shyly, she brushed her hand against the skirts of her Clarence blue afternoon dress. "Thank you, Weymouth."

"Ladies, are you ready to depart?"

Moira assisted Beth into a pelisse of Bishop's blue, then perched a Gypsy hat on her golden brown hair and tied the matching ribbons with a flourish. Her lady now complete to a shade, the maid stepped back.

As he offered one arm to Lady Julia and the other to Beth, George wondered when he would have the opportunity to propose. He would prefer to make his offer before they told their tale, but that might not be possible.

On the way back to Bellingham House, Lady Julia's conversation was lively, but Beth was very quiet. *Was she worried about explaining her absence to her uncle?* When he assisted the ladies from the carriage, George gave Beth's hand a gentle squeeze and smiled reassuringly when she glanced up at him.

As they surrendered their outerwear to Hargrave, Beth posed a question. "Will Moira be asked to give an account of our . . . our . . ."

"Our adventure?" George supplied, determined to present their families—and Society—with a positive interpretation of events. "I daresay she will. Henry, too." After asking the butler to have Henry join them in the morning room, George escorted Beth and Lady Julia down the hallway. Moira trailed behind.

The scene in the parlor was much as he had left it, although Isabelle was no longer present. Pausing in the doorway, he looked down at Beth's great-aunt. "Would you like to introduce your niece to my relatives or shall I?"

"I will." Smiling, Lady Julia led her niece toward his aunts. George made a beeline for Beth's uncle.

"Lord Castleton, will you permit me to pay my addresses to your niece?"

The question seemed to startle the earl. "Fallen in love with her, have you?"

"I am fond of her, sir, and we are friends, but my primary concern is that her reputation has been tarnished by her disappearance."

"If I understood your letter correctly—and I thank you for notifying us of Beth's whereabouts and her injury—you had nothing to do with my niece's disappearance."

George resisted the urge to run his finger under his collar, which, for some inexplicable reason, suddenly seemed much too tight. "I was not directly responsible, but it was because of the schemes of Arabella and her cousin to trap me into marriage by kidnapping my niece that Beth was abducted." He clasped his hands together behind his back to keep from tugging at his cravat. "Also, Beth has spent several weeks in my company with only a maid as chaperone."

"You are an honorable man, Weymouth. You have my permission to make an offer, but the decision will be Beth's alone."

"Thank you, sir." He breathed a sigh of relief as Beth, having completed the circuit of introductions, approached her uncle.

The earl stood and enveloped his niece in a hug. George crossed the room to apprise his father of his intentions.

While Lady Matilda poured tea and Lady Richard passed plates of cakes and other delicacies, Beth strove to reduce the lump of trepidation in her stomach from the size of a boulder to something a bit more manageable. The Winterbrooks had been kindness itself, but her courage seemed to have deserted her. George caught her eye and smiled. An ember of valor flickered alight in her soul.

Lord Bellingham glanced from her to his son. "Who will begin the tale?"

Beth set her cup aside, smoothed her skirts, then clasped her hands in her lap. "I suppose I should start, since my abduction, and Isabelle's, occurred first." She told of leaving the inn at Reading, of the events she later dreamed.

When she finished, her uncle complained that he didn't understand why she'd been abducted. Since Isabelle wasn't present, George explained that Beth had been hit over the

head by one of Sir James's men in the mistaken belief that
she was the child's governess. Beth resumed the narrative
with her awakening at Gull Cottage six days later, ending
with her time pacing the book room, reciting theorems and
calculating square roots—which won her an admiring
glance from Lord Bellingham and a proud smile from
Uncle Charles. When the marquess asked how she and Isabelle had gotten from Oxfordshire to Scotland, Henry said
he believed they had been taken by carriage to Southamp-
ton, then by yacht to Drummore.

Lord David and Aunt Julia began speaking simultaneously, but George's brother deferred to the lady. Aunt Julia
spoke with a twinkle in her eye and a deal of vivacity. "I
was sleeping soundly in the coach, dreaming of a needlework pattern that wouldn't come right. When I awoke, I
was in a grubby cottage, tied hand and foot, and lying on
a straw-filled mattress with a handsome young man. A very
enterprising young man, too, for he turned so that our
backs were to each other and asked me to try to undo the
knots in the rope binding his hands."

"Which she did, more quickly than I would have thought
possible." George's brother took up the story, explaining
how they had untied each other's bonds then released the
coachmen. A note nailed to the inside of the door, where
it could not be missed, said that Isabelle would be returned
unharmed in a few days, provided Lord David did not alert
the authorities. No mention was made of Beth, but the
Castleton coachman, although wounded, had seen her carried off with the little girl. Their carriages had been outside
the cottage, the horses in a nearby pasture. Believing that
further messages from the kidnappers would be delivered
to Lord David's home, he and Aunt Julia had traveled
there, from whence she had dispatched a groom to Castleton Abbey with a letter for the earl.

Lord David waved an arm, inviting the next person to
give their explanation. "Wait. George, confirm something
for me, please?"

"If I can."

"I am certain I already know the answer, but did you or
did you not send me a note shortly before Isabelle was
kidnapped telling me you'd injured your arm and asking us
to come to Dorsetshire?"

"I did not. I did, however, receive a similar note, purportedly from you, asking me to come to Oxfordshire."

"So that is why you and Isabelle had luggage and I did not," Beth exclaimed. "I must confess, I thought it most unfair that the two of you always looked elegant and fashionable while I had to wear an increasingly shabby carriage dress."

That drew an apologetic smile from George. Lord Bellingham and Uncle Charles looked grim as the charges against Arabella and Sir James mounted.

George's part was next. He described his abduction and the conversation in which Arabella had explained the scheme she or her cousin had concocted (their exact roles were still a mystery), his request to Beth to spirit Isabelle to safety, and the assistance of Moira and Henry. He skipped over the confrontation in the parlor, merely saying Beth returned because he hadn't given her adequate directions, and described Henry's courageous action that allowed them to escape, although not unscathed. Then the race up the Mull, the decision to go to Elston's lodge, and Moira and himself removing the pistol ball from Beth's shoulder. He detailed their route from Stranraer to London, explaining that snow in Scotland and rain in England had slowed their travel.

When George finished, there was silence for nearly a minute, then a chorus of exclamations. A few questions were posed, which he answered. Beth was amazed that he had, without lying, presented the tale in such a way that their behavior seemed unexceptional. Except for James's and Arabella's, of course. George had said little about her fever and their time at Hawthorn Lodge, but he had given a complete, if not detailed, recounting of all that had occurred.

After Moira and Henry were thanked and dismissed, Lord Bellingham questioned the wisdom of hiring servants who had shown such disloyalty to their former mistress. George averred they had demonstrated their devotion to their new employers in many ways. Beth concurred then, impetuously, posed a question. "Lord Bellingham, if Lady Matilda were to . . . to undergo a sea change and take to scheming and abduction, would you be surprised if her servants deserted her?"

"I daresay I would not. Your point, Miss Castleton." The marquess's grin was identical to his eldest son's.

The lighthearted moment was destroyed when Uncle Charles asked, "What is to be done about Sir James and Lady Arabella?"

George rose and paced back and forth in front of the fireplace. "I have given the matter a great deal of thought. I cannot bring them to book for their crimes without airing a lot of dirty linen in public and ruining Beth's reputation. Since I refuse to do anything that might harm her, I will do nothing except send Arabella's chaise to her father, with a letter detailing her cousin's actions—and hers. I don't know if Hartwood can keep them in line, but I want him to know what they did."

Uncle Charles frowned and rubbed his chin, an action characteristic of deep thought. "I daresay you are right that we cannot charge them for any of their crimes without involving Beth and damaging her reputation. Certainly I cannot charge Sir James for abducting her, nor Lady Arabella's footman for attempted murder, without the world and his wife eventually learning all that transpired." In a mutter he added, "More's the pity."

"Do you think they will make another attempt?" This from Lord David and Lord Bellingham simultaneously.

George raked a hand through his hair. "I doubt that Sir James will; I believe he achieved his objective, if not the desired result. But Arabella may decide to try again, in some other way. She is desperate to marry, for wealth and social position."

"Social position?" scoffed Aunt Julia. "She is divorced; she has no standing in Society."

"That is not entirely true, ma'am," Lady Richard countered politely. "There are some people who still receive her, believing—"

"Believing Arabella's fanciful delusions, do you mean, Caro? Ha!" Aunt Julia dismissed such misguided persons as unworthy of her attention.

Lord Bellingham cleared his throat. "Arabella's lack of social position is not our concern. How can we protect George, Isabelle, and Miss Castleton from further harm at Arabella's hands?"

Lady Matilda looked at her brother as if he had lost his

wits. "The solution is simple. David must keep Isabelle close—and safe at home. George must be alert at all times and armed to defend himself. Miss Castleton . . . Miss Castleton should—"

Smiling an apology for her rudeness, Beth interrupted. "Since my abduction was accidental, I do not believe I am in danger, even if Arabella tries again."

Lady Richard started to speak, but a Look from Aunt Julia silenced her.

The clock on the mantel chimed the hour, and Lord Bellingham rose to his feet. "I am a poor host to invite guests then leave, but I am overdue at Lords." As Uncle Charles struggled to his feet, the marquess crossed the room to stand in front of Beth. She started to rise, but he waved her back to her seat, taking her hand and bowing over it. "Miss Castleton, I am delighted to have made your acquaintance. I understand from your great-aunt and uncle that you are a very talented musician. I hope you will join us soon for an informal evening of music."

"I would enjoy that, Lord Bellingham. Very much. And I am pleased to have met you after hearing Weymouth sing your praises. You deserve all of them and more."

"Thank you, dear girl." The marquess turned to his heir, blue eyes atwinkle. "A bit chary with your compliments, were you, my boy? Remind me later to take you to task." With a charming smile and a bow for the company, Lord Bellingham left the room. He was followed by Uncle Charles, who completed a whispered conversation with his aunt, then made his *adieux.*

Lady Matilda rose and crossed to the bellpull. "I will ring for a fresh pot of tea, and we can have a comfortable coze. Perhaps, Lady Julia, you will tell us your plans for Miss Castleton's come-out."

George darted a look at Aunt Julia and received a slight nod in return. "While we wait for the tea, Aunt Tilly, I will take Beth up to see Isabelle." He looked at his brother. "Did I tell you that your daughter asked Miss Castleton to be her honorary aunt?"

"I don't believe you mentioned it, George." Lord David smiled at Beth. "Thank you, Miss Castleton, for your role in rescuing my daughter and your kindness to her. And welcome to the family, so to speak."

After receiving Lady Julia's silent acquiescence to his unspoken request, George stood. He wanted a deep breath to calm his nerves—he had never proposed marriage before—but his cravat was choking him again, making even normal breathing difficult. Walking to the sofa on which Beth was seated next to her great-aunt, he mutely offered his hand. Taking it, she rose and excused herself. He tucked her hand in the crook of his arm and escorted her from the room.

Think, you idiot! You cannot make your offer in the nursery. Nor can you propose without words.

Beth looked at him inquiringly, as if puzzled by his silence. "That wasn't nearly the ordeal I feared it would be. I thank you for bearing the burden of most of the explanation."

He tugged at his cravat, ruining the *trone de amour* he had chosen in honor of the occasion. "Since you bore the pain, the least I could do—"

"Weymouth, stop lambasting yourself over my injury. It was not your fault."

"Yes, it—"

"It was *not* your fault." Her glare warned him not to dispute her.

Having decided to make his proposal in the gallery, which was at the opposite end of the second floor from the nursery, George led Beth to the stairs.

"Won't Isabelle be taking a nap now?"

"Perhaps. If she is, I will show you the portraits of my ancestors."

"Very well, but if the resemblance between them is as marked as between you and your father, you can just point to one painting and be done with it." A teasing smile accompanied her words.

George laughed—and felt his tension easing. "Looking at my father is like looking in a mirror and seeing myself at two-and-sixty." He smiled down at her, wondering if she thought him handsome. "There isn't such similarity of features in all my relatives. Some children favor their mothers, as David does."

"Yes. Your brother resembles your cousin."

"You think David looks like Dunnley?" George winced at the incredulity in his tone.

"No, like Captain Middleford."

"Hmm . . . I suppose he does, at that." When they reached the third story, George turned left, toward the gallery.

"Beth." He stopped several paces from the first portrait. *Lord, he hadn't been this nervous facing French cannons!*

She slipped her hand from his arm, walked to one of the padded benches lining the walls and seated herself, then patted the space beside her. When he sat, she touched his sleeve. "What is troubling you, Weymouth?"

"Nothing is troubling me, I am merely a bit nervous." She glanced up at him, silent but obviously willing to listen.

He took a breath—as deep as the torturous cravat would allow—and clasped her left hand in his right. "Beth, will you do me the great honor of becoming my wife?"

Chapter 11

~

*B*eth's hand jerked in his, but that and a delicate gasp were the only signs of her startlement. Her beautiful blue eyes searched his face.

"Why, George?" The bald, unadorned question demanded an answer.

Feeling like an errant schoolboy called before the headmaster, he sought an acceptable reply. "We are friends, aren't we, Beth?" She lowered her gaze to her lap but nodded her agreement. "We like and respect each other." Another nod. "I trusted you to save Isabelle, and you trusted me to treat your wound and escort you to London." He paused, but there was no sign of acknowledgment this time.

Panicked, he continued building his argument—or sounding the death knell of their friendship. "At Stranraer and on our journey, we spent many hours together unchaperoned. If word of that gets out, your reputation will be ruined—"

"Stuff and nonsense!" The words exploded from Beth as she jerked her hand from his and rose to her feet. "You know as well as I do that you did nothing dishonorable. Never—not for one second since we met in the book room at Gull Cottage—has your behavior been less than gentlemanly."

She paced away, then whirled to face him. He thought he saw the glimmer of tears in her eyes, but she was too far from the branch of candles for him to be certain. "You told me then that you wanted to marry for love. I agreed to help so you wouldn't be forced to marry a woman who wanted only your title and fortune."

She stalked toward him, and he stood quickly. Stopping in front of him, she poked his chest with her finger. "So now you are going to allow yourself to be forced into marriage with me?" Another jab. "Because Society might gossip?" Poke, poke. "Because of a misguided sense of honor?" The tears spilled over, and she turned her back to him.

Gently grasping Beth's shoulders, George turned her into his embrace. He rubbed his cheek against her hair as she cried into his ruined cravat. When her sobs had dwindled to sniffles, he handed her his handkerchief. "No one," he said, his voice quiet but firm, "is forcing me into anything. 'Twas my choice to offer for you. I asked for, and received, your uncle's permission to pay my addresses to you.

"Beth, we are friends. Good friends, with shared interests. We could have a very happy marriage."

She stepped back, out of the circle of his arms. "Perhaps we could, but it wouldn't be the love match we both wish for."

"In time it might become a love match."

"How could you come to love me when you don't even trust me?"

He jerked as if stung. "*What?* Of course I trust you!"

"If you trusted me, you would admit that your sense of honor compelled you to ask for my hand. Not friendship, not the belief that we could have a happy marriage, not the possibility that, in time, the marriage could become a love match. Only honor."

She mopped away a new freshet of tears. "I am not belittling your honor. I wouldn't like you half so well if it weren't such an integral part of your character. But honor is not enough. For either of us."

Beth took a deep breath—no choking cravat hindered her—and looked him in the eye. "Lord Weymouth," she said formally, "I am very sensible of the kindness of your offer, but *my honor* compels me to decline. I do not believe we would suit."

She curtsied, then left the room. Feeling as if the weight of the world had been heaped upon his shoulders, George sank down on the bench. *She did not believe they would suit? Then why was he so disappointed by her refusal?*

* * *

Beth walked from the gallery, past the staircase, and into the opposite hallway. Weary to her bones, she leaned her forehead against the wall and let the tears flow. She had lost a friend—her dearest friend—and she could blame no one but herself.

Frustrated, she pounded her fist against the wall. A door down the hall opened, and Isabelle's head popped out. "Aunt Beth!" The little girl ran to her, hugging her about the knees. "Did you bang on the wall?"

An older woman followed Isabelle. Beth wiped away tears with the back of her hand. "Um, yes, I did. I—"

The child grabbed her hand and guided her toward the open door. "You ought to have knocked on the door, but we heard you anyway." Isabelle gestured with her free hand. "This is Abby, my nanny. Abby, this is Aunt Beth, my honorary aunt."

The nanny, a plump, kindly looking woman, dropped an awkward curtsy. "Mrs. Abbott, my lady."

"I am pleased to meet you, Mrs. Abbott. I am Miss Castleton."

As soon as they stepped into the nursery, Isabelle's nanny scrutinized Beth from head to toe. "I believe, Miss Castleton, you must have gotten a speck of dust in your eye out there in the hallway. Let me get you a damp cloth."

Beth smiled her thanks when the woman returned. "Thank you."

She put the cloth to good use while Mrs. Abbott said, "Miss Isabelle has been telling me how you and her Uncle George saved her from the mean lady and a bad man. It sounds as if you had quite a . . . a . . . ."

"It was quite an adventure."

Mrs. Abbott "hrmphed," as if adventure wasn't the word she'd had in mind. As Isabelle chattered about her reunion with her papa and all she had done this afternoon, Beth felt herself relaxing. Here, she didn't have to worry about a tarnished reputation, disappointed relatives, or misguided senses of honor. She let herself forget, for a short time, all her worries.

A knock on the door heralded the arrival of nursery supper. Repressing a sigh, Beth rose to her feet. "I had best go downstairs. My great-aunt—and yours, poppet—

will be wondering where I am." She kissed and hugged Isabelle, reminding her of her promise to call.

After saying her good-byes, Beth walked slowly down the hallway to the stairs. No light came from the gallery, so George must have gone elsewhere. She stood with her hand on the newel post, gathering her composure. And her courage. It wouldn't be easy to face him again, but a meeting was inevitable. Now was not the time to mourn their lost friendship.

She descended the stairs, unseeing, her thoughts darting this way and that. When she reached the first-floor landing, she nearly collided with Lord David. "I beg your pardon, sir. I wasn't watching where I was going."

"The blame is mine, Miss Castleton, for racing up the stairs completely oblivious to the fact that someone else might be using them." His smile was rueful. "My aunts sent me up to tell you and George that it is nearly time for dinner."

"I . . . I did not realize we were invited to dinner. I am not suitably attired."

"My aunts issued the invitation an hour or so past, and Lady Julia accepted, on her behalf and your own." His gaze swept her from head to toe. "We aren't dressing this evening, and you look very pretty just as you are."

Beth dipped a curtsy. "Thank you, kind sir. Are our aunts in the same room as earlier?"

"Yes." Lord David studied her for a moment, his head tilted to one side. "Is my brother still in the nursery?"

"He . . . he wasn't a few moments ago when I left."

"Then I will have to search him out." His grin was as charming as George's. " 'Tis a reversal from our usual roles."

Why had Beth been crying, David wondered as he made his way to his brother's room. He'd thought, along with his aunts and Lady Julia, that George had escorted Beth from the morning room to ask for her hand. Was she unhappy because he didn't offer or because he had?

Arriving at his brother's chamber, David entered without knocking. George was in the dressing room, talking with Perkins, his valet. David stood in the doorway and watched his brother tie his cravat. No *trone de amour* this time, just a simple mail coach. When the knot was complete and a stickpin in place, he spoke. "If you don't cease dawdling, big brother, you will be late for dinner."

George started and glanced at the clock. "I didn't realize it was so late." He nodded dismissal to his valet. "I am not very hungry this evening."

"You, not hungry? The aunts will be up here to dose you quicker than the kitchen cat can lick her ear. Lady Julia, too, probably."

"Lady Julia is still here?"

"Yes. Miss Castleton as well. After the two of you came upstairs, the aunts invited Lady Julia and her niece to stay for dinner. The three women have been chattering nineteen to the dozen all afternoon." David grinned and attempted to lighten his brother's mood. "I have learned Interesting Things. Not to mention a collection of *on dits* that will entertain all of Oxfordshire for months."

George rolled his eyes. "One can only imagine."

David reached out and touched his brother's arm. "If you don't stop fiddling with your cravat, you are going to ruin that knot." Then, after a moment's hesitation, "Do you want to tell me what happened?"

"I offered for Beth. She refused."

"There is more to it than that, I think. I encountered her on the stairs on my way up. She had been crying."

George sighed and dropped into a chair. "Yes, but I don't know why. I wish to hell I did."

"Did she give a reason for refusing?"

"She gave several, in fact." George dragged his hands through his hair. "She said I had behaved honorably and that she wouldn't allow anyone—or anything—to force us into marriage. Said her honor compelled her to decline my offer."

"Do you love her?"

"Beth is a good friend. I am fond of her and feel protective of her. We could have a happy marriage."

"I daresay you could, but it wouldn't be a love match."

George crossed his arms over his chest, his rising chin indicative of his contrary mood. "In time it might become a love match."

"Perhaps." David shrugged, surprised his brother didn't

realize he was in love. "Now, you'd best comb your hair and hie yourself to the morning room."

The dratted butterflies were back. They fluttered in Beth's stomach worse than ever they had at Dunnley Park. After weeks in George's company with barely a flicker, they had chosen tonight to emerge from hibernation.

She had been fine until he arrived. No, not fine, but relatively composed. The very second he appeared in the doorway, all the butterflies in southern England had gone on a rampage.

George avoided her gaze as he apologized for his tardiness. Eyes still averted, he spoke quietly with Aunt Julia. When the butler announced dinner, George flicked a glance in Beth's direction, but offered one arm to her aunt, the other to Lady Matilda.

"Miss Castleton?"

Beth started when Lord David addressed her. He offered his arm to escort her to the dining room, then extended the other to Lady Richard.

In his father's absence, George sat at the head of the table. Aunt Julia was on his right, with Lord David beside her. Beth was on George's left, Lady Richard on her left. Lady Matilda sat opposite George. With such a small group, conversation was general. Beth replied when spoken to—and breathed a prayer of thanks when their hostess rose to lead the ladies to the drawing room.

Beth contributed little to the talk about needlework, not from lack of interest but because she was rehearsing an apology to George. *Had she really poked him in the chest, not once but several times? Then cried like the veriest watering pot?* He probably wouldn't want to listen to her apology, but she would make it all the same.

The gentlemen joined them half an hour later. Lord David persuaded the older ladies to play whist with him; George crossed the room to join her on the sofa.

"Beth?"

"Weymouth?"

They shared a hesitant smile at their simultaneity, then he indicated she should speak first.

"Weymouth, I apologize for my behavior earlier. I . . ."

It was . . ." Her hands writhed against her skirts as she attempted to gather her scattered wits. George reached out and clasped her right hand in his left—and the butterflies went into a frenzy. "It was very bad of me to rail at you like that, then drown you with my tears. I hope that, some-day, you will be able to forgive my lack of manners."

"You have no need to beg my forgiveness, Beth. It is I who must apologize for upsetting you. I didn't realize you would find my proposal so offensive—"

"Your proposal was not offensive, only the fact that you were forced to offer."

"No one forced me to offer!"

"No person did, but would you have proposed if you knew my reputation was safe from any possible blemish?" She paused for scarcely a second. "I don't believe so. Your sense of honor compelled you to propose, and I no more want you forced into a loveless marriage with me than with Lady Arabella."

"The two are not even comparable, my dear. I like and respect you. I trust you and admire you. For Arabella I feel nothing but contempt."

"That is as may be, but—"

"But nothing." He rubbed his thumb against her knuckles. She darted a glance at him from beneath her lashes and saw a slight frown creasing his brow. "Have I . . ." He tugged on his cravat. "Can we still be friends, do you think?"

"I would like that above all things."

"As would I." He heaved a sigh, apparently as relieved as she. "Can I tempt you into the music room for a duet or two, my friend?"

"I don't have my violin. I don't even know where it is."

"You could use my father's violin." He rose, pulling her to her feet.

"Not without his permission, but I would like to hear you play."

Still holding her hand, George led her from the room. "Is there something in particular you would like to hear?"

"Bach's Cello Suite in G, if you know it. I have found, much to my surprise, that he is not very well-known in this country."

"I do, indeed, know it, but I am too tired to do it jus-tice tonight."

"Do you, too, feel as if this day has lasted for, oh, a fortnight or so?"

"Yes. It seems impossible that we have been in London only eight hours."

George was reading in the library, his feet stretched toward the fire and a brandy in his hand, when his father returned. "Did the vote go as you wished, sir?"

"Yes, just." After pouring himself a brandy, his father sank into an adjacent chair and stretched out his legs. "What are you reading?"

"*Sense and Sensibility* by A Lady."

"A delightful book. Have you read the author's newest offering?"

"I didn't know she had one."

"It came out a month or so ago. *Pride and* . . . something." The marquess waved a hand toward the shelves.

"I must remember to tell Beth. She is extremely fond of *Sense and Sensibility* and will be delighted to know the lady has written another book."

"Speaking of Miss Castleton, am I to wish you happy?"

"No, sir. Beth declined my offer."

"She refused you?"

At the incredulity in his father's voice, George felt a smile tugging at his lips, which he hid by raising his glass. "She did, sir. Said she had no more wish to see me forced into marriage with her than with Arabella."

"It is not at all the same thing!"

"I agree, but Beth doesn't see it that way."

"An uncommon—and honorable—young lady." His father sat in silence for a minute, gazing into the fire. "I hope, for Miss Castleton's sake, there is no gossip about her disappearance."

"I intend to speak to Lord Castleton and Lady Julia in the morning, to ask them to impress upon Beth the possible consequences of her refusal."

"It is possible that Castleton won't want an alliance with our family."

George's eyes slewed to his father. "He allowed me to propose, and he has always been cordial to me at the races and at Tatts."

"I forgot your racing connection with him."

"Sir, why do you think the earl might not wish an alliance with us?"

The marquess shifted in his seat. "Several years ago, back in '08, Castleton and I had a rather unpleasant—and public—disagreement."

George could not imagine either man behaving so improperly. "What kind of disagreement?"

"It happened at a meeting of the Royal Society. We both were scheduled to read papers. Mine was first. Part way through, Castleton stood up and accused me of stealing his paper. I responded rather heatedly that I had done no such thing. He walked up to the dais, slapped his paper down on the lectern, and dared me to explain how my paper could be identical to his if I hadn't stolen his work."

"Were the papers identical?"

"No. The subject was the same, as were the initial calculations, but there was a divergence in methodology about halfway through. The conclusions were different, but similar." The marquess paused to sip from his glass. "Honesty compels me to admit that if he had read first, I might have thought as he did. But I would not have created an uproar at the meeting with a public accusation."

"I assume Sir Joseph Banks was presiding. What did he do?"

"He and several other members read both papers, questioned the two of us as if we were collegians sitting for an examination, and concluded the work was done independently. Which, of course, it was. Then he demanded Castleton apologize."

George winced. "Not one of Banks's wisest decisions. Which paper was it?"

"The first one predicting comet orbits." The marquess sighed. "To this day, I am not certain Castleton accepts that it was just coincidence."

"Are both papers published in the Proceedings? I would like to read them."

"They are." The words were accompanied by a wave toward another shelf. His father drained his glass and rose, saying, "I am for my bed."

George followed suit. His father patted him on the back, then hugged him. "I am glad you are safely home, son."

*   *   *

The next morning, at an hour suggested by Lady Julia but generally considered too early for calls except upon one's nearest and dearest, George sat in the library at Castleton House. He explained to the earl that Beth had refused his offer and expressed, as diplomatically as possible, his concern that her inexperience with Society may have led her to the wrong decision. Lord Castleton listened politely, agreed that naïveté may have influenced his niece's decision, and reiterated that the decision was Beth's alone.

A few more delicately worded questions brought George the assurances that Beth's relatives would speak to her about the consequences to her reputation if there should be gossip about her disappearance, and that they would notify him if they heard any such gossip, although the earl was of the belief that they would likely be the last to hear. Then George repeated his offer, saying that Beth might accept it any time this Season.

"Only this Season?" the earl quizzed.

"I will be very much surprised, sir, if your niece isn't betrothed—perhaps even wed—by the first of June. As her friend, I will endeavor to assist by introducing her to all the eligible gentlemen of my acquaintance."

"That is very kind of you, Weymouth."

George prepared to take his leave, but the earl waved him back into his seat and asked which of his horses were entered in upcoming races. Castleton was a rival, but theirs had always been a friendly competition. Even so, George answered cautiously.

Finally the earl said, "Getting information out of you is like searching for water in the desert."

George grinned. "I suppose I have only to ask and you will tell me all your secrets."

Castleton chuckled. "Not bloody likely."

During the ensuing conversation, George learned a great deal about Beth, including the fact that Castleton, who was known for being very particular about his horses, allowed her to ride and train his jumpers.

When a knock on the door heralded the arrival of the earl's man of business, George bid his lordship farewell. As he followed the butler into the hallway, George congratulated himself on having accomplished all he had intended, and more.

Chapter 12

❧

*B*eth descended the stairs with a light heart, having survived two hours at the modiste with her sanity intact. And a substantially increased wardrobe. She had lost count of the number of gowns Aunt Julia had ordered for her, delighting instead in spring gowns in pastel colors instead of shades of mourning or half mourning. Beth was ready for a pot of tea, then an hour or so in the music room.

As she reached the bottom stair, she saw George emerge from the library. He wore a charcoal gray morning coat, light gray pantaloons, a dark blue vest, a cravat tied in a style she hadn't seen before, and gleaming Hessians—and he looked even more handsome than usual. She pressed a hand to her stomach to calm the butterflies before greeting him. "Good morning, Weymouth."

"Beth! Good morning. I was just about to ask North if you were in."

"As you see," she said, smiling. "Would you like to join me for a cup of tea, or do you have an appointment elsewhere?"

"I would be pleased to join you, as I am charged with several messages for you."

"Are you? I am glad we returned from the modiste in time for me to hear them." She requested a tea tray from the butler, asked him to invite her aunt to join them, then led the way to the morning room, wondering why George had been closeted with her uncle. She sat on a sofa and offered him a nearby chair.

"The modiste, eh?" he quizzed. "And what wonders did you find at Madame Whomever's shop this morning?"

"Untold delights, Weymouth," she replied, grinning, as Vetch, Aunt Julia's hatchet-faced dresser, entered the room to chaperon their meeting. The maid took a seat near the door and plied her needle mending a torn flounce.

"As many as that? Then I daresay you ordered a new gown or two."

"Indeed I did. I shall spare you a description of each one and—" Beth laughed as a look of profound relief flickered across his face.

"I enjoy hearing you laugh, even if it is at my expense." She must have looked disconcerted by his remark because he added, "It is very musical, your laughter, like an arpeggio."

Flustered, and completely at a loss for words, Beth was relieved to see North enter with the tea tray. She fixed a cup for George, offered scones and cake, poured her own tea, then redirected the conversation to more prosaic grounds. "You said you had messages for me?"

"I do." He leaned back in his chair and crossed one elegantly clad leg over the other. "First, David and Isabelle would like to know if they may call this afternoon."

"I am not certain of Aunt Julia's plans." Raising her voice slightly, Beth queried the maid. "Vetch, do you know my aunt's plans for the afternoon?"

" 'Tis Wednesday, Miss Castleton. Lady Julia is always At Home on Wednesdays."

"Thank you." Beth turned to George. "I would be pleased to receive Lord David and Isabelle this afternoon."

"Second, my father invites you, Lady Julia, and Lord Castleton to join us for dinner and an informal musical evening on Tuesday next. Your aunt will receive a formal invitation from Aunt Tilly this afternoon, but my father is all eagerness to hear you play and charged me to deliver the message this morning, if possible."

"I would enjoy that excessively, although I fear I shall fall short of your father's expectations." She sipped her tea. "What will we play?"

"You and I could perform some of the duets we played at Dunnley Park."

"But we practiced together before performing there!"

"We can practice beforehand here, too." George set his

cup and saucer aside. "Since you don't know your aunt's plans, I will call this afternoon and we can work out a time then."

"Very well. Your father will play, also, won't he?"

"He will. Do you know the Bach concerto for two violins?" Beth nodded. "My father is extremely fond of it but can rarely find someone with whom to play it. You would make him very happy if you offered to perform it with him."

"Which part does he play?"

"To answer that, I would have to hear them."

"I could play them for you, if you like. And if you have the time."

George smiled. "I would and I do."

"Do the other members of your family play or merely listen?"

"Aunt Tilly learned to play the harpsichord as a girl, but I cannot recall that I have ever heard her do so. Aunt Caro is a competent pianist and probably will perform. David plays the viola, but only under duress."

A smile tugged the corner of her mouth as she asked, "Will Lord David be, ah, persuaded to play Tuesday?"

George grinned. "I think we can count on my father to exhort my brother to perform." Pitching his voice a bit lower than usual, he gave a creditable imitation of Lord Bellingham. "Quartets, my boy, are much more interesting than duets."

Beth placed her cup and saucer on the tray and rose. "In that case, we'd best adjourn to the music room so you can tell me which quartets I might be called upon to perform, as well as what part of the Bach concerto your father plays."

Shortly before two o'clock, Beth entered the drawing room. All through luncheon, Aunt Julia had discussed the callers they were likely to have this afternoon. Beth, as was her wont when faced with the prospect of conversing with people she didn't know, was trying to convince herself that she wasn't shy and that she could talk to anyone about anything.

It wasn't working.

It never did, because it wasn't true.

She had done everything she could think of to bolster

her confidence. She was wearing her favorite walking dress, a pretty shade of pink that Moira had assured her was all the crack. Her hair was styled a bit more elaborately than usual, curls tumbling from a knot high on the crown instead of her usual smooth bun. And she was looking forward to a drive in the park with George later in the afternoon. He had extended the invitation before he left this morning, and her aunt, who deemed him an unexceptional—and highly eligible—escort, had readily given her consent.

All she had to do between now and then was survive two hours of callers. Preferably unscathed.

Hearing footsteps on the stairs, Beth sat on a sofa near the window and picked up her embroidery. Aunt Julia had not yet appeared, so she hoped this first caller was someone with whom she was acquainted. And someone who would not quiz her about her month-long absence. Fortunately, her visitors met both criteria.

North cleared his throat to draw her attention, then intoned, "Lord David Winterbrook and Miss Isabelle Winterbrook."

Isabelle was halfway across the room before Beth rose to her feet. "Aunt Beth, Aunt Beth!"

She smiled a greeting to Lord David and bent down to hug the little girl. "Hello, poppet. How nice of you and your papa to call on me. Will you sit beside me and tell me what you have been doing since last I saw you?"

As the child clambered onto the sofa, Beth offered Lord David a chair. After seating himself, he said, "Mostly Isabelle has been looking forward to calling upon you, Miss Castleton. As have I, so that I might thank you again for . . . ah, for bringing her home safely."

"I was happy to do so, sir. Isabelle is a delight. She—"

Aunt Julia entered the room, greeted the visitors, and sat on the sofa opposite. Isabelle, after a wobbly curtsy, went to sit beside her, leaving Beth to entertain Lord David. He was an attractive man of average height with reddish-brown hair, light blue eyes, and a smile of singular sweetness. She learned that he and Isabelle would stay in Town until the middle of next week, then return to Oxfordshire, where he managed one of his father's estates. Shortly after the arrival of another group of guests, he and his daughter departed, but not before Lord David assured

Beth that if ever he might assist her, she need only ask and he would do everything in his power to aid her.

Before the end of an hour, she had lost count of the number of times she'd fended off questions about her absence. Her reply, that she had been visiting friends in the country, was readily accepted by most, but some rudesbys—including a patroness of Almack's—pressed for details. Beth hadn't expected such an interrogation. Stretching the truth, she described, without names or locations, a house party in Scotland and another in Cumberland. That she had been bleeding and feverish through the first, and that the second had been of only one night's duration, was no one's business but her own.

As the most persistent inquisitor launched a new series of questions, Viscount Dunnley was announced. The tall, handsome, elegant peer was a welcome addition to any lady's drawing room. He was also one of the few people Beth knew well enough to call friend. In the flurry of greetings, she murmured "save me," and George's cousin gallantly came to her rescue. A pointed query about her son caused Lady Rag-Manners to recall an urgent appointment. Beth stifled a sigh of relief and gave the viscount a heartfelt smile. "Thank you, Dunnley. Another question from her and I would have run screaming from the room."

He smiled and sat beside her on the sofa. "My pleasure, Miss Castleton." Accepting a cup of tea, he glanced about the room. "Lady Julia has, as always, drawn quite a crowd this afternoon."

"Is it like this every week?" Beth bit her lip, dismayed.

"Twice a week, actually, but you will become accustomed to it."

"I doubt that, although I will be better prepared for their questions next time."

The viscount flicked an invisible piece of lint from the sleeve of his bottle green coat. "I had lunch with Weymouth. Thank you, Miss Castleton, for all that you have done for my family."

"Anyone would have done the same."

"No, ma'am, they would not. If ever I might be of service to you, you have only to ask." He must have sensed her discomfort because he shifted the subject slightly. "At the least, you may depend upon me as a dancing partner, for drives in the park, and as an escort. Provided your aunt gives her permission, of course, and I believe"—his gray eyes twinkled—"Lady Julia considers me acceptable."

A giggle escaped Beth at the understatement. Dunnley was one of the leaders of the *ton,* very proper and highly eligible. "Yes, my lord, she does. As do I."

"I hope you also consider me a friend."

"I do, sir, and am honored by your friendship."

He set his cup and saucer on the table. "Such elegant graciousness will serve you well in Society."

"I beg your pardon?" she stammered, discomposed by the seeming non sequitur.

"I was complimenting your manners, ma'am."

Beth goggled. *He, who was famed throughout the* ton *for the elegance of his manners and address, was complimenting hers?* "Th-thank you. Coming from you, that is a compliment, indeed."

He arced one tawny eyebrow in inquiry. Beth was spared further reply when Miss Cathcart approached and directed a question to the viscount. Several other young people joined them, and the conversation become general.

At the end of half an hour, Dunnley took his leave, but not before inviting her to drive in the park with him tomorrow afternoon. Aunt Julia gave her consent, a time was decided, and the viscount departed with a bow and a charming smile. *My word,* Beth thought, astonished, *I have not yet appeared in Society and I have already received two invitations to drive in the park.*

A question from Lord Selwyn brought Beth out of her reverie. "Miss Castleton, will you tell us about America?"

It was a nice, safe subject, and she latched onto it gratefully. "Is there something in particular about which you are interested in hearing, my lord?"

It appeared there was not; the young lordling was only trying to make conversation. Fashion was the request of Miss Broughton and Lady Christina Fairchild. Miss Spencer wished to know about social events. Beth endeavored to satisfy both requests.

"Have you ever seen a red Indian?" asked a blonde miss whose name Beth couldn't remember. Before she could answer, the young lady's green eyes widened nearly to the size of saucers. Curious to know what—or whom—had elicited such a reaction, Beth turned and saw George bowing over her aunt's hand. " 'Tis Weymouth," Miss Blonde confided in a breathy whisper. "He is one of the premier catches on the Marriage Mart. My mama says he may be looking for a bride this Season, since it is past time he settled down and set up his nursery."

Beth found it amusing that Society thought it could dictate such things, but she maintained a neutral expression. "Really?"

The young lady nodded emphatically. "Oh, yes. Mama says a gentleman of thirty or more is ripe for the plucking, since his family will be pressuring him to marry."

Beth didn't think much of the chit's mama, whomever she might be, for preaching such drivel. The gentlemen in the group shifted uneasily, so she changed the subject. "Since I am unfamiliar with Society, I hope you will tell me some of the amusements I can look forward to in Town."

As she listened to a veritable flood of recommendations and suggestions, the butterflies in her stomach took flight. 'Twas only a small meadowful today, thank goodness, but Beth knew they signaled George's approach. Glancing up, she found him a pace away from her chair. "Good afternoon, Weymouth," she said, smiling.

He bowed to the group and returned her smile. "Good afternoon, Miss Castleton. Are you ready for our drive?"

"Oh, unfair, George!" chorused Mr. Brewster and Lord Howe, both noted Corinthians.

"How did you manage to steal a march on the rest of us, Weymouth?" queried Sir Henry Smythe.

George nodded to the first two gentlemen and answered the third. "I had the pleasure of meeting Miss Castleton last month at a house party hosted by my cousin."

"And we were able to further our acquaintance later in the month at a house party in Scotland," Beth told the group.

George's eyes widened slightly, but he gamely followed her lead. "Indeed we were."

She smiled at the group of young ladies and gentlemen. "It has been a pleasure meeting you all. I hope we will have an opportunity to talk again soon." Then, turning to

George, "Only allow me to run upstairs for my bonnet, and I will be ready for our drive."

George took Beth's elbow, escorting her across the room to take leave of the guests surrounding her aunt and then out into the hallway. "I shall wait for you downstairs."

Five minutes later she joined him, wearing a spencer of a deep rose color that complemented her dress, a bonnet whose ribbons matched the spencer, and gloves of blush pink. She was lovely, and George was proud to be her escort for her first promenade in the park. Proud and honored.

Belatedly remembering he had a gift for her, he reached into the pocket of his caped driving coat. "This is for you, Beth."

"Why, thank you, Weymouth." She smiled up at him as her elegant, long-fingered hands traced the contours of the package. "It feels like a book."

"You needn't guess the contents," he teased. "Open it."

"Very well." The string defeated her until North produced a penknife. Then she unwrapped the brown paper. "It *is* a book. *Pride and Prejudice* by A Lady." She opened the front cover and leafed through the first few pages. "It is by the author of *Sense and Sensibility!*" Beth's smile was dazzling in its brilliance, lighting her face and her beautiful blue eyes. "Thank you. I shall enjoy this excessively."

She reached out and squeezed his arm. A jolt, rather like one of Sir Humphrey Davy's electrical shocks, traveled from George's arm to his toes. "You . . . ah . . ." He shook his head, trying to rattle his brains back into order. "You will have to tell me if you like it as well as *Sense and Sensibility*."

Tucking her hand in the crook of his arm, he led her outside. His curricle was parked in front of the house, his tiger at the horses' heads.

"What beautiful, and beautifully matched, horses!"

He stood with her at the curb, basking in her admiration of his favorite pair. When she had looked her fill, he assisted her to the seat, then climbed up beside her. "Let 'em go, Jim." The lad clambered up behind.

As he turned onto Upper Brook Street, George wondered why his conversational skills—and his wits—seemed to have deserted him. Both had been perfectly functional in the drawing room. Recalling something Beth had said there, he darted a look at her and quizzed, "A house party in Scotland?"

Her smile was mischievous. "At Stranraer, of course." The smile faded as she turned to look at him. "Weymouth, you would not have believed the rudeness of some of the ladies who called today! It wasn't enough for me to say I had been visiting friends in the country. They wanted to know where and with whom and . . . and heaven only knows what else." Alarmed, he darted a glance at her. "They had to settle for a tale of a house party in Scotland and another in Cumberland, with no names or locations given."

"Where was Lady Julia whilst you were being interrogated?"

"Busy with a roomful of callers." Beth bit her lip, something he had noticed she did in times of stress. "Fortunately for me, your cousin arrived just as the worst of them was launching a new series of questions, and he sent her to the rightabout."

"I am glad to hear it. Who was this busybody?"

"Lady Smithson, I think. Or maybe it was Lady Moreton." With a wave of her hand, Beth dismissed them both. "Whichever one has a son named Rupert."

"Lady Moreton."

"I wasn't prepared for their probing. Nor did I expect so many callers. And Dunnley said it is like that every week. Twice a week," she added with a grimace.

"Lady Julia is very popular. As for their questions, well, you are unknown in Town, so the old tabbies want to look you over."

"Looking wouldn't be so bad; an inquisition is another matter."

George turned into Hyde Park. "It is behind you now. Smile, and pretend you are enjoying my company."

A dazzling smile blossomed on her lovely face. "That, sir, is no pretense."

As she dressed for Lord Bellingham's dinner and musical evening, Beth reviewed the past few days. It seemed impossible that she had been in London for only a sennight. Since

Aunt Julia's Wednesday afternoon At Home, which Beth counted as her first appearance in the *beau monde,* she had been for six drives in the park, with five different gentlemen (George having taken her twice), taken four morning rides in the park (one with her uncle), been to the Opera House and a play at Drury Lane, and attended a dinner party, two routs, a *soirée,* and a very chilly Venetian breakfast. Not to mention two visits to the modiste, two additional mornings of shopping on Bond Street, and scores of afternoon calls and callers.

She had been deemed "a pretty, well-behaved gel" by the Dowager Duchess of St. Ives, pronounced "a delightful young lady" by Lady Throckmorton, and complimented on her manners and deportment by Mrs. Drummond-Burrell. George and Dunnley had told her that the gentlemen styled her "the American Beauty" and considered her a Diamond of the First Water.

It was enough to turn a young lady's head—if said miss didn't have to steel herself for each appearance in Society.

The worst was past, Beth supposed. She'd been presented at the Queen's Birthday Drawing Room in January, her pedigree and prospects were known, and, at the advanced age of three-and-twenty, she wasn't viewed as a threat by the other young ladies making their come-outs. They were happy to give her, often quite condescendingly, their views of life in Society, and the gentlemen therein.

Her first appearance at Almack's and her come-out ball were still to be faced, but she refused to fret about them now. Tonight she would enjoy a delightful evening of music with George and his family. Her only worry was that Lord Bellingham would be disappointed by her performance.

She'd practiced for at least an hour every morning and had twice rehearsed with George, but the month without her violin had had an effect and her shoulder injury made playing difficult, even painful sometimes. That was something she was determined that no one would know. Not tonight. Not ever.

Wearing a blush-colored evening gown, her hair dressed in the curls-tumbling-from-a-knot style Moira assured her suited her well, Beth pulled on her gloves, donned the evening cloak her maid had chosen, and picked up her violin case.

*   *   *

Arabella and her cousin had traveled from Drummore
to Carlisle to York in search of Weymouth. When they
reached the latter city, Jamie had declared their effort a
wild-goose chase and asked her to marry him. She'd considered it; Jamie had a comfortable fortune and was an inven-
tive and eager lover. But he preferred Yorkshire to London
and was relatively unknown in Society, so he could not help
her regain her place in the *ton*. He also was five years
younger and a bit possessive, so she had declined his proposal. He had taken her rejection well and, after telling her
to write him if she changed her mind, departed for home.

Undeterred by her cousin's desertion, Arabella had continued all the way to Stamford without finding a trace of
her quarry and was now retracing her route north. Will was
a good coachman, and he had other attributes she enjoyed,
but he was a chaw-bacon. How he could have allowed Weymouth to escape in her carriage, leaving her stuck with this
lumbering old monstrosity, she didn't know. But he had,
and she was, and she didn't have the funds to hire a better
one. She was so badly dipped that she'd had to sell some
of her jewelry in Carlisle this morning. She needed to find
Weymouth quickly and force him into marriage. And she
wouldn't be so nice about it this time.

As if she didn't have problems enough, one of the wheels
had broken a few miles outside of Dumfries. Will had un-
harnessed two of the horses, and she and her coachman
had ridden off in search of an inn and a wheelwright, re-
spectively, leaving Tom with the carriage and the other
horses.

Will waved a hand, indicating an inn a short distance
down the road. As they drew closer, she saw it was a large,
reputable-looking establishment, the Rose and Crown. Unfortunately, at the moment, she didn't look at all respectable.

Will helped her dismount, then approached an ostler,
presumably to ask the location of the nearest wheelwright.
He could worry about that horrid coach; she wanted a
room, a meal, a bath, and a soft bed with clean, dry sheets.

She entered the inn only to be told that "her sort" wasn't
welcome there. Glaring at the proprietor, she said, "I am

Lady Arabella Smalley, and I want a room for the night and a private parlor."

"Aye, and I'm ole King George hisself" was the insolent reply.

She would have liked to storm out of the inn, but she was unlikely to find a better reception at another establishment. "I am Lady Arabella Smalley, daughter of the Earl of Hartwood. My coach—"

Will stepped inside the door. "My lady, I be orf to the 'wright. I'll return—"

"Just go." Peevishly, she waved him off, her attention on the innkeeper. "As I was saying, I need a room and a private parlor."

"I'll see the color of your money first."

She stomped over to the desk, ripped open her reticule, pulled out several coins, and slapped them down. "There. Satisfied now?"

"Reckon I am."

"Then show me to a room and have a maid prepare a bath."

"Sign the book first."

As he slid the register across to her, a familiar name near the top of the facing page caught Arabella's eye. *Weymouth!* Signing her name, she considered the best method of getting information from the innkeeper. "I see that a friend of mine was a recent guest of yours. Do you recall when the Earl of Weymouth stayed here?"

"Two, three weeks ago it was."

"Who was traveling in his party?"

"What's it to you who his lordship traveled with?"

She slid a coin across the desk. "I will reward you well for any information you give me about the earl."

Greed lit the man's eyes. "Lemme think. There was the earl, his wife—"

"You must be mistaken. Weymouth isn't married."

"The lady was ill, he carried her inside, and the little girl, what called him uncle, called the lady aunt. Sounds married to me," the brazen fellow said.

He couldn't be married! "What did the woman look like and who else was with him?"

The man shrugged. "She looked like a lady. Brown hair."

Arabella took out another coin, which jolted his memory. "As for rest of the party, there was the niece, a maid, and his lordship's man. Another gentleman and his man joined them late that night."

A few more questions and another coin gleaned little additional information. Arabella paced her room as she pondered what she'd learned. *The woman must have been the governess, but why would Weymouth's niece call her aunt? Ah, of course! She must be a poor relation, given house room in exchange for taking care of the child. The maid was definitely Sinclair and the manservant, Henry. But who was the gentleman traveling with them?*

His identity didn't matter, she decided. She could use this information, appropriately altered, to force Weymouth to marry her.

With a sly smile, Arabella planned the tale she would tell the *ton*.

Chapter 13

❦

*B*eth looked forward to the coming evening with both pleasure and dread. She worried about a new venue—Almack's—and the usual difficulty of conversing with strangers and people she didn't know well, but she looked forward to the dancing. It was one of her favorite pastimes. She loved the music and the patterns of the dances. That the movements of the reels and country dances made any but the most trivial conversation impossible was no drawback as far as she was concerned. She was getting better at social chitchat, but she still didn't enjoy it.

George had proven a wonderful friend, introducing her to people, both ladies and gentlemen, with interests similar to her own. They seemed to understand about her shyness as well. Perhaps he had warned them; perhaps they had sensed it. However it had happened, Beth was grateful to have a group of interesting, convivial people with whom to chat at routs or between dances at a ball.

Her uncle was her escort this evening, with George gallanting Aunt Julia. Uncle Charles couldn't dance because of his injured hip, but he wanted to be her champion for her first appearance at Almack's. He would praise her to the patronesses then sit with Aunt Julia, he'd said; Weymouth could do the dancing honors.

George could partner her only twice, of course, but many of her other dances were already bespoke. Dunnley had claimed two; his brother, Captain Middleford, another; Lords Howe, Selwyn, and Durwood had each requested one; as had Mr. Brewster, Sir Henry Smythe, Sir Kenneth Peyton, and Mr. Radnor. Several of those gentlemen,

George had told her, rarely graced the hallowed halls of Almack's.

Why they were doing so tonight was a mystery to Beth. George had told her, in his teasing way, that she was All the Crack. One of the Rages of the Season, in fact. She hadn't known if he was serious, and still didn't know if it had been Spanish coin, but she would not question a benevolent fate. It would be a pleasure to dance with each of the gentlemen—even Captain Middleford, who seemed to have two left feet—and not to have to worry about being a wallflower.

She would have to sit out the waltzes, of course. No young lady could take part in the new dance some deemed scandalous until she received the nod from one of the patronesses. Aunt Julia had told her that permission was almost never granted during a young lady's first appearance at the assembly rooms. Beth was not concerned about the waltzes. She would enjoy watching others perform the lovely dance, and she would have a partner for most of the other sets. What more could a tall, shy, nearly on the shelf American wish?

Moira lovingly placed the last curl, bent to tie the ribbons of Beth's dancing slippers, then motioned for her to stand. When the skirts of the white silk gown were settled to the maid's satisfaction, she tied the cornflower blue sash. Beth put on the pearl necklace that had belonged to her grandmother and the matching earrings Uncle Charles and Aunt Julia had given her. The poem about bridal apparel came to mind, for some reason, and Beth smiled. She had a new gown, an old necklace, and a blue sash. She was missing something borrowed and a sixpence for her shoe, but she was more than satisfied with her appearance. She was merely a spinster making her first bows at Almack's, not a bride.

After a quiet word of thanks to Moira, Beth pulled on her gloves, looped her fan and reticule over her wrist, picked up her evening cloak, and left the haven of her room.

The knocker sounded just as she reached the first-floor landing, so she stepped back, out of view. When North opened the door, George stepped inside and Beth's breath caught in her throat. He was wearing a dark blue swallow-tailed coat, a silvery gray vest, white knee breeches, and an elaborately tied cravat, with a *chapeau bras* tucked under one arm. She had never seen him in formal evening wear before, and he looked . . . She couldn't find a word that did him justice. Wonderful. Handsome. Splendid. All fit, as they always did, yet they didn't quite describe him.

Her stomach was strangely calm—until her heart dropped through it to her feet. Or to his feet. Shaken, her composure in shreds, she raced back to her room, then sank down on the chaise longue in front of the fireplace and covered her face with her hands. *She was in love with George! Not just in love with him, she loved him, heart and soul.*

She was roused from her reverie some time later by a knock on the door. "Beth?"

"Yes, Aunt Julia."

Lady Julia opened the door to her niece's chamber. "Why are you sitting here in the dark, darling?" Leaving the door ajar so the light from the hallway would enter the room, she crossed to the hearth and lit the candles on the mantel. "Is something wrong?"

"Yes. No." Beth paused and took a deep breath, as if trying to calm herself. "Nothing is wrong, precisely. I just realized something that . . . came as a bit of a shock."

Lady Julia crossed to stand in front of her niece, tipping her face upward. *Something was very wrong.* Beth was pale, her features drawn, her eyes anguished. "Would you like to tell me about it?"

Beth bit her lip. "No. Not right now."

"Will you be able to attend Almack's or would you prefer to stay at home?"

"I would prefer to stay here, but there is no real reason not to go."

"Are you certain, darling?"

Beth clasped her hands together as if in prayer. "Y-yes. I just need a few moments to compose myself."

"Shall I stay with you or would you prefer to be alone?"

"Alone, I think."

"Very well." Bending, she hugged her niece. "I will wait for you downstairs in the drawing room, with your uncle and Weymouth."

Lady Julia returned to the gentlemen. "Something has

upset Beth. I found her sitting in her room in the dark.
She is pale as a wraith and deeply distressed."

"Did she say anything to you?" Castleton asked.

"When I asked her if something was wrong, she said yes,
then no, then that she'd just realized something that came
as a bit of a shock."

"Whatever could it be?"

"I don't know. She didn't want to tell me, at least not
now. When I gave her the choice of staying at home or
going to Almack's, she said there wasn't a reason not to go,
but that she needed a few moments to compose herself."

"Do you think it would be better for Beth to stay
home?" Weymouth asked.

Restless, her heart aching for her niece, Lady Julia paced
from one end of the room to the other. "I don't know.
I . . . I just don't know."

"If she wants to go, and feels able to, perhaps it would
be better for her to be out among people."

"But you know how shy she is, especially with strangers."

"Yes, ma'am, I do. I also know that many of her friends
will be there tonight. Most of her dances are already bespoken, so the patronesses won't have to introduce unknown
gentlemen to her as partners. Both of you, whom she loves
dearly, will be there to support her. As will I. We—"

George turned at the sound of a soft footfall on the
stairs. A second later Beth appeared in the doorway. She
looked as if she would shatter into a million pieces if anyone, or anything, touched her. And she was breathtakingly
beautiful. He wanted to fold her in his arms, to protect her
and take care of her. He settled for walking toward her
with both hands outstretched. "Beth, how lovely you are
this evening."

She grasped his hands like a drowning man grabbed the
rope that would pull him to safety. "Thank you, Weymouth." Her glance flicked up to a point just below his
chin, then down again.

What was this? Beth always looked the person she was
speaking with in the eye, even if she had to tip her head
back to do so. That forthrightness was one of the things he
most admired about her. Why was she avoiding his gaze
tonight?

Tucking her ice-cold hand in the crook of his arm, he

escorted her to a chair. As her uncle complimented her appearance, George poured her a glass of wine. The hand she reached out to accept it trembled, but she steadied herself enough not to spill a drop.

He exchanged a worried glance with Lady Julia, then returned to scrutinizing Beth. After a small sip, she set the glass on the table beside her chair and said, in an overly bright voice, "I am sorry I kept you waiting. I daresay it is past time to leave."

"Are you certain you wish to go, darling?" Lady Julia inquired.

Beth bit her lip, then nodded. "Yes, I . . . Yes."

She was pluck to the backbone. Whatever was bothering her—and there was definitely something—she was determined to meet her obligations. She was *sans pareil:* courage, honesty, intelligence, and integrity, all in one beautiful person. George didn't think he'd ever admired a woman more. Nor liked one half as much.

"You will do the Castleton name proud tonight, Beth," the earl averred. "I am certain we haven't had such a beauty in the family since . . . since—"

"You'd best be planning to say '61, Charles," Lady Julia said, her tone acerbic.

George chuckled, as did Beth. The earl frowned. "I was going to say '66. Weren't you three-and-twenty in '66, Aunt Ju?"

"Uncle Charles," Beth exclaimed, her tone scandalized but her eyes dancing, "you should know better than to inquire a lady's age."

The earl smiled sheepishly. "Of course I do. But," he added in a conspiratorial tone, "I think she will forgive me since my number would make her younger."

"Hush, the pair of you." Lady Julia crossed to Beth's chair and extended a hand to her niece. "Come, darling. Let's dazzle the *ton*."

Beth was finding Almack's a bit overwhelming. The room was enormous, about one hundred feet long and perhaps forty feet wide, with tall Palladian windows and huge chandeliers. It was decorated with columns, pilasters, classical medallions, and mirrors, much like any ballroom, but it didn't feel like any other in which she'd been. Not that she'd set foot in many of them, but something about the assembly rooms seemed different.

They had been met at the top of the grand staircase by Mr. Willis, run the gamut of the patronesses, and found seats along the wall. She'd danced the opening minuet with George, the cotillion with Lord Dunnley, and reels and country dances with various partners. Between sets she'd conversed with friends and acquaintances and been introduced to a score or more of people.

Now she was listening to the chatter of Lady Christina Fairchild, the youngest of the ladies making their come-outs this Season. Tina was a dark-eyed, raven-haired beauty with an impish smile and a vivacious manner and, despite the difference in their ages, one of her particular friends. At the moment, Tina was scheming to be granted permission to dance the upcoming waltz. With Viscount Dunnley, of all people. Beth hid a smile, glanced around to be sure no one was within hearing distance, then interrupted her friend mid-spate, before she said something even more outrageous.

"Tina, I hate to disrupt your plotting, but Aunt Julia told me that young ladies are almost never granted permission to waltz their first evening."

"Mama said the same, but I could be an exception to the rule."

"I think you were born the exception. To every rule," Beth teased.

Tina grinned. " 'Tis vastly more entertaining than being like everyone else."

"And more likely to land you in the briars."

"Oh! Oh!"

"What are—" Beth saw Lady Sefton approaching, accompanied by George and a young man she didn't know, all arms and legs and coltish grace.

Lady Sefton stopped in front of them and smiled. "Lady Christina, Miss Castleton, are you enjoying yourselves this evening?"

"Yes, Lady Sefton," they chorused.

"Miss Castleton, may I present Lord Weymouth to you as a suitable partner for the waltz?"

"Th-the waltz?" Beth felt the flush of color in her cheeks. "Thank you, my lady." She forced a smile for the countess, but her heart sank. *Waltz with George? Lud, she was doomed.*

"Lady Christina, His Grace of Aylesbury will escort you to the refreshment room."

"Yes, my lady. Good evening, Your Grace." Tina curtsied to the duke, then took his arm. "Enjoy your waltz, Beth."

Enjoy it? She wasn't at all certain she could endure it. At least, not without making a cake of herself. Biting her lip, she looked down at the floor, seeking a measure of composure.

"Beth?"

She started. "I am sorry, Weymouth. I . . . I was woolgathering." To deflect his attention from her nervous state, she said, "I thought you were going to partner me in the last country dance."

He smiled. "I was, but I would prefer to waltz with you."

"You realize that I have never waltzed in public before, don't you?" *Stupid! Of course he knows, he just saw to it that you were given permission to do so.*

"Yes, I do." His beautiful blue eyes searched her face. "Are you enjoying yourself this evening?" Smiling, he admonished, "The truth this time, please."

"I think I am. It is an intimidating place, Almack's. Especially with so many people I don't know. But I am getting better at social chitchat, and I adore dancing."

The music began and he held out his hand. "Now you can add another dance to your repertoire."

George was an excellent partner, as she had noticed many Corinthians were. The athletic grace that served them well in their sporting activities translated, in a ballroom, into deft, sure movements that bolstered a lady's confidence and allowed her to relax and enjoy herself, without fear of missed steps or crushed toes. George was the best of the Corinthians, on the dance floor as elsewhere.

Waltzing with him was heaven and hell and all the delights and torments in between at once. Heavenly to be held in the arms of the man she loved. Hellish to know he did not return her regard. Delightful to float around the room as if dancing on a moonbeam among the stars. Tormenting because the dance would end far too soon.

"Beth?"

"Hmm?"

"It is customary to talk with your partner, my dear."

She darted a glance at him, saw the smile in his eyes. "Perhaps I am minding my steps."

"Do you take me for a flat, O Musical One? You feel the music in your bones and sinews. You wouldn't be such an excellent dancer if you did not."

"Thank you, Weymouth." She smiled shyly up at him. "You are a wonderful partner." After a moment's pause she suggested, "Perhaps I was studying your cravat."

A baffled expression flickered over his face. "What?"

"You didn't believe that I was minding my steps—which, in truth, I was not—so perhaps you will believe I was studying your cravat. Which, in fact, I was." Rather, she mentally amended, I was staring at it in a daze. "I don't believe I have seen that particular arrangement before. What is it called?"

"En cascade." He caught her gaze, his own bemused. "Beth, why are we discussing my cravat?"

"Perhaps because I am dizzy with the pleasure of waltzing," *with you,* she added silently, "and cannot think of a more intelligent topic of conversation. What would you like to discuss?"

Involuntarily, the muscles in George's arms tightened, drawing her a bit closer. *You. I want to know all about you. I want to know who or what upset you earlier this evening. I want to know if you like and admire me as much as I do you. I want to know your hopes and dreams.*

He couldn't say any of that; he probably shouldn't even *think* half of it. He swallowed and racked his brain for something they could discuss. "Tell me what amusements you would enjoy in Town. Do you want to see the Egyptian Hall or Elgin's Marbles? Would you like to attend a performance at Astley's Amphitheater or the exhibit at Somerset House? Would you prefer to hear a lecture at the Royal Mathematical Society or a play at Covent Garden or Drury Lane? Would you like to go to Vauxhall or the Botanical Gardens?"

"All of them." Beth's eyes sparkled as brightly as her smile. "I want to see them all."

He smiled in return, delighted she had recovered from

her earlier upset. "Are there one or two you would especially enjoy?"

"The Mathematical Society, Somerset House, Astley's, and . . ." Her brow wrinkled. "Was the Opera House in that list?"

"If it wasn't, it should have been."

"Also the Opera House and the theater."

He whirled her into a turn as the music reached a crescendo. "There is a Mathematical Society meeting next week. I think you would enjoy it, and I would be honored to escort you. My father will be presenting a paper." He wondered if she knew about the disagreement her uncle and his father had had.

"I would like it above all things! When will you give a paper?"

"The meeting after next most likely."

All too soon, the music ended. He bowed and Beth curtsied, then he tucked her arm in his to escort her to her great-aunt.

"Thank you for waltzing with me, Weymouth. It was . . . exhilarating."

He hid a smile; he was supposed to thank her for the dance. "It was my pleasure, Beth. Would you like a glass of lemonade?"

"Yes, please."

Deep in conversation with the Dowager Duchess of St. Ives, Lady Julia smiled at them. George pointed to the refreshment room; Lady Julia nodded permission.

He looked down at the lovely lady walking beside him. Despite her fears, Beth had made quite a splash this Season. He knew, from conversations with friends and acquaintances at his clubs and at Jackson's, Manton's, and Angelo's, Beth had many admirers. It was such a pleasure, Lord Howe said, to hear a young lady talk about something other than fashion or the weather. Young Selwyn praised her kindness and lack of complaint. And Brummell acclaimed her "bright spirit" and gracious manner.

While they drank their lemonade, George asked her impressions of her partners and people she had met tonight. Beth had an instinct for quickly and accurately assessing people, and he enjoyed her witty, but never unkind, character sketches. He had introduced her to a number of his friends, but judging from her conversation, the perfect husband had not yet appeared.

As they strolled back to Lady Julia, he inquired the identity of her next partner. Beth bit her lip. "Sir Edward Smithson. I . . . I took an instant dislike to him when we were introduced, but I had no reason to refuse to dance with him."

"I would say your reaction shows your good sense. We called him Nasty Ned at school, and nothing he has done since indicates a change in character."

"Oh dear."

When they reached her great-aunt, Beth smiled up at him and thanked him prettily for the dance and his company. Smithson arrived and led Beth to join a set. The sight of her on the arm of such a shagbag had George gritting his teeth. Crossing his arms over his chest, he leaned against the wall. If the rotter crossed the line or upset her, George vowed he'd darken Smithson's daylights.

Beth's success at Almack's was followed by equally noteworthy appearances at routs, drums, balls, and musical evenings. Her come-out ball was a sad crush, much to Aunt Julia's delight and Beth's astonishment. Since Uncle Charles could not dance, the Marquess of Bellingham, the highest-ranking gentleman present, was her first partner. Uncle Charles cut up stiff about that, for some inexplicable reason, but all were relieved that neither the Regent nor his brothers had arrived early and claimed the honor.

She was enthralled by the Royal Mathematical Society meeting, listening in enraptured fascination to discussions of the current work of various members. She and George arrived early, and Lord Bellingham allowed her to read his paper before times, while they set the schedule for the next meeting. She earned the marquess's eternal gratitude when she returned his paper with a penciled note in the margin indicating a small error that propagated throughout his calculations and the correct solution detailed on the back of the page. When he acknowledged her assistance, she stammered and blushed seven shades of red, never having imagined such public acclaim. She won the devoted admiration of a gentleman bemoaning the dearth of information in his area of interest by informing him that Thomas Jefferson had written a paper on the subject last year, then summarizing the results. And she was saddened, on the way home, to learn of the disagreement between her uncle and Lord Bellingham.

When Beth recalled the dread with which she had viewed the prospect of a Season, she could but laugh at herself for being such a ninnyhammer. Aside from the queries about her delayed arrival in Town, everything had gone splendidly. She was, inexplicably, a success. Her shyness, her age, her height, her nationality—all the things she had worried would be a hindrance—seemed to matter not a whit. There was nothing to prevent her from enjoying a wonderful Season.

On a rainy Monday afternoon in early April, she was sitting in the morning room reading *Pride and Prejudice* to Aunt Julia, who was embroidering, when the Marquess of Elston was announced.

Beth greeted him with a beaming smile. "Elston, how lovely to see you again!"

"I am equally delighted to see, Miss Castleton. Good afternoon, Lady Julia. You both look wonderfully well."

Aunt Julia waved him to a chair. "We are in fine fettle. I am enjoying watching my darling girl cut a dash in Society."

Beth blushed. "Aunt Julia!"

"Well, child, I am and you are."

North entered with the tea tray. Aunt Julia poured out, and Beth offered the marquess a selection of cakes. After he had been served, Elston turned to her. "I was very sorry to miss your come-out ball, Miss Castleton. Especially after having reserved a dance."

"I know that you have other obligations right now, my lord. As for your dance, you may claim it any time."

"Do you attend Lady Throckmorton's ball this evening?" She nodded. "Then I request the first minuet and the third waltz, if you have not already promised them."

"Both are free, unless the third waltz is the supper dance." She hesitated, then said, "If Weymouth hasn't returned from Dorsetshire, you may have the third waltz even if it is the supper dance, if you'd like."

The marquess gave her one of his rare smiles. "I would be honored, Miss Castleton. If George makes a timely arrival, and I daresay he will, you may put me down for anything but a reel after supper."

She returned his smile with a shy one of her own. "Thank you."

"Is George expected back today?"

"He hoped to be."

"Is my errant friend your escort his evening? I would be pleased to stand in for him."

"Dunnley is doing the honors tonight." Aunt Julia's wry tone evidenced her enjoyment of her charge's success.

Elston was as elegant, urbane, and charming as ever, but Beth wondered at the air of sadness that hung about him like a dark cloud. After half an hour he took his leave. As she walked him to the door, he said, "If you should see George before I do, tell him I saw Arabella at an inn in Stevenage yesterday, headed for London. Tell him to be on his guard."

Chapter 14

Arabella arrived in London seven weeks and a day after Weymouth escaped from Gull Cottage. That he had ruined the lovely scheme she and her cousin had concocted was dastardly enough. That he had taken her carriage, her maid, and her majordomo, leaving her with an angry uncle, a surly footman, a beef-witted coachman, and a temperamental chef demanding his wages, added insult to injury. Now, armed with the information from the innkeeper in Dumfries, she would spread a tale of betrayal and broken promises with herself as the woman scorned. That the story was cut from whole cloth bothered Arabella not at all. Her only aim was to wed Weymouth, by fair means or foul.

As the ancient coach meandered its way south, she'd had plenty of time to plan her campaign. She would establish herself in her father's townhouse, then visit a few quidnuncs, telling them—in strictest confidence, of course—of her plight. In a day or so, the news would be all over Town, and Weymouth would be forced to offer for her.

The first setback occurred when she descended from the carriage and noticed the knocker was on the door. She hadn't expected her father to be in London, but since she'd always been able to wrap him around her little finger, except in the matter of her allowance, she deemed it only a minor annoyance. As she walked to the door, she pondered whether to tell him her tale. Best not, she decided. The role of outraged father was not for the Earl of Hartwood; after having sat through every minute of the divorce proceedings in Lords, he knew her too well.

Arabella was taken aback when Jeffers, her father's starchy butler, informed her that her father had been expecting her for weeks and had given orders that she was to appear before him the moment she arrived. The earl was in his study, Jeffers added, as she walked toward the staircase.

"I will see my father later, after I have eaten and changed clothes."

A door down the hallway opened. "No, Arabella. Now!"

"Really, Father, you cannot expect—"

"I expect a daughter with some semblance of manners and decorum. Since you have neither, and since your recent behavior has been nothing short of criminal, you cannot expect to be given the courtesies due a lady." The Earl of Hartwood's cold tone conveyed his contempt, his clipped speech revealed his fury.

She blinked in astonishment. He was the very picture of an outraged father—except for the fact that his anger was directed at her. Realizing that the butler, a footman, and a maid were watching and listening in rapt fascination, Arabella changed direction, her steps slowing as she neared her father.

The earl closed the door with quiet vehemence, then crossed to sit behind his desk, stabbing his finger in the direction of the chair before it. Arabella sat. Smoothing her skirts, she reviewed his words and planned her response to this second setback.

"Really, Father," she said, a hint of amusement in her voice, "I cannot imagine what you think I have been doing, but—"

"It was not necessary for me to exercise my imagination. Weymouth told me of your actions."

What had Weymouth told him? Surely not the truth! "What are you talking about, sir? I haven't seen Weymouth for some time."

The earl took out his pocket diary. "Not for nearly seven weeks, I believe."

"I . . . I cannot recall, precisely."

"Allow me to refresh your memory." His tone was icy.

She shrugged. "If you feel it necessary, but—"

"I do." His anger unabated, her father proceeded to give an exact accounting of her actions—and her cousin's.

"Did Jamie—"

"What the devil does your crazy cousin have to do with this?"

So Jamie hadn't betrayed her. "Not a thing," she lied. "He is my second cousin, and he isn't crazy." In fact, during their time together, she'd realized there was much to admire about the younger cousin she had heretofore ignored, not the least of which was his devotion to her.

"That is debatable, but if he was not involved, it is irrelevant. Although I cannot help but wonder why you introduced his name into the conversation."

Arabella scrambled to find an acceptable answer. "I saw Jamie recently. He might have . . . ah, deduced—"

"As I said before, Weymouth told me what you did. Your uncle corroborated part of the tale. And informed me of the lies you spouted to gain his participation."

She averted her gaze, well aware of her father's abhorrence of lies and liars.

"What did you hope to gain by involving Miss Castleton in your schemes?"

Confused, Arabella looked at her father. "Who?"

"Beth Castleton." Apparently her expression reflected her bemusement. A muscle jumped in her father's left cheek before he explained, "The Earl of Castleton's niece and ward."

"You are mistaken, sir. I am not acquainted with Castleton's niece—"

"Miss Castleton is the young lady abducted with Weymouth's niece."

"The child's governess is Castleton's niece?" Arabella asked, incredulous.

Her father's glare was withering. "No. You told Weymouth she was Isabelle's governess, but Miss Castleton was only attempting to save the child."

How could Jamie's men have made such an error? With an effort, Arabella refrained from dropping her head into her hands. It was bad enough that her father knew what she had done. That Weymouth's entire family, the Castletons, and at least one other gentleman knew sounded the death knell to her plan. She would not be able to trap him into marriage now. Not after this debacle. *Who would have imagined Weymouth would come to London and in-*

form his family of his abduction? Or that a young lady would aid a total stranger?

She would find a way to come about. Find another man to . . .

"Did you hear me, Arabella?" the earl thundered.

"Ah, no, sir. I was contemplating—"

"Contemplating your apology? Considering your choice of exiles?"

Apology? Exile? "What are you talking about, Father?"

His voice was as cold and hard as steel. "About the apologies you will give Weymouth, Miss Castleton, Lord David Winterbrook, and Lady Julia Castleton—"

"Lady Julia?" she inquired, not understanding why that lady deserved an apology. Miss Castleton was her ladyship's great-niece or some such, but surely her father didn't expect her to beg forgiveness from that grande dame for the accidental abduction of her relative. "You want me—"

"I expect, nay, I demand that you apologize to Weymouth for abducting him and for scheming to trap him into marriage. To Miss Castleton for her abduction, the five days she spent unconscious afterward, and the pain and injury she suffered when one of your men shot her. To Lord David for kidnapping his daughter. And to Lady Julia for leaving her tied up in a filthy cottage and for her anguish during her great-niece's absence."

"But—"

"After you have done all that, you may choose one of my estates in which to serve out your banishment from Society."

"What—"

The earl stood. "You have a day or so to formulate your apologies. I will make all the arrangements to have them heard."

"But—"

"No buts, Arabella. You *will* pay the consequences for your actions."

Her father's inflexibility left her with few choices. She needed time to think. Needed a new plan. She stood and left the room without a word.

An hour later, after a bath and a meal, she ordered the newspapers for the past week brought to her sitting room. Miss Castleton was frequently, and favorably, mentioned in the Society news. The chit was having a spectacular Season, despite the fact she'd been missing for several weeks. Perhaps even more surprisingly, she wasn't engaged to Weymouth, even though she'd spent a week—or more—in his company with only a maid for chaperone. Despite his determination to marry for love, the earl was too honorable not to have proposed. Which meant the wigeon must have refused his suit.

Arabella's smile was wicked as she planned her revenge. Since she couldn't have Weymouth as husband, she was determined that he wouldn't have the love match he wanted. She would tell the *ton* the truth: Weymouth and Miss Beth Castleton had traveled together as man and wife. The tale would spread through the *beau monde* like fire through a dry forest, and the earl would be forced into a loveless marriage with a woman who must despise him. It was, Arabella thought, a just retaliation for the ruination of the lovely scheme she and Jamie had devised.

Calling for a maid to help her dress, she pondered the best scandalmongers. Lady Moreton, Mrs. Windham, and Lady Smithson would have the story in circulation by sundown. Society's penchant for scurrilous gossip would take care of the rest.

Beth, her aunt, and Viscount Dunnley surrendered their outerwear to the Throckmortons' footmen and joined the throng on the stairs.

Aunt Julia raised her lorgnette and peered at the crowd. "What a crush! Esther must be delighted."

"Lady Throckmorton is nearly as popular a hostess as you are, Lady Julia." Dunnley's voice dropped to a conspiratorial whisper. "But your suppers are far superior."

Aunt Julia beamed a smile at the viscount, patting the arm to which she clung. "Thank you, dear boy."

They inched their way upward, greeted their host and hostess, and, after being announced by the butler, entered the ballroom. It seemed to Beth that their entrance attracted more stares than usual, but she dismissed the notion as foolish. Dunnley had escorted them several times this Season, so there was nothing in that to cause comment. He was very handsome in evening attire, the black of his coat a stark contrast to his tawny hair and the white of his linen.

Aunt Julia was her usual, elegant self in lavender silk with
a dainty lace cap perched on her silver hair. Beth looked
down at her apricot silk gown. She had been pleased with
her appearance in the cheval glass in her room, and she
still had gown, slippers, gloves, and shawl, all in their
proper places. *If there were any extra stares, 'twas only because we are all in looks.*

After escorting her aunt to a seat amid the dowagers and
duennas, Beth and Dunnley stood beside her, watching the
country dance being performed and commenting on the
attire of others. There were a plethora of lovely gowns,
embroidered waistcoats, and intricately tied cravats to admire, as well as some less successful ensembles. A number
of Beth's friends and admirers stopped by to confirm
dances they had previously requested. Lady Throckmorton
had given the ladies a little card listing the order of the
dances. Long before the set ended, Beth's card was full. If
George did not attend, she would need to find a partner
for the cotillion he'd bespoken, but Lord Elston would take
the third waltz, which was the supper dance, if his friend
did not appear.

Several of the young ladies making their come-outs this
Season, who had arrived too late to dance in this set, complimented Beth on her gown and received her admiration
in return. Plans were made for shopping expeditions and
promenades in the park, and an excursion to Richmond
Park later in the week was discussed. The latter would, of
course, depend on the weather. England could not rely
upon sunny days in early April, much to the dismay of
Society's hostesses. In the last week alone, a Venetian
breakfast, a garden party, and an evening at Vauxhall Gardens had been postponed because of rain. The uncoopera-
tive weather was, Miss Spencer declared, enough to give
one a megrim.

Elston joined the group, after greeting Aunt Julia and
the older ladies seated nearby. Beth glanced at her card
and saw that the first minuet was next.

"Yes, Miss Castleton," he said with a wry smile, "I left
it a bit late. I did not expect such a tangle of carriages
outside, nor such a crowd on the stairs. I have been too
long in the country, I expect." Nodding at her card, he

added, "A clever idea. Lady Throckmorton could start a new fashion."

When the set ended, the gentlemen dispersed to find their partners. Elston offered his arm to lead her onto the floor. "You look lovely tonight, Beth."

"Thank you, sir. You are very handsome as well." She was more pleased that he'd finally addressed her by name than by the compliment.

They moved through the patterns of the minuet, one of her favorite dances, chatting amiably. As he escorted her back to Aunt Julia, Elston said, "I don't know if George has returned. I left a note for him at Bellingham House but have not received a reply. Since the third waltz is the supper dance, I shall hope to partner you then. If George cuts me out, have you a dance for me later in the evening?"

"Have you promised the second country dance after supper?"

"I have requested no dances except with you."

"Elston, such talk could turn a lady's head!"

"That of a simpering miss, perhaps, but not yours."

She sighed theatrically. "I don't even know how to simper."

A smile tugged the corner of his mouth. "You needn't learn. Simpering is vastly overrated." He bowed over her hand and thanked her for the dance. Lowering his voice, he inquired, "Has George's absence left you without a partner for another set?"

"Yes, for the first cotillion, but I am not concerned about that, only worried about Weymouth." She bit her lip, opened her mouth, then closed it again without saying a word.

"What were you going to ask?"

"You said you hadn't yet promised any dances. Would you think me terribly forward if I asked you to dance with some of the other young ladies whose cards aren't likely to be full?"

"I would think you quite wonderful for looking out for your friends. Whom do you recommend for my next partner?"

She glanced around the room. "Miss Broughton. Do you know her?"

"No, but I assume she is the brunette in white standing next to Mrs. Broughton." Beth nodded. "Then I shall take myself off to request an introduction and ask your friend to dance."

He turned to go, but stopped when she said, "Thank you, Elston. Harriett is rather shy, but a delightful girl. She likes music and reading."

While Beth danced and chatted with her friends, George sat in a private parlor of the coaching inn in Aldershot and brooded over a snifter of brandy. Earlier in the day, an idiot coachman tooling blindly down the center of the road had nearly collided with him. To avoid an accident, George had swerved to the side, a maneuver that damaged a wheel of his curricle and nearly landed him in a ditch. The wheel had been repaired, but too late for him to reach London for the Throckmorton ball.

Since there was little moon tonight, he had chosen to stay in Aldershot. He would resume his journey at dawn, reaching London in time for a final rehearsal with Beth before Mrs. Broughton's musicale. Provided that she hadn't given up on him for standing her up tonight, that is. She wouldn't have the slightest difficulty finding partners for the dances he'd reserved, but he had no substitute for her bright presence.

He'd spent a lot of time at Winterhaven Manor thinking about her, wondering what she was doing. *Face it, George, you missed her. Just as you are missing her now.* Too weary to ponder the whys and wherefores of such an unprecedented occurrence, he drained his glass and trudged up the stairs to his room.

Elston returned several times throughout the evening to ask Beth to recommend partners for him. He returned the favor just before the first cotillion by introducing her to Captain Ashton, who had served in his regiment in Portugal. The captain, whose left arm was in a sling, declared himself honored to partner her in the absence of Major Lord Weymouth, but devastated that he could not dance. She was happy to sit out the set with the good-natured captain and listen to his stories—much edited, she suspected—of adventures on the Peninsula.

There seemed to be a greater than usual number of ladies gossiping behind their fans, but since Beth wasn't interested in gossip, she didn't regard it. She danced and chatted, then danced some more, thoroughly enjoying herself. Partway through the evening, she was astonished to see Elston stop abruptly in front of two matrons and converse rather heatedly with them. Beth didn't know either lady. Perhaps they were relatives of his, taking him to task for not calling on them when he arrived in Town. Even so, it was rather a shock to see the elegant, urbane, normally unflappable marquess in such a pother.

George had not arrived when the music began for the third waltz, so Beth danced with Elston and went to supper on his arm. They shared a table with Tina Fairchild and Lord Howe, Harriett Broughton and Mr. Radnor, and Dunnley and Miss Spencer. Lord Howe and Mr. Radnor regaled them with a tale of a race in which one horse refused to start and another ran in the wrong direction. Several of the group were to perform at Mrs. Broughton's musicale the next evening, so they compared selections to ensure that there would be no repetitions.

Tina, an excellent pianist, dismissed her choices with an airy wave. "A Mozart sonata and a folk song."

Harriett Broughton, shy but with lovely voice, admitted to "a Handel aria and a Scottish ballad." Dunnley was singing two madrigals as part of an octet. Beth had rehearsed a duet with George and a trio with him and his father. When queried, she said merely that she hadn't yet decided what to play. Harriett was aghast, having practiced her pieces dozens of times in the past fortnight, and even Tina shuddered at the idea of waiting until the last minute to choose. Dunnley gave her a knowing look and a nod of approval. When they rose from the table, he whispered, "I am certain George will do everything in his power to return in time to perform with you."

As they walked back to the ballroom, Elston asked if she was to play a duet with George. When she told him what they'd planned, he said, "Regrettably, I can't take his place tomorrow as I did tonight. I am a violist, not a cellist. I know a duet for violin and viola and would offer to play it with you, but that would solve only half of your problem."

"I didn't know you played the viola!"

He smiled. " 'Tis a deep, dark secret known only to a select few."

"I am honored to be among them. Were you to perform with me tomorrow, your secret would be revealed, so I shan't take you up on your very kind offer."

His smile deepened to reveal a dimple in his left cheek. "I am relieved. I would have to stay up all night practicing if you did."

"I would enjoy playing with you some other time. As for tomorrow, I can perform any number of solo pieces if estate business delays Weymouth's return."

Sir Edward Smithson approached Beth between dances. "Miss Castleton? Are you really Miss Castleton?"

"You know very well who I am. Your mother introduced us at Almack's."

"But are you really Miss Castleton?"

"You speak in riddles, sir." She turned and walked the few steps back to Aunt Julia, wondering if Nasty Ned was foxed.

Dunnley strolled toward her. "Beth, is all well? You look a bit perplexed."

"I just had the most bizarre conversation with Sir Edward."

The viscount arced one tawny eyebrow in inquiry, but Beth dismissed the baronet and his words with a wave of her hand. She traded impressions of the ball with Dunnley until Mr. Brewster, her next partner, arrived.

Sir Edward approached her again as couples were taking the floor for a country dance. This was the set she'd promised Elston, but he had already partnered her twice, since he'd stood in for George for the supper dance. As the baronet requested the dance, a gentleman she didn't know came hurrying toward her. The stranger bowed and said, "Miss Castleton, please forgive my tardiness. Elston just reminded me I am promised to you for this set."

The unknown man was about thirty, not much taller than she, and rather plain, but she was certain any friend of Elston's would be a far more amiable partner than Nasty Ned. Aunt Julia was a few feet away, deep in conversation and unaware of her niece's dilemma. Beth searched for Elston, who nodded toward the stranger. She smiled at her rescuer. "I thought you had forgotten me, sir."

"Never, Miss Castleton. I merely lost track of the dances." Sir Edward stalked off as she took the stranger's arm and allowed him to lead her onto the floor. When they were out of earshot, he introduced himself. "I am Fairfax, and pleased to make your acquaintance."

"Thank you for rescuing me, Your Grace."

"Elston intended to introduce me to you, but was detained in conversation by his godmother." The music began. "He bid me come to your aid when he saw Smithson approaching you." The pattern of the dance parted them. When next they came together, the duke asked, "Was it really a rescue?"

She nodded. "As valiant as a knight of yore."

He seemed to stand taller as he circled her and moved back into line. They exchanged comments as the steps permitted. When the set ended, Fairfax escorted her back to her aunt, then bowed and thanked her for the dance.

"Thank you, Your Grace, for your chivalry."

By the end of the evening, Beth felt like one of the animals in the Tower menagerie. People *were* staring at her, although she couldn't imagine why. She'd checked her appearance in the ladies' withdrawing room, but there were no rips in her gown nor anything else that should attract such attention. *What could it mean?*

Dunnley came to escort her onto the floor for the last dance, a waltz. "Have you enjoyed yourself this evening, Beth?"

She moved into his arms as the music began. "Have you noticed anything unusual tonight?"

"Other than George's absence and Elston's first appearance in Society this Season?"

"Yes, other than those things."

"I cannot say that I have, but I spent the last hour in the card room." He studied her face. "What is troubling you?"

She bit her lip. "Perhaps it is just my imagination."

"You are not overly fanciful, my dear. What seems unusual to you tonight?"

"I . . ." She shook her head.

"Come, child, tell Uncle Theo all about it," he invited.

"Uncle Theo?" she queried, smiling a bit.

The gray eyes twinkled. "Do you question the uncle or the Theodore?"

"The uncle, although I didn't know your given name. Everyone, even your relatives, calls you Dunnley."

"That is because at school I became less than fond of my name." At her wide-eyed look of inquiry, he explained. "Some . . . ah, unflattering nicknames can be bestowed on a boy named Theodore."

"That is unfortunate. It is a strong name, and an unusual one, and suits you well."

"I shall take that as a compliment, I think."

"It was meant as one," she replied, then changed the subject to forestall further questions.

When the dance ended, the viscount escorted her back to Aunt Julia, who was talking with Elston. After they said their good nights to those nearby, the marquess offered his arm to escort Aunt Julia to their carriage. Beth wondered if the attention was merely an example of Elston's excellent manners or if her aunt wasn't feeling well. *Had Aunt Julia noticed the stares directed at her great-niece?*

Beth was surprised when Elston joined them for the ride back to Castleton House. This was more than good manners. What, she wasn't sure. And she wasn't at all certain she wanted to know.

Dunnley and Elston accepted Aunt Julia's offer of a brandy and joined them in the drawing room. Beth loved her great-aunt dearly, and valued her friendships with both men, but she wished they would take themselves off to their respective beds so that she could seek hers. She had the headache and wanted quiet and solitude in which to ponder this strange evening.

After a quarter hour, Elston and Dunnley departed, saying that they would see the ladies tomorrow evening at Mrs. Broughton's musicale. Beth bid her aunt good night and escaped to the haven of her bedchamber.

As he walked downstairs, Elston debated telling Dunnley what he had heard this evening. He didn't know Dunnley all that well, the viscount being a few years younger, but the man was George's cousin and a leader of the *ton*. He was also one of Beth's friends. In George's absence, the viscount was a logical ally.

When the butler closed the door of Castleton House behind them, Elston made his decision, "Dunnley, have you a few minutes? I would like your advice on something."

A look of surprise flickered across the younger man's face. "I would be pleased to help you, if I can. Shall we go to White's?"

"Somewhere more private would be better. My house is just a block down Upper Brook Street."

The viscount acquiesced with a nod. As they strolled along, Elston asked, "Do you know when George will return?"

"He planned to be back today. I am certain that he will do his best to return tomorrow. He is to perform with Beth at the musicale."

"So I understand. I look forward to hearing her play. George told me she is extremely talented."

Dunnley nodded. "That she is. Even more so than George or Bellingham, in my opinion."

"Good Lord! I have performed with most of the violinists and cellists in the *ton* and consider Bellingham to be the best, with George a close second and Sherworth a more distant third."

"I didn't know you played. I am only a singer and a music lover, but I agree with your assessment, except to rank Beth higher than my uncle."

Elston answered the unspoken question as they entered the foyer of his townhouse. "I am a violist."

After a footman had taken their coats, hats, and gloves, the viscount said, "Satisfy my curiosity, please, and tell me where you would rate yourself in that list of talented performers."

Elston pondered the question as he led the way to the library. "Sixth or seventh, perhaps."

"I shall look forward to hearing you perform someday. And perhaps sometime you will share the other names in your ranking with me."

He waved the younger man to a chair in front of the fireplace, then poured two snifters of brandy. "If you like." After handing Dunnley a glass, Elston sat in the other chair and sipped his brandy. "Do you know anything about George's visit with me in Scotland in February?"

"I know most of the tale, including his companions and the reasons that led to that visit."

"Did you hear or see anything unusual tonight at the Throckmortons?"

The viscount crossed one leg over the other. "No, I didn't, but Beth asked me much the same thing during the last dance."

"Did she? Why?"

"I don't know why; she wouldn't say." The younger man frowned. "But something was troubling her during the last dance. What did you hear, Elston?"

"A vicious—and false—rumor about Beth and George was making the rounds tonight."

"What kind of rumor?"

"That they traveled as husband and wife from Scotland to London."

"Good God!" Dunnley set his glass aside. "From whom did you hear it?"

"I heard it twice. The first time, I overheard Lady Cathcart telling it to Mrs. Phillips. When I confronted her, Lady Cathcart said she'd had it from Lady Smithson. Later, my godmother questioned me as to the possible validity of the tale. She'd heard it from Lady Moreton."

"I spent the last hour or so in the card room and didn't hear a whisper of it. Which means the gossip was started by a woman, probably late today."

"What makes you say that?"

"The fact that it hasn't reached the men yet." The viscount rubbed his chin. "The real question is, who would start such a rumor and why?"

"The why is obvious: Someone wants to ruin Beth."

"Beth is, much to her surprise, one of the most popular young ladies making their come-outs this Season. As well liked by the other girls as by the gentlemen."

"Could the rumor have been started by the mother of a less favored girl?"

Dunnley picked up his snifter and drank before answering. "It must have been started by someone who knows Beth and George were in Scotland and that they traveled together to London. I didn't think anyone outside of their immediate families and you and I knew the latter fact."

"Arabella and Sir James know."

"They know Beth and George left Gull Cottage together, but how could they know the rest?"

"They need not know it to spread false rumors."

"I suppose not." Dunnley swirled the brandy in his glass. "It doesn't make sense, though. Arabella wants to marry George. Spreading this rumor won't aid her cause, since it will force him to offer for Beth."

"He would have done so when they reached London. Did Beth refuse him?"

"Yes, because she didn't want him forced into marriage with her." The viscount shifted in his chair. "Do you intend to tell Beth and Lady Julia about the gossip?"

"This," Elston said, his tone wry, "is where I need your advice. I know how Beth deals with pain, the repercussions of abduction, and the hardships of travel, but not how she would take this. Lady Julia needs to know, but Beth . . ." He lifted a hand, palm upward, in supplication.

"Beth will be upset by the gossip, and very hurt. It will undermine her confidence, which, at times, falters inexplicably. But she will take a deep breath, put on a brave smile, and face the *ton*'s scandalmongers."

Dunnley took another fortifying sip. "You traveled with Beth and George, so you can refute the rumors. I will do what I can, but since he is my cousin, my arguments won't have the same impact as yours."

"Damnation!" Elston slammed his glass down on the table, shattering the delicate crystal. "When I find the author of this rumor, I will wring his or her neck."

The viscount placed his snifter on the table and rose. His face grim and his voice harsh, he said, "You will have to stand in line—behind George and I."

Chapter 15

George arrived in London as the church bells chimed noon. At Bellingham House he received a warm welcome from his father, his favorite cousin, and his best friend. After his parent's hearty slap on the back, Dunnley's fervent handshake and Elston's muttered "Thank God," George said, smiling, "I was only gone for a week. Not quite the prodigal son."

"We are glad to see you, my boy. Join us for luncheon, and we will tell you the latest news." Then, in afterthought, "I trust you got everything sorted out at Winterhaven Manor?"

"I did, yes. As for joining you, I am in no state to grace the dining room. My aunts will take one look at me—"

"Your aunts are out. Wash and change if you must, but join us."

It was more command than invitation. George acquiesced with a nod. "Give me ten minutes."

As he climbed the stairs, he pondered his father's unlikely choice of luncheon companions. Bellingham knew them both, of course, and quite well—Dunnley was his nephew by marriage and Elston was his heir's best friend and a frequent participant in their musical evenings—but George doubted that his father had ever shared a meal with just the two of them.

Eight minutes later, after a hasty wash and a quick change of clothes, he took a seat in the dining room. A scant two minutes after that, subsequent to Elston opening his budget and Dunnley reporting that the rumor had been the talk of all the clubs that morning, George was out of his chair, storming around the room.

On his third circuit, his father blocked his path and grasped him by the shoulders. "We feel the same, son. That is why we are here. Sit down, calm down, and think."

George rubbed his hands over his face and returned to his seat. After offering a silent prayer of thanks to the Almighty for his wonderful family and friends, then damning the scandalmongering malefactor to hell, he harnessed his anger and set his mind to finding the best solution to the problem.

If there *was* a solution.

Elston had done his part, staunchly refuting the gossip with the truth: He had traveled with George from Scotland. Bellingham and Dunnley had denounced the rumor as a lie, but with less success. George knew that nothing he said would make a whit of difference. The gossipmongers would not believe him if he swore the truth to the Archbishop of Canterbury, with one hand on the Bible and his hope of heaven in the balance. The quidnuncs did not care about accuracy, nor that the tale would destroy an innocent young lady's reputation.

Who the devil would spread such a story? And why?

Elston favored Arabella as the culprit, despite Dunnley's argument of illogic. But neither Arabella's wish to wed him nor her cousin's plot to grant her heart's desire had been rational, so George was not prepared to discount their participation. Especially since the rumor started the day she arrived in London.

The difficult but unanimous decision not to charge Arabella and Sir James with forgery, abduction, and attempted murder, so as to spare Beth's reputation, was for naught. She would be the Talk of the Town. By God, if Arabella was responsible for the rumors, he would lay charges against her! Not that doing so would help Beth.

Nothing could save Beth except marriage. To him.

As his father, his cousin, and his friend formulated plans, George pondered the best way to convince Beth. She had refused him before, the night they had arrived in London, because she didn't want him forced into marriage. He had accepted her decision then, since they had behaved honorably, although not within the canons of propriety, and because no one but themselves, their families, and Elston knew they had traveled together with only a maid as chap-

erone. That was no longer the case. He had to find a way
to persuade her to accept his suit.

He knew she wanted to marry for love, as he did. Unfortunately, when he met Beth that first morning at Dunnley
Park, he had not experienced the *coup de foudre* by which
his parents, aunts, grandparents, and great-grandparents
had known their loves. He was fond of Beth. He admired
and respected her. He valued her friendship. And he had
missed her this past week. That, however, was not the love
that poets—and at least three generations of Winterbrooks—proclaimed.

George believed the affection, the admiration and respect, and the friendship he and Beth shared would be the
basis for a good marriage. Even a happy one. He'd thought
so a month ago, before he'd become so fond of her. He
was even more certain now. But how to convince Beth?

He could approach the matter rationally, citing her ruined reputation. Castleton and Lady Julia would, undoubtedly, add their arguments to his. He could appeal to her
sense of honor, since his would be questioned if he did not
marry her. Or he could try to persuade her that friendship
and affection would lead to love.

None of those seemed quite right, somehow. The first
two because they would, in essence, force her into a marriage she didn't want. The latter because . . . probably because he was not absolutely certain he believed it.

Perhaps a combination of all three would work . . .

"George? George!"

Startled from his musings, he glanced at his companions.
His father and his cousin looked mildly annoyed, Elston
slightly perplexed. Abashed, George tugged at his cravat.
"My apologies. I—"

"This is no time to be woolgathering, son."

"I wasn't, sir. I was considering the best way to convince
Beth to marry me."

"Surely you don't think she will refuse you!" Bellingham
exclaimed, aghast.

"She did last time. She thought, quite rightly, that my
proposal was offered to satisfy honor. What is there in this
to make her think differently?"

"Circumstances are different now. She is, or soon will
be, the talk of the *ton*."

George raked a hand through his hair. "That is, unfortunately, true. But my proposal still has its basis in honor, not love."

"Beth is a lady of honesty and integrity," Dunnley explained to his uncle. "She knows, as do her relatives, that George behaved honorably. For her, that is sufficient. Society's gossip won't sway her overmuch, since she knows it is all lies."

"But she will be ruined!"

"Very likely she will—unless we find a way to thwart the scandalmongers."

"How?" George and his father asked in unison.

The viscount toyed with his wineglass as he considered the matter. "The first thing to do is trace the gossip to its source. If the rumor was started by a young lady jealous of Beth's success this Season, then she must be confronted and forced to confess. And to apologize, publicly. If—"

"How—"

Dunnley raised a hand to halt the question. "If, however, the gossip came from someone who saw Beth and George traveling together, without a proper chaperone, the story will be more difficult to refute."

George pushed his chair back from the table but did not interrupt his cousin. "Assuming that to be the case, they must have been seen at an inn in Scotland, since the rumor claims they traveled together from there to London. Elston was with them from Stranraer to Brough and can attest to the fact that Beth and George did not travel as man and wife."

"I spent the morning doing just that," the younger marquess said, "but it didn't stop the slander."

"Gossip does not die an instant death," the viscount reminded them. "You are known as an honest, honorable man, Elston. Your denial will make people—men, at least—think twice before repeating the tale."

"Those who know and like Beth will repeat your words when they hear the gossip," George said, devoutly hoping that would be the case.

Bellingham nodded in agreement. "Your refutation won't spread as quickly as the rumor, Robert, but it will help to stem the tide."

George slammed a fist against the table. "Damn it, it is

so bloody unfair! Beth did nothing wrong. Nothing! She was kidnapped by accident and shot whilst helping me. And now she is suffering again because of her good deeds."

Pacing around the room helped to vent some of his ire. After three circuits, he braced his hands against the wall, his muscles knotted with tension. Finally, he took a deep, calming breath and turned to face his companions. "Do the Castletons know about the gossip?"

Elston and Dunnley exchanged a glance before the viscount answered. "They didn't seem to last night, although Beth asked me, during the last dance, if I had noticed anything unusual at the ball. Which I hadn't."

Elston added, "Dunnley and I plan to call on Lady Julia this afternoon and apprise her of it."

"Tuesday isn't one of her At Home days," George pointed out.

"No, but she will likely be there to chaperon your rehearsal with Beth," his cousin said.

"Zounds!" George pulled out his watch. "I need to leave in ten minutes."

Elston and Dunnley volunteered to track the rumor. After they spoke to Lady Julia, they would call on Lady Moreton and Lady Smithson, since those matrons, both notorious gossips, had been named as talebearers last night. From there they would follow the trail, wherever it led.

George retrieved his cello and his father's violin from the music room, then departed for Castleton House in his curricle, his instrument on the floor, his feet holding it in place. His father, Elston, and Dunnley followed in their own carriages. They would speak with Lady Julia, giving George time alone with Beth. Later, his father would join them for a rehearsal of tonight's program. George was eager to see Beth, but dreaded the conversation they must have.

Lady Julia was descending the staircase as North admitted them to the house. She greeted George fondly and smiled at her unexpected callers. When he requested a private word with Beth, Lady Julia scrutinized him before waving him in the direction of the music room and escorting her visitors to the morning room. George smiled wryly at her departing back. Since she usually entertained callers in the drawing room, he could only suppose that Lady Julia wanted to be nearby if her great-niece needed her. He hoped the shocking news his luncheon companions were about to convey wouldn't be too much for the dear lady.

George took a deep breath, wiped his suddenly clammy palms surreptitiously on his pantaloons, then picked up his cello and walked down the hallway to the music room. As he approached, he could hear Beth playing a lively, lilting air. He eased the door open and stopped, enchanted, watching and listening. She stood in front of a window that looked out on the small garden behind the house, her eyes closed and her body swaying gently in time to the music. Dressed in a simple white round gown and haloed by sunlight, she looked like an angel. Surely no member of the heavenly host was lovelier or could create sweeter music.

Feeling as if a large fist was squeezing his heart, he leaned against the door frame. Beth was as innocent and angelic as she appeared, yet someone wanted to destroy her, to crush her gentle spirit. As his anger flared anew, he closed his eyes and let the music wash over him. Several minutes later, soothed, he opened his eyes and stood erect. He must have made some small sound because Beth's eyes flew open and she turned toward the door.

A dazzling smile lit her face. "Weymouth, you are back!" She placed her violin and bow on a table and walked toward him, hands outstretched.

"As you see." He mustered a smile for her. "I am sorry I wasn't here last night—"

She waved his apology aside, the look in her beautiful blue eyes telling him she required no explanation for his delayed return. Grasping her hand, he raised it to his lips, brushing a kiss against her knuckles.

Her cheeks flushed a delicate rose at the unprecedented salute. Ducking her head, she gently pulled her hand from his clasp. "Is your father not joining us?"

"He will be here shortly."

She offered him a chair then sat on the sofa. "Did your business go well?"

"Yes." The word emerged more curtly than he'd intended, and he winced inwardly at the hurt expression that clouded her face.

He closed his eyes for a moment, grappling with his emotions. "Beth, there is something I need to tell you."

"I am listening." Her voice was calm, but the expression in her eyes was wary.

God, but he hated this! Hated being the cause of her distress. He stood, then paced the room, searching for the right words.

Suddenly, she was standing in front of him. She reached out and touched his coat sleeve, looking up at him with concern. "What is wrong, George?"

He told her. She paled, then swayed as if he had planted her a facer. He pulled her into his embrace, holding her close as he finished his explanation. Her arms crept loosely around his waist as she listened, but she didn't say a word. Tremors shook her slender frame. He rubbed one hand up and down her spine, wishing he could bear the pain for her.

Finally, she raised tear-drenched eyes to his. "Wh-who would spread such a lie? And why?"

He cradled her face in his hands, wiping away her tears with his thumbs. "I don't know who or why. Yet. But we will find out."

She groped for her handkerchief. "We?"

He handed her his, waited while she mopped her face and delicately blew her nose, then led her to the sofa. Seating himself beside her, he took her left hand in his right, absently rubbing his thumb against her knuckles as he explained. "Elston and Dunnley will pay calls this afternoon on two ladies who were spreading the rumor last night. From there, they will work back to the source of the gossip."

"Who told the tale last night? That is, who will Elston and Dunnley visit?"

"Lady Smithson and Lady Moreton."

Beth started. "Do those names surprise you?" he asked, searching her face.

"N-not exactly. I have noticed Lady Smithson's fondness for *on dits,* and it was Lady Moreton who asked such probing questions at Aunt Julia's first At Home. That Lady Smithson was spreading the rumor does, perhaps, explain a strange conversation I had with her son last night."

"Oh? Tell me about your encounter with Nasty Ned."

"I had two, actually. The first one was after supper, between sets. He came up to me and said, if I remember correctly, 'Miss Castleton? Are you really Miss Castleton?'

To which I replied that he knew very well who I was. Then he said, 'But are you really Miss Castleton?' I told him he spoke in riddles and walked away."

She raised her eyes to his. "If he heard the gossip from his mother yesterday, that would explain his questions, would it not?"

"Yes, I suppose it would." When she didn't say anything more, he prompted, "Tell me about the second encounter."

"He asked me to stand up with him in a country dance for which I did not have a partner. I—"

"What?" he quizzed. "Your dances are usually taken within minutes of your arrival."

"This was the second set I had promised Elston, but he partnered me for the supper dance instead."

George winced. "I am sorry, Beth. I—"

"Hush. You have already apologized for your absence." She squeezed his hand gently. "As I was saying, I didn't have a partner, and Sir Edward asked me to dance. I didn't want to stand up with him but had no reason to refuse. The Duke of Fairfax came gallantly to my rescue, and I danced with him instead."

"Fairfax? I didn't know you were acquainted with him. He wasn't in Town when I left."

A mischievous look chased some of the bleakness from her eyes. "I wasn't. The duke said Elston reminded him that he was promised to me for the dance, so I knew the marquess had sent him. Aunt Julia was deep in conversation and unaware of my dilemma. I looked around for Elston, and he nodded toward Fairfax, so I smiled at the duke and told him I thought he'd forgotten me. Sir Edward stalked off, then His Grace introduced himself and we danced."

"Miss Castleton," George exclaimed in accents of mock reproach, "I am shocked that you would take the floor with a complete stranger."

"Oh, pooh. Any friend of yours or Elston's is certain to be nicer than Sir Edward."

"I am honored by your confidence, Beth," Elston said from the doorway, where he stood with Lord Bellingham.

Beth rose to her feet, blushing to be caught with George holding her hand. How had that come about? she wondered. "Good afternoon, my lords." Walking toward them, she spied the case in Elston's hand. "Are you going to perform with us this evening?"

"Perhaps" was the enigmatic reply.

After she invited the two marquesses to be seated, Lord Bellingham took over the conversation. "If the two of you have no objection, I thought we might expand our program for this evening a bit."

"I have none, if you think Mrs. Broughton will not mind. What were you thinking to add? A quartet?" Beth looked a question at Elston, wondering if he truly wanted to play in such a public forum, and received a reassuring nod in reply.

Lord Bellingham smiled, blue eyes atwinkle. "Mrs. Broughton will be flattered beyond measure when the best of the *ton*'s musicians make her musicale one of The Events of the Season. Which is just what I propose we do."

Beth bit her lip. It would be lovely if Mrs. Broughton's musicale was remembered because of the exceptional music, dreadful if the cause was the presence of the notorious Miss Castleton.

Her fears must have been writ large upon her countenance because George's father asked, with kindness in his eyes and voice, "Do you trust me, Beth?"

"Of course I do, Lord Bellingham!" she exclaimed, shocked that he might think otherwise.

"I am fond of you, child, and would do nothing that might hurt you. Tonight I want to remind the *beau monde* that you are beautiful, intelligent, honest, talented, kind-hearted, and as innocent as a babe in arms."

Flattered by his high regard, and decidedly flustered by such a sweeping compliment, she looked down at her hands, folded in her lap. "Thank you, sir. Er, my lord. I shall do whatever you think best. Provided Aunt Julia and Uncle Charles have no objection."

"Lady Julia has already given her permission. And it is perfectly acceptable for you to address me as 'sir.' We are friends, are we not?"

Beth met Lord Bellingham's eyes. "I am honored by your friendship, sir." She glanced at George and Elston. "By the friendship of all three of you."

Smiling his approval, Bellingham stood. "Then, as

friends, you will call us by title, and we will call you Beth. Now, to work."

"You have not yet told us what you plan, sir," George reminded his father.

"I will tell you whilst we unpack our instruments and tune them."

That evening, dressed in a white muslin gown with a pink sash and tiny pink rosebuds embroidered around the bottom of the skirt, Beth entered the Broughtons's home on Lord Bellingham's arm. George and Elston walked side by side in front of her, Dunnley and Uncle Charles, with Aunt Julia between them, followed behind. Even surrounded by her family and friends, she was in quite a state, her nerves aquake and her stomach once again the repository of all the butterflies in southern England. Her composure was a very fragile thing, likely to shatter at the first look askance or unkind word.

Bellingham, bless the dear man, must have sensed her unease. "Remember, Beth, you *are* innocent."

Did she know him better, she would have hugged him for his kindness and concern. Instead she offered a brave but wobbly smile and heartfelt words. "And you, my lord, are quite wonderful."

He smiled down at her, with George's smile. "As are you, m'dear."

Mrs. Broughton, who had always treated her kindly, frowned when she saw Beth, but addressed them civilly. Harriett, at her mother's side, greeted Beth with a hug. "I am all eagerness to hear you play. Tina and the rest of our friends are, too." Beth couldn't help but wonder if the young ladies hadn't heard the rumor. Or if they'd heard but dismissed it as rubbishy nonsense.

As she talked with Harriett, Bellingham spoke with Mrs. Broughton, explaining the alteration in their program. The widow was apparently no more immune to the Winterbrook charm than Beth, for Mrs. Broughton simpered and smiled at the marquess, accepting his changes without demur.

"Excellent." Bellingham smiled at their hostess before escorting Beth into the Broughtons's drawing room. He led her to a seat at the back, then sat beside her. "Mrs.

Broughton proclaims herself delighted at our expanded
program. And for us to perform last. The *grande finale,* as
it were."

"I only hope, sir, that I will not expire from a nervous
disorder before then."

The marquess patted her hand. " 'Tis natural to be nervous before you perform. Good, in fact. It gives your playing an extra brilliance."

"Then we shall dazzle the *ton* tonight."

"That's the spirit." Bellingham smiled and nodded
approvingly.

After the ordeal of doing the pretty, with Uncle Charles
and Elston for support, Beth felt calmer. There had been
some Looks, and a number of whispers behind fans, but
only two people had alluded to the gossip. Elston had fro-
zen them with a haughty stare and a curt denial of the
rumor.

When Mrs. Broughton walked to the front of the room
to introduce the first performer, Beth was able to relax
slightly and enjoy the music. Despite her shyness, Harriett
sang splendidly, setting a standard of excellence that would
be difficult to match. Tina nearly did so, but became flustered when she lost her place and ended badly. During the
interval for supper, Beth praised her friends, then consoled
Tina with a tale of turning a page of her music with such
force that it flew off the stand.

As they returned to the drawing room, Tina's hug and
fiercely whispered avowal of her belief in Beth's innocence
almost cost Beth her composure. She rallied, but it was a
near-run thing. Uncle Charles looked at her with concern,
then wrapped an arm around her shoulders and hugged her
to his side. She was lost then, tears streaming silently down
her face at such a public display of affection from her reserved uncle. Sinking down on the sofa, she covered her
face with her hands.

Aunt Julia pushed through the gentlemen blocking Beth
from the view of others in the room and embraced her.
"My dear, what has overset you?"

Beth wiped away tears with the back of her hand. "Kindness, Aunt Julia. And affection. Have you ever known a
sillier wigeon?"

"Thousands, darling" was the wry and loving reply as her aunt handed her a handkerchief.

Beth looked blankly at Dunnley when he offered her a glass of cool water and a napkin. "Wipe your face and bathe your eyes."

After she had done so, she thanked him, then said, "How very kind you are." She looked up at the five men shielding and supporting her. "All of you. I thank you most sincerely. And I apologize for behaving like the veriest goosecap."

Mrs. Broughton asked everyone to take their seats. George offered a hand to Aunt Julia, settled her in a chair, then sat beside Beth on the sofa. In a whisper, but with very real concern, he asked, "Are you feeling better now, sweetheart?"

Beth's reply was equally quiet. "At the moment, I feel very foolish. I fear I am turning into a watering pot." *He had called her sweetheart!*

"Because of a few tears? What balderdash. Most women would have had strong hysterics this afternoon and cowered in their bedchambers tonight." He gave her a look of approval mixed with something that, to her hopeful heart, looked remarkably like affection. "Everyone must admire your courage."

She ducked her head. "I do not feel at all brave, Weymouth."

"If you slide your hand from your lap, I will hold it under cover of your skirts and try to bolster your spirits."

She glanced around the room. Everyone's attention was focused on Lord Howe, who, accompanied by Tina, was giving a stirring rendition of "Why Do the Nations So Furiously Rage Together?" from Handel's *Messiah*. Beth moved her hand to the sofa cushion and felt soothed to the depths of her soul when George's warm, strong hand enveloped hers.

"Your fingers are like ice." He rubbed his thumb the length of her hand. "What? No comments on the shocking impropriety of my suggestion?" he quizzed.

Her voice was bleak as she replied, " 'Tis far less scandalous than that of which I am accused."

His apology was drowned by the wave of applause for Lord Howe. Beth pulled her hand from George's so that she, too, could express her appreciation for the baron's marvelous performance. As the next performer was announced, she placed her hand so that George could hold it, if he chose. Which he did, much to her comfort.

When their turn came, Beth felt composed enough to perform. She was nervous, of course, but not impossibly so. Just enough for her playing to have the extra edge Bellingham had mentioned earlier. The marquess escorted her to the front of the room, with George and Elston walking behind them.

After quickly checking that all four instruments were in tune, Beth and Elston led off with a duet for violin and viola. Beth had never played the piece before this afternoon, and she was not as comfortable with it as she would have liked, but it went splendidly, and received enthusiastic applause.

The trio with George and his father was even better; the duet with George was by far the best performance they had ever given. The fourth selection, a Beethoven quartet that they all knew but hadn't played together before today, had the audience on its feet, cheering for more. Finally, she and Bellingham played the Bach violin duet that was his favorite. At the conclusion, there was a veritable storm of applause and cries of "Bravo!"

As the ovation began to subside, there were calls for an encore. Dismayed, Beth looked at George's father; they hadn't prepared for such an eventuality. He stepped closer and whispered, "Play a solo for them."

She felt burnt to the socket but nodded her agreement. "Bach's 'Jesú, Joy of Man's Desiring'?" she suggested softly. The piece would comfort her, even if the audience disliked it.

"Excellent choice." Bellingham made the announcement, then stepped back and took his seat in the circle of chairs from which they'd played the quartet. Unwilling to risk a glance at the audience, Beth looked down for a moment, then tucked her violin under her chin, closed her eyes, and began to play.

When she finished, there was moment of silence, then a tidal wave of applause broke over her. She mustered a smile for the audience and sagged in relief. Bellingham quickly stood and put his arm around her to escort her to her seat.

Before they had taken two steps, Tina and Harriett were there, unabashedly wiping away tears before hugging and praising her. "Lord, Beth, your playing would make the angels weep," Tina proclaimed. "Even Mama was crying."

Beth glanced at Tina's mother. Sure enough, Her Grace of Greenwich was wiping her eyes with a lacy handkerchief. The duchess's smile conveyed admiration and approval, and Beth felt heartened enough to face the rest of her well-wishers.

Finally, they were in the carriages and on their way home. Beth was exhausted, too tired to participate in the conversation, or even to hear it. In the foyer of Castleton House she realized both Winterbrooks, Elston, and Dunnley had accompanied them inside. With a weak smile, she offered her excuses. "I hope you will forgive my rag-manners, but I am too fatigued even to talk. I thank you all, from the bottom of my heart, for everything you have done for me today."

With words of praise and a hug or a kiss on the cheek, they sent her off to bed.

The next morning Beth felt much restored. She had slept long and deeply, her rest untroubled by nightmares. Wearing a sunny smile and a jonquil muslin morning gown, she joined her uncle and great-aunt in the breakfast parlor.

"Good morning, darling. Are you feeling better this morning?"

"Indeed I am." Beth bent over and kissed her aunt's cheek, then turned and offered her uncle the same salute.

As she walked behind her uncle's chair to her seat on his left, the earl cleared his throat. "I was so proud of you last night, Beth. So very, very proud."

"As was I, darling," chimed Aunt Julia.

Beth unfolded her napkin as North brought her tea. She smiled her thanks at the butler, then returned her attention to her relatives. "The music went very well, and people were much less censorious than I expected."

The earl rolled his eyes. "Beth, your performance—all six pieces—was a triumph. The *ton* won't hear anything so wonderful again for a very long time."

She blushed at the praise. "Much of the credit must go to Bellingham, Weymouth, and Elston. I couldn't have done it without them. And without the two of you."

"We did nothing."

"That is not true, Uncle Charles. You are standing by me, supporting me in the midst of this scandal. That is considerably more than nothing, and means a great deal to me."

"Of course we are supporting you! 'Tis naught but a pack of lies."

"Yes, it is. But I do not believe that every uncle and great-aunt in England would so staunchly support a niece. Especially one they have known for only sixteen months."

"Time has nothing to do with it, darling. 'Tis character."

The earl nodded his agreement, then changed the subject. "What are your plans for today, my ladies?"

"I hope we haven't any," Beth replied, still a bit weary. "I could use a quiet day."

A slight frown creased her aunt's brow. "You may have a quiet morning, but we are At Home this afternoon and there is Almack's this evening."

Beth managed, barely, to stifle a groan. "Aunt Julia, could we pretend today is Thursday?"

"Why, darling?"

"Because I do not think I can endure the gossipmongers this afternoon and Almack's this evening."

"Faugh. No one who knows you could possibly believe the rumors. Your innocence was accepted last night. Today will be no different."

"I would say, rather, that my music was accepted last night." Beth saw the protest forming on her aunt's lips and added, "But I bow to your superior knowledge of Society."

The afternoon wasn't the ordeal she had feared. There were, of course, questions about the gossip, but Elston was there to deflect them, pronouncing the rumor a scurrilous lie. The dear man stayed the entire two hours while Dunnley worked to trace the source of the rumor, Ladies Moreton and Smithson not having been at home yesterday. George made a brief appearance, as did Bellingham, Lady Matilda, and Lady Richard.

Beth descended from the carriage in front of Almack's that evening with some trepidation but hopeful that the worst was behind them.

She couldn't have been more wrong.

Chapter 16

*B*eth smiled at Dunnley as he handed her down, then took Uncle Charles's arm. As the earl made his slow, painful way up the stairs, she reflected on the past few hours. George had wanted to escort her this evening, as had Elston. Her three gallant friends had argued for the privilege throughout dinner, heartening Beth considerably and amusing Aunt Julia, George's aunts, and Elston's great-aunt, Lady Lavinia Symington, who had accompanied him to Town. Both Beth's family and George's believed Dunnley the best choice for her escort, since he was not associated with the rumors, so he had been given the duty. Much to his cousin's displeasure.

George and Elston escorted Lady Matilda and Lady Richard. Due to prior commitments, neither lady had attended the Throckmorton ball or the musicale, but both were determined to lend their support tonight. Lady Matilda hadn't set foot in Almack's since her own Season; she had followed the drum with her soldier husband until his death and now lived in Northumberland, managing Bellingham Castle while her brother was in Town. Lady Richard was a more frequent visitor but had not yet attended this Season. Lady Lavinia had returned home after dinner, still sadly pulled from the rigors of the journey to the metropolis, her wardrobe too shockingly provincial for the sacred portals of Almack's.

Her uncle's sigh of relief recalled Beth to her surroundings. As they walked toward the patronesses, Beth saw George, Elston, and George's aunts standing off to one side, with Dunnley and Aunt Julia a few feet away. Lady Sefton greeted Beth and her uncle with a kind smile. Mrs.

Drummond-Burrell gave Beth a searching look, then whispered, "Hold your head up and face them down."

Beth's heart sank despite the bolstering words. *Please, God, help me to endure this.* As her uncle steered her toward their friends, Lady Jersey hurriedly crossed the room, Princess Esterhazy in tow. The countess stopped in front of them.

"Miss Castleton, I regret to inform you that your vouchers have been revoked." The words were accompanied by a smug smile.

Absolute silence reigned in the huge ballroom for several moments, then whispered conversations broke out all around them. Beth knew she was the cynosure of all eyes. Her uncle started to speak, but she squeezed his arm.

Beth looked the countess in the eye. "And I regret, Lady Jersey, that you accept, without question, such scurrilous lies as the rumor currently circulating about me." With that, she turned and walked toward the door.

Uncle Charles caught up with her after a pace or two and offered his arm. Behind her, she heard Aunt Julia castigate the countess as a fool and Elston say, "Lady Jersey, you have made a terrible mistake."

Other voices joined in, but Beth didn't listen. All her energy was focused on keeping her head up, her spine straight, and her feet moving forward. If she had to leave, she would do it with dignity. Dry-eyed, she made her way down the stairs, unaware of the people she passed and deaf to their greetings.

George watched Beth's departure from the ballroom with a heavy heart. Admiration for her and anger at Sally Jersey battled for supremacy. When Beth and Castleton reached the stairs, George allowed the anger free rein. He turned on the countess, only to find that Lady Julia, Elston, and Dunnley were before him.

"You are a fool, Sally!" Lady Julia exclaimed.

Before the patroness could reply, Elston addressed her with all the hauteur at his command. "Lady Jersey, you have made a terrible mistake. I traveled with George from Scotland, and I assure you, he and Miss Castleton did not travel as husband and wife."

The countess's smile faded. "But—"

"But nothing." Dunnley went on the attack. "I traced the source of the gossip. The rumor was started, out of spite, by a woman whose advances Weymouth spurned."

So it had been Arabella. Why was still a mystery, but . . .

"Who?"

The viscount arced a tawny eyebrow. "Does it matter?"

Lady Jersey shrugged. "Perhaps. Perhaps not."

"Lady Arabella Smalley." With a scornful look, his cousin queried, "Do you choose to believe her or Elston?"

"Arabella is not known for veracity; Elston is. Of course I will believe him."

Elston's bow to the countess was a mockery. When he spoke, his voice was cold. "Then I will tell you again. The gossip about Miss Castleton is a tissue of lies." He offered his arm to Aunt Caro and walked to the door.

George found Aunt Tilly standing beside him. They, too, left the room without a backward glance, Dunnley and Lady Julia close behind.

As they reached the stairway, Mrs. Drummon-Burrell exclaimed, "I told you it was a lie, Sally!" A roar of conversation followed them down the stairs.

When they arrived at Castleton House, they found Beth and the earl in the drawing room. Castleton's arm was around his niece, holding her close beside him on the sofa. Beth's expression was haunted, and she drooped against her uncle like a flower deprived of water, but to George she was beautiful.

The earl didn't rise to greet the ladies. With a smile of apology, he waved them all to seats. Lady Julia offered brandy or tea. George walked to the decanter and poured a full measure for each of the gentlemen, then carried a snifter to Castleton, who smiled his thanks before downing a bracing draught.

When the butler entered with the tea tray, Beth roused as if from a trance. As she glanced around the room, George caught her gaze. She extended a hand to him.

"Oh, George."

He crossed to her, raised her hand to his lips. "I am so sorry, Beth."

Castleton fumbled for his cane. George helped him stand, whispered that he wanted to speak privately with Beth

sometime this evening, then took the earl's seat on the sofa.
Beth leaned her head against his shoulder, as she had done
with her uncle, and George slid his arm around her waist.
"I am so sorry, sweetheart."

She raised her head and looked at him. "It isn't your
fault that Lady Jersey chose to believe the rumor."

"I would say that if it weren't for me, there wouldn't be
any gossip, but you would argue. So, instead, I will tell you
that you were magnificent."

"Truly?" At his nod, she added, "I was determined to
leave with as much dignity as I could muster, my head
held high."

"That you did, my darling," Lady Julia praised.

"In spades," added Aunt Tilly.

Dunnley's grin was wicked. "You should have seen Sally
Jersey when His Haughtiness of Elston was through with
her."

The marquess's eyes opened wide, eyebrows rising. "I?
You delivered the killing blow."

Beth clasped her hands together tightly and looked down
at her lap. "If you don't mind, I would prefer not to discuss
it. At least, not tonight."

"Very well, darling." Lady Julia rose, crossed to her
niece, and kissed the downturned head. "I am going downstairs to see what kind of supper I can contrive. Join me
in the morning room, if you wish." One by one, the rest
of the party followed her from the room.

George looked down at Beth—and felt as if a giant fist
was squeezing his heart. She was so brave, so very beautiful. She was also, at the moment, bewildered and hurt. He
hugged her, wanting to comfort her, and to shield her from
all harm.

With his free hand, he covered hers. "Beth, we need to
discuss what happened tonight."

She sighed, then unclenched her fists and entwined the
fingers of one hand with his. "If we must."

"Lady Jersey is now aware, as is everyone present tonight, of her mistake."

"I do not find that particularly comforting, Weymouth.
She enjoyed the Scene she created."

"Probably she did, but she did not like the one that
followed." Beth made no reply but did not protest when

he described what happened after she left the assembly rooms.

She stirred at the end of his recitation and looked up at him. "Arabella began the rumor? But she was so determined to marry you in February that she—or her cousin—arranged to kidnap your niece and abduct you. It would better suit her purpose if she spread a story that you and she had traveled together."

George rejoiced at Beth's rallying spirits. Only she would look for logic in the face of social catastrophe. "Elston could, and would, refute that as a lie."

A touch of bleakness entered Beth's voice. "His refutations do not travel with the same speed as the gossip."

"They will now," George averred, rubbing his thumb across her knuckles. "Sally Jersey has offended many with her malicious tongue. They will be delighted to spread the tale of her comeuppance."

"That will not restore my reputation."

"Not completely, no, but it will help."

"Is there anything that will entirely reestablish it?"

"Yes, there is."

Her gaze slewed to his. "What?"

"Beth, will you do me the very great honor of becoming my wife?" He tightened his hold on her. And prayed for a positive response.

"Weymouth—"

To give himself time to present his arguments, he tried to divert the refusal he imagined was forming on her lips. "I much prefer when you call me George."

She blinked. Several times. "Have I ever done so?"

"A few times." *When you were hurt, or upset.* "We are friends, are we not?" Without giving her time to answer, he rushed on. "I have known you only two months, yet you are my closest friend, except for Dunnley, whom I have known since he was a babe, and Elston, whom I have known for nearly twenty years."

Beth looked at the man she loved, heart and soul, and listened for the words that would allow her to accept his proposal.

"I am very fond of you, Beth. I admire and respect you. I want to help you, and to protect you. And I believe, I truly believe, we could have a happy marriage."

She waited in vain. The words never came.

Locking her gaze with his, she asked, "Do you love me, George?"

"I . . ." He leaned back against the sofa cushions and, with his arm still wrapped around her, pulled her head against his chest. Untwining their fingers, he stroked his hand over her hair.

Beth felt safe and warm. Comforted and cherished. *Say yes. Please, say yes.*

"I have told you how I feel." His fingers tangled in the curls of her topknot. "Is that love?"

His fingers tightened, breaking the ribbon, and her hair tumbled down, spilling over his cravat and waistcoat. "It isn't what the poets proclaim, nor what my parents and grandparents experienced." He smoothed her hair over her shoulders, then bestowed a gentle kiss on her forehead. "I may not love you, Beth, but we could have a happy marriage."

She closed her eyes against incipient tears. Fondness and friendship weren't enough. She would not settle for anything less than love—on both sides.

She lay against his chest for several moments, fighting for composure and drawing strength from his warm, solid presence. Then she took a deep breath and pushed herself upright. "George, I am very sensible of the honor you do me. I thank you for the friendship and affection which prompted your offer, but I will not see you trapped in a marriage where you do not love." After giving his hand a gentle squeeze, she stood and walked from the room.

George lifted a hand to halt Beth's departure, but she did not look back. As she crossed the threshold, the fist that had been squeezing his heart jabbed a flush hit in the breadbasket. He couldn't quite believe that punch was the cause of the tears in his eyes.

Chapter 17

The next morning, several hours before was proper, the Castletons had unexpected visitors. Beth watched, wide-eyed with shock, as North ushered Lady Jersey, Princess Esterhazy, Lady Sefton, and Mrs. Drummond-Burrell into the morning room. Beth rose to her feet, helped her uncle stand, then curtsied to their guests. As her great-aunt invited the ladies to be seated, Beth wondered what ill their presence boded.

She was pleasantly surprised to find they brought no bad news. She was shocked nearly speechless when Lady Jersey apologized, then reported that Beth's voucher had been reinstated. Beth found her voice in time to accept the apology with more grace than it had been offered. Lady Jersey flushed and, at Lady Sefton's prompting, stated that she would beg Beth's pardon again, in a public forum. Aunt Julia said next Wednesday at Almack's would do very well, Lady Sefton nodded her approval, and Lady Jersey gritted her teeth, then left with obvious relief, the princess once again in tow.

As Aunt Julia offered refreshments and Mrs. Drummond-Burrell and Lady Sefton settled in for a coze, Uncle Charles made his excuses and escaped. Beth wished she might do the same. After tea and scones were served, Lady Sefton turned to Beth and spoke kindly. "Miss Castleton, I hope you won't think me an interfering busybody, but I cannot help but wonder why Weymouth did not deny the rumor. And why he has not confronted Lady Arabella."

"I cannot answer for Lord Weymouth, my lady. Perhaps he did not think he would be believed. Or that Lord Elston's refutation would be sufficient."

"Has he, or have you, confronted Arabella?"

"I have not, ma'am. I have never even been introduced to her. As for—"

"What?" interposed Mrs. Drummond-Burrell. "This is infamous! Arabella slandering an innocent young girl she doesn't know?"

"I have never slandered anyone, ma'am, but I daresay it must be easier to slander a stranger than a friend." Beth's tone was wry.

Both patronesses chuckled. After a restoring sip of tea, Mrs. Drummond-Burrell said, "Maria is right, you know. A confrontation with Arabella would clear the air and remove this . . . shadow from your reputation."

Beth's right shoulder rose in a tiny shrug. "There is little I can do."

"Perhaps not, but Weymouth can."

"Weymouth is an honorable man. I am certain he must have good reasons for what he has, or has not, done."

Mrs. Drummond-Burrell "hrmphed" then muttered, "If he is so honorable, why hasn't he made you an offer?"

"Clementina!" Lady Sefton was clearly shocked.

Beth ducked her head. "He proposed, but I did not accept."

"Why not?" the patronesses asked, Mrs. Drummond-Burrell reprovingly, Lady Sefton more kindly.

"Because I do not want him forced into marriage with me by circumstances over which he has no control."

Lady Sefton set down her cup and saucer. "My dear, you have a stronger sense of honor than any woman I have ever met. And a deal more than many men. I shall do whatever I can to help you."

"Thank you, my lady." Beth scrambled to her feet and curtsied.

As the countess took her leave of Aunt Julia, Mrs. Drummond-Burrell stood. When Beth completed a second curtsy, that august dame grasped her by the shoulders, kissed her cheek, and whispered, "You were quite wonderful last night." Then in a normal voice, "You can count on my assistance."

Beth stood, immobile with astonishment, as the patronesses departed. Then she walked to the music room and picked up her violin, pondering, as she played, the advantages and disadvantages of a confrontation with Lady Arabella.

Thursday afternoon Arabella endured a thundering scold from her spinster aunt, Lady Beatrice Smalley. Lady Beatrice had repeated Arabella's story about Weymouth and Beth Castleton traveling together as husband and wife earlier in the afternoon while making calls and had been humiliated at Lady Grenley's when the Marquess of Elston had soundly, and quite publicly, denounced the tale as a lie.

"How could you could have gotten the story so tangled, Arabella?" Aunt Beatrice demanded. " 'Twas Elston, not Miss Castleton, who traveled with Weymouth from Scotland."

Arabella listened in silence, her fists clenched. *What rotten luck, that Elston was the unknown gentleman who had traveled with the earl!* Most people would believe the marquess, but if she could keep the rumor in circulation a few more days, her scheme would see fruition. The chit would be ruined, and Weymouth would have to offer for her. Arabella thought it a fitting revenge: The determined-to-marry-for-love earl wed to a woman who despised him for his role in her ruination.

How best to . . .

"Arabella!"

"Yes, Aunt Bea?"

"Pay attention. Do you think I should call on Miss Castleton and apologize or wait until I see her at some function?"

Apologize? Good Lord. "Are you likely to see Miss Castleton soon?"

Her aunt sorted through the stack of invitations on her desk. "I daresay she will attend the Duchess of St. Ives's masquerade tomorrow night. Lady Julia and the duchess are great friends."

Oh, it was perfect! She could attend the masquerade and spread the rumor herself. "If you are planning to attend, I think tomorrow night is soon enough."

"Of course I am planning to attend! Everyone who is anyone will be there."

"Well, then, Aunt, if you will excuse me, I have . . . the headache."

Instead of going to her room, Arabella headed for the attics. There were trunks of old clothes up there. Surely she could find a costume that would fit.

The Earl of Hartwood entered the house as his daughter ascended the stairs. The sly smile on her face boded ill for someone and after spening the afternoon at his club, where gossip and scandal had been the predominant topics, he was certain he knew whom it was. "Arabella!"

She turned, her face wiped clean of all expression. "Yes, Father?"

"I have made arrangements for your apologies to be heard Saturday afternoon at Bellingham House."

"Yes, Father," she said obediently, then resumed her climb.

Hartwood watched, liking her current smile even less than the previous one. Something had to be done to control his errant daughter, but demmed if he knew what.

Chapter 18

❦

*F*riday evening the *beau monde,* except for the members of the Queen's Light Dragoons, flocked to the Duchess of St. Ives's masquerade. As they joined the throng on the stairs, Beth's trepidation about facing the *ton* resurfaced. She hoped the mask and costume she wore would grant her a measure of anonymity, and minimize the number of stares she received. Everyone would know her as soon as she spoke, of course, but for a time she might enjoy herself.

She was dressed as Euterpe, the muse of music, in a flowing white Grecian robe with musical notes embroidered in gold thread, white kid sandals, and a white half mask. Aunt Julia wore the elaborate dress of her youth, with wide plum-colored skirts, a heavily embroidered bodice, a loo mask, and high-heeled, buckled shoes. Dunnley, their escort for the evening, was in his usual black and white evening attire, with a domino. The viscount had proven himself a staunch friend, standing by her through the scandal and tracking the source of the rumor, but Beth wished George, or even Elston, were here tonight. Both of those gentlemen, however, felt obligated to attend the regimental dinner, even though they had resigned their commissions nearly two years ago. They had promised to stop by later, if they could, but, selfishly, she wished for their support now.

As they inched their way up the staircase, Beth listened to Dunnley and her aunt speculate on the identities of those ahead of them. They had determined nearly a dozen by the time they reached the ballroom and greeted the duchess and her son, the current duke.

Despite the incident at Almack's two nights ago, or perhaps because of it, most of Beth's dances were claimed before Dunnley led her onto the floor for the opening minuet. Many people came by to tell her they hadn't believed a word of the gossip. She thanked them all, yet was certain many had not only given credence to the tale, but also helped to spread it.

After about an hour, she began to relax. The rumor, and the accompanying stares, seemed in abeyance tonight. With a light heart she danced, chatted with her friends between sets, and made plans for the coming week. The oft-postponed trip to Richmond Park was scheduled for Tuesday, provided it didn't rain. Which, Mr. Brewster said, it surely would, since the excursion had already been deferred three times for that reason. The ladies were more optimistic, and planned accordingly. They did, however, choose an alternate setting for their picnic—the ballroom at Greenwich House—to ensure there would be an entertainment to look forward to on Tuesday even if the weather was inclement.

After waltzing with the Duke of Fairfax, who was dressed as a cavalier, Beth promenaded around the room with him. As they neared the center of the room on the side opposite where Aunt Julia was seated, Beth smiled at Mrs. Kincaid, who was wearing an ivory round gown with a lovely tartan shawl and talking with a short blonde woman who nearly overflowed the bodice of her shepherdess costume.

It was then that the trouble began.

George glanced around the large dining room, wishing they would finish the speeches and serve the next course. He was seated near one end of a long table, next to Colonel Morton; the men who had served under him ranged down both sides, in much the same formation in which they had marched on the Peninsula. George had spoken with each man earlier, and had offered to help two who had been invalided out find work. He'd wanted to come tonight, wanted to honor old Dr. MacInnes and to congratulate him on his upcoming retirement. But now that he had done so, George was ready to leave.

Restless, he shifted in his seat. *How had such windbags ever accomplished anything?* He didn't even have the consolation of comparing his state of ennui with Elston, who sat at the next table, surrounded by the men who had served under him. Bored with the verbal pomposity, George leaned back in his chair and let his mind drift.

He wondered if Beth was enjoying the masquerade ball, hoping that her friends and admirers hadn't deserted her and that the *ton* had adjudged her innocent after Elston's repeated refutations of the rumor.

Repressing a sigh, George wished he was at St. Ives House with Beth. He would much prefer to be there with her. He enjoyed being with her anywhere. He would rather be with her than with . . .

He jerked erect in his seat. *Lord, he was an idiot! A beef-witted, bacon-brained fool. A mutton-headed numskull. The slowest slowtop ever born.*

He would rather be with Beth than with anyone.

With a hand that wasn't quite steady, he reached for his wineglass. *He loved her, had loved her since . . .* He wasn't certain when. It hadn't been a *coup de foudre* but a more gradual progression from admiration and respect to friendship to love.

He raked a hand through his hair. *He had traveled with her from Stranraer to London and twice proposed marriage without realizing he loved her.*

Did she love him? Recalling how happy she'd been to see him when he'd returned from Dorsetshire, how she'd reached out her hand to him after the fiasco at Almack's Wednesday night and let him embrace her, he believed she did.

Then why had she refused his offer that night? He remembered how wonderful it felt to hold her. Surely he could remember their conversation.

She'd asked if he loved her, and he, like the caper-witted idiot he was, had danced around the question. Then she had refused him, politely and with great dignity, saying, "I will not see you trapped in a marriage where you do not love."

He nearly groaned aloud. *She'd refused him because she believed he didn't love her. Dear God! He had to go to her, to declare his love and beg her to marry him.*

George gave the prosing palaverer holding forth in front of the room a glare that ought to have felled him but, unfortunately, didn't, then settled back in his chair and prayed for the interminable dinner to end.

*   *   *

Beth smiled at Mrs. Kincaid and was dismayed to see that lady's stricken expression. *She believes the gossip.* Beth kept her head high even as her heart sank. As she and the Duke of Fairfax walked past, Beth heard the blonde shepherdess say, "I tell you, Weymouth and Miss Castleton traveled from Scotland to London as man and wife."

Trembling, Beth slipped her hand from the duke's arm and turned to confront the slanderer. "How dare you spread such a lie!"

The voluptuous blonde raised an eyebrow. "Are you speaking to me? I assure you, Miss Whoever-You-Are, it is not a lie."

Beth ripped off her half mask. "I am Miss Castleton. And I assure you, madam, that I did not travel from Scotland to London, nor anywhere else, as Lord Weymouth's wife."

"An innkeeper says differently."

"Then he is a liar."

The duke removed his mask and stepped forward to stand beside her. "Perhaps the innkeeper was paid to say so by someone trying to discredit Miss Castleton?"

The shepherdess did not remove her mask. "Who would wish to do so? And why should you care, Fairfax?"

"I cannot imagine why anyone would do such a horrible thing. I care because dishonesty and deceit are repugnant to me. Two honest, honorable men refute the rumor you would spread." The duke's countenance turned haughty. "Perhaps it is you who wishes to harm the lady. You hide behind a mask; we do not."

"Of all the ridiculous—"

Mrs. Kincaid placed a hand on the shepherdess's arm, cutting off her tirade. "I told you it wasn't true, Arabella, but you refused to listen."

Beth stiffened. "Lady Arabella Smalley perhaps? I can well believe you wish to discredit me. After all, I can expose your criminal actions—and your cousin's—to the full view of Society. And a court of law."

The gasps and whispers that followed were Beth's first indication that the confrontation had drawn a crowd. She kept her eyes on Arabella, even as Dunnley came to stand beside her and placed his hand at the small of her back.

The blonde paled but blustered on. "Criminal? You must be mistaken. I have done nothing wrong."

Beth arced an eyebrow. "You do not consider forgery, three abductions, and attempted murder wrongful acts? I daresay most people would disagree with you."

"Beth!" Dunnley hissed, in warning or alarm, under the cover of another bout of gasps and whispers. She heard him, and understood his concern, but she would not back down now. The *ton* should know what Lady Arabella and Sir James had done, and that George had behaved honorably.

The duke stepped toward the shepherdess. "Will you remove your mask and answer the question, madam, or shall I remove it for you?"

"I am capable of removing it myself," the woman snapped. Then she reached up and, with seeming reluctance, pulled it off.

"It would seem you are capable of much more than just that," said a male voice from the crowd around them.

"Did she say abduction?" asked another.

The voluptuous shepherdess was indeed Lady Arabella Smalley. Beth pinned the blonde with her gaze and spoke clearly enough to be heard by everyone in the ballroom. Her voice trembled, although not nearly as much as her knees. "Lady Arabella said she has done nothing wrong. I know differently. My question to her, which she has yet to answer, was 'Do you not consider forgery, three abductions, and attempted murder unlawful acts?' "

"I . . . I . . ." The miscreant's fists clenched. "I did not abduct or attempt to murder anyone."

"Not directly, but you and your cousin ordered your servants to do it."

"No, I—"

Beth's cold voice was a contrast to her white-hot anger. "You forget, madam, that I am not the only one who knows of your crimes. There are four others, five if you count the child, who can attest to your actions."

"But I didn't—"

"Shall I assist your flagging memory?" Beth asked, her voice rich with scorn. "After forging a note to Lord David Winterbrook, purportedly from his brother, your servants

abducted Isabelle Winterbrook and me on the eighth of
February. I was not one of your intended victims; your men
thought I was Isabelle's governess when I went to her aid
after they felled Lord David with a blow to the head. I,
in turn, received a knock on the head that rendered me
unconscious for five days.

"Next, after another forged letter, your men abducted
Lord Weymouth on the thirteenth of February. Your intent
was to force him into marriage. You threatened to hide
his niece where no one would ever find her if he did not
marry you.

"Do you deny those actions, Lady Arabella?" she demanded, ignoring the mutterings of the crowd.

Like a cornered animal, the blonde snarled at her ac-
cuser. "No! I only wish Jamie's men had killed you. You
ruined all my lovely plans."

Beth flinched, but her voice was even when she spoke.
"I helped to do so, certainly, but I did not act alone. When
Weymouth explained the situation to me, I agreed to try
to spirit his niece to safety. Two of your servants, disgusted
by your actions, volunteered to help us. Your butler ordered your carriage made ready, and your maid helped me
get the child outside. I was—"

"Why did you come back inside? You ruined everything!"

"Why I returned to the house is irrelevant. I was shot
by your footman. Weymouth was his intended target, but
your butler threw off his aim."

"No—"

Beth gritted her teeth. "Do you deny that your footman
shot me? Or that it was by accident?"

"It was an accident. He wasn't supposed to shoot
anyone."

"He cocked the pistol and aimed it but didn't intend to
shoot?" she asked rhetorically, her tone sarcastic. Beth had
to wait several moments for the titters and the muttering
of the crowd to die down so she could be heard. "Your
footman shot me, but Weymouth and I escaped with the
help of your butler. Weymouth carried me to the carriage
where his niece and your maid awaited us. Your butler and
footman ran out of the house. While your footman was

reloading, the butler climbed onto the box, and Weymouth drove off. Is that not correct, Lady Arabella?"

"Yes, but—"

"You and your servants, and possibly your cousin, gave chase. Fortunately, you did not find us. We stopped so the pistol ball could be removed from my shoulder, staying for a week at a hunting lodge belonging to the Marquess of Elston, with your maid and his housekeeper as chaperones. Elston traveled with us from Scotland, which is why he is able to refute the lying tale you have been spreading."

Dunnley spoke to Lady Arabella, his tone cold and condemning. "Do not think to deny that you were the source of the rumor. I tracked the gossip, and the three women who first circulated the tale named you as the originator."

"But the innkeeper said she and Weymouth traveled as husband and wife!"

"I traveled with Weymouth, his niece, your former maid and butler, and Lord Elston," Beth repeated. "The maid, the child, and I shared a room. If the innkeeper said otherwise, he lied. Four people, five if you count the child, will corroborate what I have said. Do you accuse Weymouth, Elston, your former servants, and me of lying, Lady Arabella?"

When that lady made no response, Beth said, "I await your answer, ma'am. Shall I repeat the question for you?"

The deceitful divorcée glared at her but didn't reply.

"Since that question appears too difficult for you, I will ask a different one. Why did you spread the rumor? If you hoped to force Weymouth into wedding you, that tale does not advance your cause."

"I did it to force him into marriage with you," Arabella spat.

"With me?" Startled by the unexpected reply, Beth's voice was nearly a squeak. "But you wanted to marry him. You and your cousin ordered his abduction and his niece's for that purpose."

"Yes, I did, but when I reached London and realized how many people were aware of what I'd done, I knew I wouldn't be able to trap him into marriage. Weymouth wants a love match, but he is an honorable man. I spread the rumor to ruin you, knowing that he would offer for you,

thus forcing him into a loveless marriage." The scheming
shepherdess smiled slyly. "It seemed a fitting revenge."

Beth wanted to slap the smirk from her tormentor's face
but clenched her fists instead. "I am surprised you can recognize honor, Lady Arabella, since you have none. Weymouth proposed, but I did not accept. I refuse to allow a
man who has done no wrong to be coerced into marriage
by circumstances beyond his control.

"That portion of your scheme has failed, and will continue to fail. On the other hand"—Beth sighed—"you may
well have ruined me. But you have ruined yourself as well,
by publicly admitting your crimes. I hope you enjoy the
results of your efforts."

Arabella blinked and glanced around. A man of about
fifty, dressed as a courtier, stepped forward and grasped
her arm. "As a magistrate, it is my duty to see you brought
to book, Lady Arabella."

"No!" The malefactor tried to pull away, but the man's
grip was too strong. The Duke of St. Ives took her other
arm, and Beth watched as the cause of her distress was
escorted, kicking and screaming, from the room.

Weary to her bones, Beth turned to face the chattering
crowd. She wanted to find Aunt Julia and leave, as quickly
as possible.

"Miss Castleton," a man at the back called, "why was
Lady Arabella not prosecuted for her actions?"

The Duke of Fairfax took her hand and bowed over it.
In a voice that must have carried to the farthest reaches of
the house, he asked, "Miss Castleton, may I have the privilege of dancing with the most honest and honorable lady
in all of England?"

'Twas either dance or answer questions. Beth chose the
former. As the musicians began a waltz, she curtsied to the
duke, then allowed him to lead her to the floor.

They danced alone, the cynosure of every eye in the ballroom. "Thank you, Your Grace. You are very kind."

"You are as brave as you are beautiful. Such courage
should be recognized, and applauded."

"Gossiped about, and not necessarily favorably, is the
more likely result."

"Hmm." Then, several turns later, "Shall I try to end
near the door so you can escape the questions?"

"Near the duchess, please, so that I may apologize before I leave."

He glanced over her shoulder. "The duchess and Lady Julia are standing near the doorway. Dunnley is there as well. Your ordeal will soon be over."

"Thank goodness."

When the music ended, they were but a few steps from the duchess—and the door. Beth mustered a wan smile for Fairfax when he thanked her for the dance. Turning to her hostess, she curtsied deeply. "Your Grace, I am so very sorry—"

"You needn't apologize, child. You behaved honorably and honestly." The duchess's gnarled hand clasped Beth's. "Too much so, I fear."

"Ma'am?"

The duchess squeezed her hand gently, then released it. "Make your escape before this crowd descends upon you."

Beth curtsied again. Dunnley, who had been talking quietly to Fairfax, stepped forward and offered one arm to her, the other to Aunt Julia. With her head held high, Beth turned and left the room, ignoring the shouted questions that trailed them down the stairs.

In the carriage on the way to Castleton House no one said a word. What could they talk about, Beth mused, other than the fact that her honesty had ruined her reputation beyond hope of salvaging? 'Twas her own fault for confronting Lady Arabella, and Beth was determined that no one else would suffer for her folly. The only way to ensure that was to leave London.

She would do so tonight, she resolved. Where she would go, she did not know. Castleton Abbey would not serve; the gossip would reach there in a day or so. A scandal was inevitable. She'd admitted to traveling hundreds of miles in the company of two gentlemen and staying at inns with those men with only a maid for chaperone. Oh, there would be a scandal, all right.

Leaving would be hard. So hard. She was not only departing from the metropolis, but from her darling great-aunt and uncle, her wonderfully loyal friends, and from George. Tears pricked her eyes, but she fought them back. Later she could weep for the man she loved. Now, in order to spare him, she must leave him.

Chapter 19

***

W hen George and Elston reached the St. Ives masquerade shortly after midnight, the receiving line had long since dispersed. Standing side by side in the doorway, more handsome and distinguished than usual in their full dress uniforms, they looked for their hostess. And for Beth. The duchess saw them and hurried toward them as fast as her rheumatic knees would allow. She extended her hand to George first, despite the fact that Elston's rank was higher, and spoke before he could greet her.

"Weymouth, you should have been here earlier," she said, breathless after her rush across the room.

He bowed over her hand. "I regret that I had a previous commitment, Your Grace."

"As did I." Elston captured the duchess's ring-bedecked hand and made his obeisance.

"I don't mean the ball. You should have been here to support Miss Castleton when she confronted Lady Arabella."

"Bloody hell," George muttered. The duchess's expression conveyed her shock at hearing such profanity, but she did not reprove him.

Elston offered his arm to their hostess. "Allow us to escort you to a seat, Your Grace, then you can tell us what happened."

When they were seated in a quiet alcove with the diminutive duchess between them, George requested, "Please tell us what happened, Your Grace."

Listening to the tale of Beth's confrontation with Arabella was like . . . like . . . He couldn't think of a sufficiently torturous comparison. It was wonderful to hear one of the highest-ranking members of Society laud Beth's honesty and courage, horrible to know that his love had endured such a scene without his support. Their hostess didn't know how it had begun—Fairfax or Mrs. Kincaid could tell them that, she said—but she rejoiced in the ending: Arabella carried off by Sir Thomas Hodge to be charged for her crimes, and Beth honored by Fairfax.

George propped his elbows on his thighs and covered his face with his hands. "Why did she do it? Castleton, my brother, and I chose not to prosecute Arabella and Sir James because we feared a public recounting of the events would damage Beth's reputation. Why—"

The duchess poked his arm with a bony finger. "What else was she to do, Weymouth? Stand there and allow the Smalley chit to spew her lies?"

"No, but—"

"There are times when one cannot back down, or stand silent. This was one of them."

"How badly has Miss Castleton's confession damaged her reputation?" Elston quietly voiced George's fear.

The duchess thought for several moments before replying. "I don't know. Beth made it clear that Weymouth's behavior was honorable, and that he offered for her but she declined. There may be some high sticklers who look down on her for traveling such a distance with two men, and staying at inns with only a maid for chaperone, but what else could the dear girl have done?"

What else indeed?

Their hostess rose to her feet. "Come, you will want to talk with Fairfax and Mrs. Kincaid."

When they stepped out of the alcove, they were greeted by a swarm of people buzzing like bees. Or locusts. Some sort of plaguey pestilence. George prayed for Job's patience.

"Weymouth, is it true that Arabella Smalley abducted you and tried to force you into marriage?"

"Weymouth, did Miss Castleton really help you escape from Lady Arabella?"

"Weymouth, why didn't you charge Arabella with her crimes?"

Those questions and a number of others were shouted at him. George crossed his arms over his chest and waited for a chance to speak.

He wanted to be with Beth, to tell her he loved her and ask her to marry him, but it was too late to call on her tonight. Instead, he would do what he could to repair her reputation.

Finally, the crowd realized that he couldn't answer their simultaneous questions and drifted into a restless silence. The best thing to do, George thought, was to tell his side of the tale. That would answer most of their queries. He wished he knew what Beth had said, but she was too forthright not to have told the truth.

"I was abducted on the orders of Lady Arabella Smalley and her cousin, Sir James Weldon, who also kidnapped my niece and Miss Castleton. Arabella intended to force me into marriage by threatening to hide my niece somewhere no one would ever find her if I refused. Fortunately for me, Miss Castleton, who had been unconscious for nearly a week from a blow to the head during her abduction, regained consciousness the morning I was delivered to Arabella. When Miss Castleton heard my dilemma, she agreed to take my niece away, thus allowing me to refuse Arabella's offer without fear of harm befalling the child."

He told of Arabella's servants volunteering to help, Beth's return to the house, Henry's timely assistance, and the footman shooting Beth. He described the race to safety and their stop at one of Elston's properties so Beth's injury could be treated, praising the marquess and his staff for their assistance during Beth's illness.

Elston took up the tale, telling of his decision to travel with them and share coachman's duty with George. They had arrived in London twenty-three days after Beth was shot, his friend reported. Although the marquess hadn't said so, most would believe he was with them the entire time.

George told of the mutual decision of himself, his brother, and Beth's uncle not to prosecute Arabella and her cousin, their reasons for that decision, and the steps he had taken to ensure that Arabella and Sir James would not succeed if they made another attempt. He confessed that he'd offered for Beth the night they arrived in London, but she'd refused him because they both knew he had behaved honorably.

The guests probably knew more than he did about Arabella's rumor campaign. The incident at Almack's and Sally Jersey's subsequent apology were common knowledge. As for his second proposal, that was no one's business but his and Beth's.

What could he say to persuade the ton *not to condemn Beth?* "You have now heard the story twice. If any of you would disparage Miss Castleton for traveling with Elston and me with only a maid for chaperone, I ask you to consider this: If your daughter or sister found herself in the same situation as Miss Castleton, would you want your relative to behave differently? Perhaps to wring her hands helplessly while a child was threatened and I, or some other gentleman, was forced into marriage with a woman like Arabella Smalley? Would you want your relative to cry pretty tears in the wilds of Scotland instead of returning to her family using the best means available? Should she allow herself to be slandered by a woman with no morals? Or would you want your female relatives to behave with honor and honesty as Miss Castleton has done?"

"Bravo, George!" Elston whispered as the duchess beamed a smile of approval.

"I favor a hasty retreat," George muttered. "Preferably with Fairfax. What say you?"

"Lead on, O Fearless One."

George walked toward his host and hostess, ignoring the murmuring crowd. After thanking the St. Iveses for their assistance to Beth and himself, he glanced at Fairfax and nodded toward the door. Recalling Beth's words about exiting with dignity, George didn't run from the room. He just walked very fast.

Beth made her plans, such as they were, with Moira's assistance. The steadfast Scotswoman volunteered to travel with her mistress, wherever she went. Their destination was still in question, but their bags were packed. They would leave at first light, taking a post-chaise to . . . somewhere. Between now and dawn, Beth had to decide on a location and write several letters.

Composing the messages was more difficult than she expected. Much more difficult. If there was a proper form to apologize for creating a scandal and tarnishing one's family name, Miss Milton's Academy for Young Ladies had not included it in the curriculum during Beth's tenure there. Nor had her mother, grandmother, or great-aunt covered it in their lessons on manners and social customs. Beth was on her own, with only love to guide her.

She finished the letter to Uncle Charles and Aunt Julia, then began one to George, *Lud, this was even harder than the first one!* After several false starts and a bucketful of tears, she completed it. Next, an apology to the Duchess of St. Ives for creating a scene at her ball and notes to Fairfax and Dunnley, thanking them for their support. Then, her labors completed, she drifted into a reverie, recalling the pleasant times she and George had shared, in Scotland and in London.

Scotland. That was where she would go. It was far enough away from Town that the gossip would take weeks to travel there. Picking up her pen, Beth wrote one last missive.

George arrived at Castleton House at nine o'clock on Saturday morning. North's frosty look conveyed his disapproval, but George's mission was too urgent to wait for proper visiting hours.

"Good morning, North. I know this is an extremely uncivil hour, but it is very important that I speak with the earl. And with Miss Castleton."

"The earl and Lady Julia are still at breakfast, Lord Weymouth!" the butler protested.

"Please ask if I might speak with them."

Either George looked more harried than he'd thought or North sensed his urgency. The butler nodded then walked toward the back of the house, returning in less than a minute. "The earl and Lady Julia will receive you, my lord. Come with me."

George entered the breakfast parlor and greeted Castleton and Lady Julia. Beth was not there. He felt a stab of disappointment at not seeing her lovely countenance, her sweet smile, but knew that last night's confrontation with Arabella must have been very draining for his shy little love. He hoped her sleep was untroubled by nightmares. And that she was dreaming of him.

He took the chair his hostess offered and accepted a cup of coffee. After a restoring sip, George set himself the task of removing the strained expression from Lady Julia's face and lightening the earl's glum one. "You are aware of Beth's confrontation with Arabella last night. It is unfortunate that Beth was forced to defend herself in such a public forum, and to reveal so much of what happened in Scotland in the process. But things are not, perhaps, as bad as you fear."

Castleton mumbled something that sounded like "They're worse."

"Sir?"

The earl waved a hand, telling him to continue. George complied. "When Elston and I arrived at the ball—"

"You came, Weymouth?" queried Lady Julia.

"He just said so, Aunt Ju." The earl sounded gruffer than usual. And grumpy as bedamned. "Let the man tell his tale."

George smiled at Lady Julia. "Elston and I arrived shortly after midnight. The duchess, after chiding me for not having been there earlier, told us what had happened. I was besieged with questions and, to answer them, I described Arabella's and Sir James's plot and all its consequences up to my proposal the night we arrived in London. I did not say I removed the pistol ball from Beth's shoulder, but I reported most of the rest."

He paused for another drink of coffee. "Elston, when he described our travels, gave the impression he was with us the entire time, although he never actually said so. I explained the decision of Lord Castleton, my brother, and myself not to prosecute Arabella and her cousin for their crimes and our reasons for that choice.

"At the end of my recitation, I appealed to those who might disparage Beth for traveling in the company of two gentlemen with only a maid for chaperone, asking them how they would want their daughters or sisters to behave if they were in the same situation. Elston thought my words eloquent and effective, and St. Ives declared a flush hit."

He looked at Beth's relatives and was dismayed to see

that their expressions had not lightened. "I think Beth's honor and her honesty last night won her more supporters than detractors."

"Oh, Weymouth—" Lady Julia broke off, tears streaming from her eyes.

Rising, he hurried to her and knelt beside her chair. "My lady, surely it is not as bad as that. There may be some gossip, but I believe the worst is over."

"No, it is not," she said between sobs.

At a loss, he took her hand in his, patting it consolingly, and looked to the earl. "She's gone, Weymouth," that gentleman said.

"Sir?" George frowned, perplexed. *Did Castleton mean his aunt was lost to tears?*

"North, get Vetch down here to care for Lady Julia." Castleton gripped his cane and rose. "Come to my study, Weymouth, and I will explain what has upset my aunt."

Several minutes later they sat in the study, the earl behind his desk, George in front of it. Castleton rubbed his hands over his face, then stared down at the blotter, his expression bleak. "Aunt Julia told me Beth was very upset when they arrived home last night. She said very little and soon excused herself, leaving my aunt to entertain Dunnley. This morning I came downstairs to find a letter from my niece."

Beth was gone? The realization stabbed more sharply than a French saber. And hurt just as much. *Why? Where?*

The earl toyed with a pen. "In her note, Beth apologized for creating a scandal and tarnishing the family name. She said she was leaving London in the hope that, with her gone, we would be less affected by her notoriety. She did not say where she was going, only that she would write to us so we would know she was well."

Castleton took out his handkerchief and wiped his eyes. "She said she loved us very much, and that she was sorry for all the trouble she'd caused."

George swallowed, hard. "Did Moira go with Beth?"

"The Scotswoman? Yes, she did."

"Do you think she went to Castleton Abbey?"

"No, but I sent a man to check."

"Might Beth have gone to one of your other estates?"

The earl shook his head. "Highly unlikely since she has never visited the others, but I sent a man to each of them."

"Has she a particular friend she might have gone to visit?"

"Most of her friends are in Town now. Besides, I think she would worry about the gossiping affecting them."

"Yes, she would." George raked a hand through his hair. "Do you have any idea how she is traveling or where she might have gone?"

"All the horses and carriages are in the mews, so she must have hired a post-chaise. As for where she is going, I don't know. I only wish I did."

"She might be traveling by stage or mail coach. Have you sent men to check the posting houses?"

"I have not, but only because all the men except North are off checking the estates."

"Would you have any objection to some of my father's men or mine helping to search for her?"

"Of course not! I would welcome your aid."

"Then I shall hasten back to Portman Square and set men to tracking her." George tugged at his cravat, which suddenly was much too tight. "Before I go, there is one more thing I want to ask you. I . . ."

"What is it, m'boy?"

"I am a bit of a slowtop, sir. I realized last night during that demmed dinner that I love Beth. Have loved her for a long time."

He gulped in a lungful of air. "I believe she refused my offer Wednesday night because she thinks I don't love her. I—"

"If you are asking my permission to pay your addresses to Beth when we find her, you have it. And my blessing."

George's breath whooshed out in an audible sigh of relief. "Thank you."

"At least she didn't have to tell you."

"Sir?"

The earl's face took on a pensive expression, and he smiled as if at a pleasant memory. "I didn't realize I was in love with Lady Castleton until she told me. You recognized it on your own."

George's mouth quirked at the image of the late countess

informing Castleton of his feelings. "I only wish I had realized sooner."

"Now that Arabella has confessed her actions, I think you, your brother, and I should lay charges against her and her cousin. I would dearly love to see Arabella and her cousin and servants prosecuted to the fullest extent of the law for the pain and distress they have caused Beth."

"I, too, would like to see them punished," George admitted, "but testifying against them might cause Beth even more distress. I think we should ask her opinion before doing anything. After we find her, that is."

He rose and shook Castleton's hand. "I will send men to check the coaching inns. Tell Lady Julia we will soon find Beth."

George had reached the door and was already planning which of his father's men to use and the most effective search method when the earl said, "Wait, Weymouth. I almost forgot. Beth left a note for you, too."

After accepting the letter, George placed it in his coat pocket and departed. As he drove back to Bellingham House, he wondered how he could be pleased that Beth had written him before leaving London, yet afraid to read her message.

An hour later, men were checking the posting houses. George wandered from the study to the music room to the morning room. He couldn't concentrate on the estate reports his father had asked him to look over, couldn't find a piece of music he wanted to play. Hell, he couldn't even sit still for five minutes.

He wished for the distraction of conversation, but his father was out and his aunts were bustling around upstairs, packing Aunt Tilly's belongings. A messenger had come from Bellingham Castle to report a problem that required either his father's or his aunt's presence in Northumberland, so she was preparing to leave. George knew he would find chatter aplenty if he joined his aunts, although nothing conducive to preserving his sanity. Aimlessly, he meandered from room to room, picking things up, then putting them down again.

His hand brushed against his coat pocket. Taking out the letter, he plopped down in a wing chair near the fireplace and stretched out his legs. He studied the inscription, then the seal. Finally, he opened it and began to read.

Dear George,

No doubt by now you have heard of the altercation at the St. Ives masquerade. I suppose I could have walked away when I heard Arabella spewing her lies, but I refused to do so, choosing instead to confront her with her crimes. Everyone present at the ball heard me accuse her and her cousin of the abductions of you, Isabelle, and me, and of her footman's attempt at murder. I detailed the entire plot, including the assistance of Moira, Henry, and Elston. I said that Elston had traveled with us from Scotland (but I did not say he was with us only until Brough) and told of your proposal and my refusal.

I know you did not want any of this to become public knowledge, and I apologize most sincerely for having betrayed your friendship and your trust. I hope that the consequences of my actions will not redound upon you.

Having destroyed my reputation beyond repair with my confession, I am leaving London for a time in the hope that my absence will minimize the repercussions of my foolishness for you, Uncle Charles, and Aunt Julia.

I will always be grateful for your kindness to me, and for your friendship. I am sorry I have not proven worthy of them.

Beth

The letter dropped from his hand into his lap. *Unworthy! How could she possibly think herself unworthy of his friendship?* Abruptly he stood. *He had to go to her, to tell her he loved her.* Just as suddenly, he fell back into the chair and picked up the letter. Folding his hands over it, he rested his head against the high back of the chair and closed his eyes. *Dear God, watch over Beth and keep her safe. Please help me to find her quickly. And, please, help me not to be such a fool in the future.*

"George?" Then a few moments later, "Hargrave, do you know where my nephew is?"

Rousing at the sound of his aunt's voice, George rose and crossed to the door. "I am here, Aunt Tilly."

"I just wanted to bid you farewell, dear. I never thought to say it, but I have enjoyed my stay in London."

He bent to kiss her cheek. "I am glad to hear it. Perhaps you will come back next year."

"We shall see. Please tell the Castletons and Elston and Dunnley good-bye for me."

"I will." He tucked her hand in the crook of his arm and escorted her out to the large traveling coach. "Godspeed, Aunt Tilly."

"Thank you, dear boy. 'Tis a long journey, but with Jem on the box, Willie and Nick up behind, and Clara to provide conversation, I shall do very well."

"Ah'll take gud care o' her, m'lord," the coachman promised.

"I know you will, Jem."

George, with Aunt Caro beside him, waved as the carriage pulled away. When it turned out of the square, he escorted her back into the house.

They were met in the foyer by the butler. "Lord Weymouth, several of the grooms wish to speak with you."

Perhaps one of the searchers had found Beth! "Thank you, Hargrave." Then, turning to his aunt, "Excuse me, Aunt Caro."

Several of the men had returned, but none had news of Beth. He sent them out again after they had eaten, checking the smaller inns and the docks.

By evening, George had paced a trench in the Aubusson in the study and all the men had been out twice and reported back—except one. Fred, the grizzled head groom, had not yet returned with his first report. The man was too reliable to be doing anything other than his assigned task, which left two possibilities: He had found the posting house from which Beth had departed and was following her, or he had met with foul play. George sent a cautiously optimistic note to Castleton House, then chose two men to check, first thing in the morning, the posting inns he'd assigned Fred. If they heard news of Beth or Fred, one was to report back, the other to follow.

The next day, by mid-morning, George knew the inn from which Beth had departed and that she had hired a post-chaise with a pair. Fred had left London about six hours after Beth; Henry was a day behind Fred.

On hearing the news, George called for his fastest pair to be harnessed to his curricle, then raced up the stairs to his bedchamber and quickly packed a bag. He stopped at Castleton House to share the news with the earl and Lady Julia. "I am leaving immediately. We will soon find Beth and bring her home."

But they did not find her.

They heard reports of her. She and Moira had eaten luncheon at Stevenage, then traveled north. They'd had tea in Biggleswade, but none of the ostlers or postilions remembered a young lady and her maid leaving. George sent word back to London for his father and Beth's uncle to send as many men as they could spare to Biggleswade. They would fan out from there, searching the inns in all directions.

Bellingham and Castleton between them sent ten men. A note from the earl explained that most of his men had not returned from checking his estates; he would send them when they did. He also reported Beth was not at Castleton Abbey. Late that evening, as George sat in a private parlor pouring over maps and issuing instructions, Dunnley and Elston appeared, each with half a dozen men in tow.

"What news, George?" was the marquess's greeting.

"Count me in as a searcher," said his cousin.

After thanking them both, George drew them to the table and expanded the search. "Theo, search between here and Cambridge. Robert, you take the area toward Wolverton. The earl reports that Beth wasn't at Castleton Abbey last night, but she may be headed in that direction."

"I regret that I cannot stay to assist in the search; urgent business calls me north." Grabbing a pen and paper, the marquess wrote a short note. "If you have need of additional men, send this to Elston Abbey, and my steward will provide as many as you need."

George bit back an angry retort. Elston was prodigiously fond of Beth, so his business must be extremely pressing if it took precedence over searching for her. "Thank you, Robert."

"I will be traveling the North Road as far as Darlington and will inquire after Beth at every stop. If I find her, or hear news of her, I will send Higgins back with a message."

"That will help a great deal." George consulted his lists. "Henry, since the marquess will cover the route directly north, you go west toward Wolverton and Castleton Abbey."

The stalwart underbutler, who had been training under Hargrave until he could take up his post at Winterhaven Manor, nodded. After satisfying himself that all the men knew their tasks for the morrow, George dismissed the servants and settled in for a comfortable coze with his friends.

By the end of the following week, George was haggard, irascible, and the possessor of considerably more gray hairs. Nearly forty men were searching, but to no avail. Beth and Moira had disappeared without a trace.

Chapter 20

*T*hree weeks later, George despaired of ever finding his love. They had searched the length and breadth of England, tracing every lead, but Beth's location and the route she'd traveled remained a mystery. He was in Carlisle, investigating the reported sighting of a young lady and her maid at the Spotted Dog Inn two days ago. Unfortunately, they hadn't been his darling American and her Scottish maid.

As he rode back to Solway Firth where his yacht was moored, his fears surfaced anew. *Where could she be?* If he could but see Beth, talk to her, know that she was well, he might sleep again. If he could embrace her, tell her that he loved her, he would be transported from the slough of despondency to high alt. And if she accepted his marriage proposal, he would be the happiest man in England. In all the world.

He returned the horse to the inn from which he'd hired it, then walked to the dock with leaden feet and boarded the *Dorset Dancer*. Martin Fisher, a childhood playmate and now one of his tenants, stood on deck. "No luck, sir?"

"No. It wasn't the lady I seek." George whirled, bracing his hands on the railing. "God, where can she be?" It was an anguished cry from the heart.

After several minutes Martin shifted his feet. "Where to, sir?"

"I don't . . ." Weary to his bones, George rubbed his hands over his face, then dragged them through his hair. "To Stranraer. I will feel close to Beth there. Perhaps I will be able to sleep, and to think."

"Stranraer?"

He turned and rested a hip against the rail. "We spent

a week there, a happy week, even though Beth was wounded. 'Twas where I fell in love with her."

"Was it, sir?"

"Hmm." The more he thought of it, the more the idea appealed. "Let's go, before we lose the wind."

A note of amusement entered his old friend's voice. "I daresay ye've been too worried to notice, but losin' the wind bain't a problem. There's a storm abrewin'."

George looked at the sky. "So there is. Let's be off, then."

"Gladly, sir, if ye but tell me where this Stranraer place is."

"In the Firth of Clyde. Northeastern side of the Mull of Galloway in a tidy little bay with wonderful fishing."

"Ye'd best be hopin' the storm holds off for several hours." Fisher called out orders to their small crew, then suggested, "Why don't ye go below and rest? I can get us into the North Channel, but ye'll have to pilot us the rest of the way."

"I will, when we are underway."

After about a quarter of an hour, George accepted the inevitable. "The storm will break long before we reach Stranraer. If we can get to Luce Bay, there is a cottage on the west side, near Drummore, that belongs to my father. We can put in there."

"We might be able to make that. Go below and rest, sir. I will send one of the men to wake ye when we enter the bay."

George grunted in response and headed for his bunk.

As the downpour began, he put on his oilskins and went up on deck. He hadn't slept, but he'd dozed a bit. And dreamed of Beth.

When they reached Luce Bay, he directed Martin to Gull Cottage. They could stay there, warm and dry, until the storm passed, then continue to Stranraer. The moment the ship touched the dock, George jumped off, leaving his crew to moor her and furl the sails. As he walked toward the cottage, he noticed lights in the parlor, as well as in the kitchen.

The back door was closest, so he entered through the kitchen. Mrs. MacAfee, who had been his grandmother's cook and housekeeper and now served as the cottage's caretaker, was standing at the table, kneading a bowl of dough. She turned when he opened the door, a smile creasing her face. " 'Tis aboot time ye got here, Master George."

"What, Mackey?" He bent to hug her. "My arrival is the merest happenstance, due to the storm."

"Hmph. Ye ought to hae been here weeks ago."

"Ought I? Why?"

"On account o' the lassie, ye daftie!"

"Lady Arabella? I was here, as her prisoner." He crossed to the pump to wash his hands. "Where were you then, anyway?"

She waved a floury spoon. "I dinna mean the blonde harpy. The bonny lassie."

"My niece Isabelle? I rescued her. She is safe at home in Oxfordshire."

"Glad I am to hear it, but I dinna mean the bairn."

"Who, then? Miss Castleton? The lady who helped rescue Isabelle and I," he clarified.

The housekeeper smiled. "Aye."

"I don't know where she is, Mackey. I have been searching—" He stiffened and turned toward the door, hearing—or thinking he heard—the sound of a violin. "Beth is here?"

"Aye. 'Tis what I hae been tryin' to tell ye."

On hearing the first word, he sluiced his face as well. *Beth was here! He had found her at last.* Grabbing a towel, he inquired, "How long has she been here?"

"Nearly a fortnight, I reckon. The lassie came—" He didn't hear the rest; the door to the hallway was too thick for her words to penetrate.

As he walked toward the parlor, George wondered why Beth had chosen Gull Cottage as her retreat. Her memories of the place could not possibly be pleasant. At the moment, however, her reasons weren't his primary concern. *He had found her. Finally, he had found her.*

He stood to one side of the open double doors, reveling in the sight of her. In a white muslin gown sprigged with blue, a darker blue sash, and her hair pulled back into a simple knot, she was, as always, breathtakingly beautiful.

Ruefully, he glanced at his own apparel: bottle green coat, damp cravat, buff waistcoat and pantaloons, rain-spotted Hessians. She might catch her breath—at the smell of him. There was a faint whiff of horse underlying the prevailing briny fragrance. It wasn't the best fashion in which to woo a lady, but he didn't even consider returning to the *Dancer* to change. He was afraid Beth would vanish if he so much as blinked.

She was facing the windows, her eyes half closed. He tiptoed into the room and sat in a chair by the door. Watching her, listening to the music she played, he felt content for the first time since that thrice-damned regimental dinner, when he'd realized he loved her.

She finished the piece she was playing—Mozart, he thought—and, after a short pause, began another. He'd never heard her play it before, although it was one he knew well. One she often requested he play. It was an unusual choice for her instrument, and very difficult for the violin's shorter bow, but she gave a creditable performance for half of the first movement. Then, with an impatient "tcha," she stopped, laying her violin on the console table between the windows.

He must have made some sound because she turned, the bow dropping from her hand when she saw him. "George?"

He stood and walked toward her, then stooped to pick up her bow. Wordlessly, he held it out to her, wondering at the wariness that had replaced the blaze of joy in her eyes.

Equally silent, she took it, then turned and placed it on the table. "What are you doing here, Weymouth?" she asked over her shoulder.

"Wh-what am I doing here?" He glanced around the room. It was, indeed, the parlor of Gull Cottage. Which was one of his father's properties. "It seems to me I should be asking you that question."

Why was he here? Beth bit her lip and pressed a hand to her stomach, seeking to calm her tumultuous thoughts and the cavorting butterflies. Hoping her voice would not betray her, she turned to face him. "I daresay you will. Several others, as well. But since I have already posed the query, perhaps you will be kind enough to answer before you begin your interrogation."

"I . . . I . . ." He paused, raked a hand through his hair. "Beth, I have been looking for you for a month!" The words tumbled out with the force of an explosion. "Along with about forty other men."

She gaped at him. "But—"

"Sweetheart, your aunt and uncle were frantic with worry when you left. As was I."

"But I told them—and you—why I was leaving."

"Yes, you did. We, however, did not agree with your decision, nor with the reasons behind it."

"They did not create a scandal and tarnish their reputations beyond repair. Nor did you." She took a deep breath, hoping to level her wobbling voice. "Neither did you betray a friendship and breach a trust."

He stepped closer and took her hand in his. "You did not do any of those things, my love."

"Oh, but I did. I—"

"I know what happened at the St. Ives masquerade, Beth. The scandal and tarnished reputation belong to Arabella, not you." He raised her hand to his lips, kissed the tips of her fingers. "You did nothing—nothing!—to betray our friendship and the trust I reposed in you."

The kiss tingled from her fingers, up her arm, and all the way down to her toes. Wide-eyed, she looked at the man she loved with all her heart. "Weymouth—"

"George," he interposed, with a smile. "I like it much better when you call me George."

Was he trying to drive her daft by smiling like that and interrupting her explanation? Beth huffed out a breath. "George, then. You would not say that if you knew what happened at the ball. I—"

"I know what happened. I had it from the duchess herself the moment I arrived, and from Fairfax later."

"You came to the ball?" She winced inwardly at the squeak in her voice.

"Yes, I did. I told you I would come after that demmed dinner."

His disparagement of the regimental celebration puzzled her. "Did you not enjoy the reunion?"

"No!" He took a deep breath, then let it out slowly. "It was pleasant enough for a time, but far too long, although there was one very good thing that came out of it. The dinner is not important, though. You are. And what happened—or did not happen—at the masquerade."

She looked down at the carpet, a lovely Axminster with a pattern of roses. "I have been trying to tell you what happened at the ball. I confronted—"

He cupped her cheek with his free hand—the one that wasn't rubbing her knuckles. "Sweetheart, both the duchess and Fairfax have excellent memories. They reported your conversation with Arabella nearly verbatim. You need not put yourself through the anguish of reliving it."

She scuffed the toe of one slipper against the carpet, thrilled but puzzled by his tenderness. And his endearments. "If they told you, how can you say that I didn't betray your friendship and trust?"

Slipping his arms around her, he pulled her close. "Because you did not."

Feeling tears prick the back of her eyes, Beth blinked rapidly. She rested against him—just for a moment, so that his warm, solid strength might bolster her flagging spirit. It felt so wonderful to be held by him that the moment stretched. Shyly, she looped her arms around his waist.

George sighed happily. *Beth felt so good in his arms. So right.* Holding her, he felt a peace and contentment that was . . . like warming oneself in front of a roaring fire on a cold day. Or pulling into a safe harbor before a storm broke. He wanted to enjoy that cozy room with the crackling fire with her. And to behold the majesty of a storm from that snug harbor with her in his arms. To share cold days and warm ones, fair weather and stormy. He wanted to share everything with her: himself, his dreams, his life. He had realized all that the night of the regimental reunion. Now, for the first time, he experienced it. And it was . . . indescribably wonderful.

He rubbed his cheek against her silky hair. In order to feel this contentment and happiness always, to love and cherish Beth as she deserved and to receive her love in return, he had to propose. Again.

At least this time his cravat couldn't choke him during his declaration. It had lost its starch, and its shape, during the storm. And this time he would offer not only his hand, but also his heart.

He kissed the top of her head. "Beth."

"Hmm?"

"As much as I enjoy holding you, love—and I do enjoy it, very much—there is more we need to discuss."

He felt her sigh more than heard it. "I suppose there is."

Stepping back, he clasped her left hand in his right. "Shall we sit by the fire?"

She nodded, then twined her fingers with his. He led her across the room and seated her on a sofa, then sat beside her, unable to decide if he wanted to see her face as they talked or to hold her. Well, he wanted to do both, but the only way to accomplish that was if she sat on his lap—and he was quite certain she wouldn't agree. Not yet, at least. He opted to see her face now and, if he was very fortunate, to hold her later.

"Beth, I know what happened at the St. Ives masquerade. I know what you said, and I think I know why you spoke out as you did. Nothing you said or did that night was a betrayal of my friendship and trust." He reached out and stroked her cheek. "Will you take my word for that?"

Wide-eyed, her gaze locked with his, she nodded.

"You think you tarnished your reputation by confessing that you traveled with Elston and me with only a maid for chaperone." He paused, seeking the right words. "Some of the highest sticklers may think a bit less of you for that, but I believe that I helped them see your actions in a different light."

"How?" she queried softly, awe and wonder in her voice.

"By asking them to consider how they would want their daughters or sisters to behave if they found themselves in the same situation." Her eyes widened further, but she didn't say anything.

"Arabella, Tom, Sir James, and two of his servants are in jail because of your courage and honesty that night. Isabelle and I are safe from the shrew's machinations, as are you. No one will take her word or Sir James's over yours, mine, and Elston's." He tucked a stray wisp of hair behind her ear. "Can you believe that, sweetheart?"

Several moments passed before she replied. "Not yet perhaps, but I want to."

"There is one more thing you must believe." He cupped her cheek in his palm. *He had to do this right. If he failed, he would lose his heart's desire and spend the rest of his life alone.* "I am a fool, Beth. I—"

"That I will never believe." A hint of a smile quirked one corner of her mouth.

He smiled in return, rather sheepishly. "Perhaps not a fool, merely a slowtop. During the regimental dinner, I realized I love you. That I have loved you for quite a long time." The beautiful blue eyes widened again, the blazing joy reappeared—and stayed. "I have searched for you since the morning you left, to tell you.

"I love you, Beth, with all my heart. I want to share my life with you, and to share yours. Please, my darling, will you do me the very great honor of becoming my wife?"

She studied his face for several moments, as if searching for the truth behind his words, then her hand tightened its clasp on his. "It is I who am honored, Lord Weymouth," she replied formally. "I would be very happy, and very proud, to be your wife." Blushing, she added, softly, "I love you, George."

The breath he hadn't realized he was holding whooshed out as he embraced her. "You have made me the happiest man in the realm." Then he pulled her onto his lap and caressed her rosy lips with his. It was a gentle kiss, soft and sweet, a declaration—and a promise—of love.

He loved her! Beth raised a hand to touch George's cheek, her lips tingling from his kiss. Ladies must covet, even crave, such sweet demonstrations of affection from their husbands. After just one, she yearned for another—and they were not yet wed! Emboldened by the knowledge that he wanted her as his wife, she brushed a kiss against his cheek, then laid her head against his shoulder, reveling in the feel of his arms around her.

Turning his head, he bestowed a kiss upon her forehead. "Tell me, sweetheart, why did you come to Gull Cottage? And how? You and Moira seemed to disappear without a trace after Biggleswade."

"I did not intend to come here; my planned destination was Stranraer."

"Stranraer? Why?"

"Three reasons, really. It is far away from London, I did not think Elston would mind, and . . ."

"And what?"

"Because I was happy there."

" 'Twas my destination as well; I knew I would feel close to you there. Fortunately for me, the storm blew up and I landed here instead." His arms tightened about her for a moment. "How did you get from Biggleswade to Gull Cottage?"

"By way of Bellingham, with your aunt."

Rearing his head back to look at her, he queried, "Aunt Tilly?"

Beth smiled at the incredulity in his face and voice. "Yes. We met her in Biggleswade. As we were leaving the inn after having tea, she was entering for the same purpose. She was . . . surprised to see me there—"

"I imagine she was."

"She asked us to sit with her while she and her maid had tea, then questioned where I was traveling and why. She, ah, suggested that we travel with her to Bellingham, saying it was sufficiently remote for any gossip to take weeks to arrive. After securing her promise not to tell anyone where I was, I agreed, although she warned me she would try to change my mind."

" 'Tis a shame she did not succeed," he muttered.

"I can be very determined." It was half statement, half warning.

"I shall keep that in mind, love." He hugged her again, rubbing his cheek against her hair. "What did you think of Bellingham? And how did you get from there to here?"

"Bellingham is beautiful, both the castle and the estate. After your aunt took care of the business that called her to Northumberland, she came here—"

His head jerked erect. "Aunt Tilly is here?"

"Yes, nephew, I am," that lady said from the doorway. "Mrs. MacAfee sent a letter after Arabella left, so I came to assess the damages." George's aunt entered the room, followed by her maid and Moira. The housekeeper, carrying a tray of tea and pastries, brought up the rear of the little procession. After seating herself on the opposite sofa, Lady Matilda looked from Beth to George. "I trust, young man, given your cozy position, that you and Beth are betrothed?"

His joyous smile was, undoubtedly, answer enough. "Indeed we are. You may be the first to wish us happy."

Tea was a celebration, as well as a recounting of all that had occurred since Beth had left London. George was very angry to learn that Elston had known her destination was Stranraer. As if fearing she'd created a chasm between the friends, Beth explained what she'd written in her note to the marquess, then demanded George's anger be directed at her.

"I cannot be angry with you, sweetheart. I understand why you left Town and, I think, why you extracted vows of secrecy from Aunt Tilly and Elston. Their silence, too." *Not to mention Elston's hurried trip north.* George sighed and rubbed his hands over his face, then dragged them back through his hair. "If I sound grumpy, it is because I am tired. I have not been sleeping well."

Beth bit her lip and reached out to touch his hand. "I am sorry, George. I thought my letters would prevent anyone from searching for me."

He smiled. "Well, I have found you now, and I shan't let you get away again."

When they were finished, Mrs. MacAfee gathered the cups and plates. "When will the wedding be, Master George?"

"As soon as the banns are read."

"Ach, laddie, ye are in Scotland. Ye dinna need banns. Nor even a minister."

"Eager as I am to marry Beth—and I am very eager—I will do so in London, with our families and all the *ton* as witnesses."

Beth's cheeks flamed at such a frank admission. "George!"

He smiled again, reaching over to rub her rosy cheek with the back of one finger. " 'Tis true, love."

"It seems almost fitting to marry here, where our adventure, and our friendship, began."

"I will bring you here on our wedding trip, if you like, but I want to marry you in Town, so all of Society can admire my beautiful bride."

After the others left the room, he pulled Beth back on his lap. "There is one thing you haven't told me, sweetheart."

"What is that?"

"When did you fall in love with me?"

"I am not sure when, exactly, because it happened gradually. I realized I loved you the evening I first attended Almack's."

He remembered that evening very well. "Is that why you were so upset?"

She laid a gentle hand against his cheek, as if to ease the hurt that had crept into his tone. "I wasn't upset, just surprised. Shocked, really. First, that I hadn't recognized it sooner and second, because I thought people fell in love simultaneously. I knew you considered me a friend, and a . . . responsibility. It seemed unlikely you would ever return my regard." She kissed the corner of his mouth before adding, "I am very happy to be wrong about that."

"What do you mean . . ." George stopped, realizing he knew the answer to his half-formed question. Beth was right, in a sense: He had considered her reputation his responsibility, so honor had compelled his first proposal. The second one, too, although that one had been tempered with affection, and hadn't occurred until several weeks after her epiphany.

"Are you going to complete your question?"

"No, love. I already know the answer."

She ducked her head. "Then, may I ask you something?"

With one finger, he lifted her chin, catching her gaze. "You may ask me anything, Beth."

She bit her lip, then laid her head on his shoulder. George knew this was either a difficult question or a very important one. He hoped he would be able to provide a suitable answer.

"Why did you give me the cut direct the first time we met?"

"What?" He jerked erect, nearly dumping Beth off his lap. Resettling them both, he grasped her shoulders and held her far enough away that he could see her face. "I have never cut you. At least, not intentionally. I don't recall meeting you before Dunnley's house party." He searched his memory but could not remember an earlier encounter. "Were we introduced before that?"

"No."

Baffled, George shook his head. "Then I don't know what you are talking about. 'Twas you who was . . . less than friendly when Dunnley introduced us at breakfast the first morning."

"I daresay you, too, would be less than friendly to someone who requested an introduction after cutting you the previous evening."

"Sweetheart, I didn't take part in the festivities the night before. I arrived late, well after dinner, and I was exhausted because I'd been up most of the two previous nights assisting my best broodmares through difficult foalings."

The hurt look faded from her face and eyes. "I don't suppose it matters anymore."

"It does to me. Tell me what happened—what I did."

"Do you remember talking with Dunnley in the drawing room when you arrived?"

"Vaguely. I was so tired by then I could barely keep my eyes open."

Beth lifted a hand and rubbed a finger between his brows. He eased his frown into a smile, then caught her hand and placed a kiss on the palm. "Tell me, please."

"Dunnley asked if you'd brought your cello. At your nod, he asked if you'd play a duet with me. You looked over at me—I was standing by the pianoforte—said 'I think not,' then left the room. It certainly seemed like the cut direct."

"I am sorry, sweetheart," he apologized, hugging her. "I don't remember any of that, except, very vaguely, talking with Dunnley. It was exhaustion . . . *My God!*"

Nearly unseated again, Beth grasped his shoulders, her beautiful blue eyes on his face. "What?"

"I don't know if you are aware that the members of my family, for several generations, have all known—or claimed to know—their loves at first sight. That is why it took me so long to realize I love you. I expected to be struck by a thunderbolt or some such thing the first time I saw my ladylove."

"Well, you did eventually realize you love me. That is the important thing, surely. But what does your belief in love at first sight have to do with your behavior at Dunnley's house party?"

Smiling broadly, George explained his revelation. "I vaguely remember talking with Dunnley. I know he asked me to do something, although I could not have said what. I refused because I suddenly felt quite shaken. I put it down to exhaustion, but I daresay it was my thunderbolt. Only I was too stupid to realize it."

"You are not stupid, George," his love averred. "If that was, indeed, your thunderbolt, you were too tired to properly appreciate it. It is too bad it didn't strike you again the next morning. If it had, we might already be married."

"That is a lovely thought." He snuggled Beth against his chest. "I understand now why you were so frosty the next morning. And why you seemed so different in Scotland and London."

"I, too, was puzzled when the arrogant, toplofty earl from the house party was so kind and friendly at Hawthorn Lodge, and ever since."

George winced then kissed Beth again. Twice for good measure. "After such an unfortunate beginning, I am amazed you gave me a second chance. But I am very glad you did, my love."

Two days later they departed for London, this time with Lady Matilda, her maid, and Moira as chaperones. George had suggested sailing, but his aunt, who was not a good sailor, refused to even consider the idea. Beth sensed his reluctance to send his yacht back to Winterhaven Manor, but he joined the four women in his aunt's capacious traveling coach without complaint.

The second day, as they walked to the carriage after luncheon, Beth placed a hand on his coat sleeve. "Are you going to ride on the box or sit inside?"

"I was planning to join you. Unless you have some objection?"

"Of course not, silly. I only wondered if you have a book you can read to us."

He smiled down at her. "Indeed I do. I finished *Sense and Sensibility* and am now reading *Pride and Prejudice*. Let me get it from my bag."

When he climbed inside, he carried a large tome and wore a rueful smile. "I packed in such a rush when I heard the report Beth might have been in Carlisle that I grabbed the wrong book from my nightstand." He settled onto the seat between her and his aunt. "This will put you to sleep in five minutes or less, Aunt Tilly." He tapped the head of his cane on the roof, signaling the coachman to start. "Beth, you may last a few minutes longer."

"What makes you say that, nephew?"

His eyes twinkling, he teased, "Say what, Aunt Tilly? That you will be asleep in five minutes or that Beth may last a few minutes longer?"

Lady Matilda's laughter mingled with Beth's. "Both."

Beth read the volume's title. "*The Proceedings of the Royal Society, 1808.* Is there a particular article you are reading, George?"

"Two, actually. One by my father, the other by your uncle."

"The articles that caused their disagreement? I would like to read them, too."

"By all means, love. You can help me determine who made the error. I am more than a little curious but have not yet found it." He put his arm around her and snuggled her against his side. "Don't look so concerned, sweetheart. Should I find it, I doubt I will tell anyone but you."

As her companions dozed, Beth read Lord Bellingham's article, then her uncle's. She found a pencil and pages of calculations in George's hand tucked in the back of the volume. After several more miles, she nudged her beloved awake with a well-placed elbow in his ribs. "I found it! Rather, I found *them.*"

"Them?" He knuckled his eyes. "They both made mistakes?"

"Do not sound so incredulous, dear sir." Smiling, she teased, "I found your mistake, too."

"At least I am in good company," he quipped. Then, "Show me, please."

And so she did.

Epilogue

On the eighteenth of June in the Year of Our Lord 1813, four weeks and two days after they returned to London, Beth and George were married at St. George's, Hanover Square. Their families and friends, as well as most of the *ton*, witnessed the joyous celebration. Lady Christina Fairchild stood up with Beth, the Marquess of Elston supported George. The Archbishop of London and George's great-uncle, the Bishop of Lymington, presided. And the Marquess of Bellingham and the Earl of Castleton smiled proudly throughout the service, once again in accord and delighted at the union of their families.

The trials were behind them. Tom and one of Sir James's servants had been sentenced to hang; the other servant would be transported, as would Sir James and Arabella. But despite her conviction and impending departure for Botany Bay, Arabella made a final, mad attempt to coerce George into wedlock. Having seduced one of the prison guards, stolen his keys, and escaped, she appeared in the church, ragged and filthy, claiming that she was with child and George must marry her. The bridegroom turned and, with one arm around his bride's slender waist and a scornful, dismissive look at the intruder, said, "Arabella, you are not a likely candidate for immaculate conception." In the ensuing laughter, the Earl of Hartwood hustled his daughter out of the church and back to Newgate Prison. Later, he apologized profusely and promised that, if the Crown was unable to keep his daughter confined, he would take over the task until she was deported.

After the wedding breakfast, the Earl and Countess of Weymouth sailed on the *Dorset Dancer* for Scotland. Beth spent the first night of her marriage alone while George helped the small crew race the yacht around Land's End and into St. George's Channel in the teeth of a raging storm. The next morning he appeared at breakfast, rueful and exhausted. When he attempted to beg her pardon, she placed a slim finger against his lips. "We shall consider today an extension of our wedding day and tonight our wedding night."

They arrived at Gull Cottage late in the afternoon. That night, snuggled in her husband's arms and happier than she could ever remember being, Beth mused sleepily on all that had occurred since her initial visit here. "The last time I slept in this bed I had a nightmare, then awoke to learn of Arabella's scheme and felt I was living one."

George's arms tightened around her. "I shall chase your bad dreams away, my love. Always."

She raised her head from its resting place on his shoulder and smiled at him. "You already have. What I meant was, it was a nightmare with a very happy ending."

The kiss with which her husband rewarded that statement was testimony to the truth of her words.

Signet Regency Romances from **Allison Lane**

"A FORMIDABLE TALENT... MS. LANE NEVER FAILS TO DELIVER THE GOODS." —*ROMANTIC TIMES*

THE NOTORIOUS WIDOW
0-451-20166-3

When a scoundrel tries to tarnish a young widow's reputation, a valiant Earl tries to repair the damage—and mend her broken heart as well...

BIRDS OF A FEATHER
0-451-19825-5

When a plain, bespectacled young woman keeps meeting the handsome Lord Wylie, she feels she is not up to his caliber. A great arbiter of fashion for London society, Lord Wylie was reputed to be more interseted in the cut of his clothes than the feelings of others, as the young woman bore witness to. Degraded by him in public, she could nevertheless forget his dashing demeanor. It will take a public scandal, and a private passion, to bring them together...

To order call: 1-800-788-6262

S317

Signet Regency Romances *from*

ELISABETH FAIRCHILD

"An outstanding talent." —*Romantic Times*

CAPTAIN CUPID CALLS THE SHOTS
0-451-20198-1

Captain Alexander Shelbourne was known as Cupid to his friends for his uncanny marksmanship in battle. But upon meeting Miss Penny Foster, he soon knew how it felt to be struck by his namesake's arrow....

SUGARPLUM SURPRISES
0-451-20421-2

Lovely Jane Nichol—who spends her days disguised as a middle-aged seamstress—has crossed paths with a duke who shelters a secret as great as her own. But as Christmas approaches—and vicious rumors surface—they begin to wonder if they can have their cake and eat it, too...

To order call: 1-800-788-6262

S321/Fairchild

PENGUIN PUTNAM INC.
Online

Your Internet gateway to a virtual environment with hundreds of entertaining and enlightening books from Penguin Putnam Inc.

While you're there, get the latest buzz on the best authors and books around—

Tom Clancy, Patricia Cornwell, W.E.B. Griffin, Nora Roberts, William Gibson, Robin Cook, Brian Jacques, Catherine Coulter, Stephen King, Ken Follett, Terry McMillan, and many more!

Penguin Putnam Online is located at
http://www.penguinputnam.com

PENGUIN PUTNAM NEWS

Every month you'll get an inside look at our upcoming books and new features on our site. This is an ongoing effort to provide you with the most up-to-date information about our books and authors.

Subscribe to Penguin Putnam News at
http://www.penguinputnam.com/newsletters